To Va

For all she mea

By the same author

The DI Mike Nash Series:

Depth of Despair

Chosen

Minds That Hate

Altered Egos

Back-Slash

Identity Crisis

Writing as William Gordon

Watering The Olives

The Last Resort

Byland Cresent - Requiem

Cover design: Val Kitson

Snow Angel

Bill Kitson

Acknowledgements

My grateful thanks to my reader, Liz Mustoe, for her appraisal of the original manuscript.
And to my wife, Val, who has edited, proofread and formatted the manuscripts ready for publication.
In addition, she has also designed the cover – she's a one-woman book factory!

Part One

The Sweet Smell of Success

DI Mike Nash greeted his boss with a smile. Chief Constable Gloria O'Donnell, known irreverently within the local force as 'God' because of her position, as well as her initials, was on her regular visit to Helmsdale station. She sat down opposite the DI, one of her favourite officers. Nash detailed the outstanding cases they had on the books 'There has been a spate of shoplifting recently but that's only to be expected with Christmas approaching. All the retailers in the town have been warned to be extra-vigilant. That's about all I have to tell you, ma'am.'

'You know I'm going on leave in a week's time?'

Nash nodded as the chief constable continued, 'Is there anything that should concern me before I leave?' She smiled and added, 'Known crime that is. I'm not asking you to become psychic.'

Nash answered immediately. 'Only the problem we've talked over several times before, ma'am. I'm talking about the drugs that are coming into the area.'

'Are you no closer to resolving the issue?'

Nash shook his head. 'We've managed to shut down a couple of small-time operators, they weren't much of a worry, but all that seems to have done is given the major supplier a monopoly.'

'Do you know who that is?'

'No, that's the most irritating part; they seem to be very clever at concealing themselves. We can't even get word from our informers. Either they don't know, which I find hard to believe, or they're too scared to let on.' Nash paused. 'I had an idea, but it is little more than that, about a couple of men who might be involved and even went to the trouble of having them watched, but without any luck. It's almost as if they knew they were under surveillance. Either that, or we're on the wrong track.'

'Did you use our own officers? Might that have given the game away?'

'No. Superintendent Fleming asked for a specialist from the Drugs Intelligence Unit for that very reason.'

'And they reported no luck?'

'As far as I was told. We got a report from their central office which seemed to imply that they didn't like being sent on a wild goose chase.'

'You didn't meet or get to speak to the officers concerned?'

'No. You know how secretive the DIU can be. Natural I suppose, to ensure the safety of their undercover officers.'

'If you have an idea of the people involved, did you think to try checking their bank records for signs of money-laundering?'

'There again, that was something the DIU handled. They simply reported nothing untoward. Very frustrating.'

'How convinced are you that you're on the right track?'

'Difficult to be positive. And with so little to go on I could be totally off course, but they're the best lead we've got – to be honest; the only lead we've got.'

'OK, leave it with me. I'll see if I can get some action before I go away.'

'When is that, ma'am?'

'We fly to California next Friday and will be back the week before Christmas.'

The chief constable phoned Nash a couple of days later. What she told him surprised Nash – and he didn't shock easily. Long after the chief had rung off he remained at his desk, thinking over the implications of what he'd heard.

Curtis Smith stared at the computer screen for a moment before pausing the recorded video captured by the concealed camera. He increased the volume to ensure he caught every word of the conversation then restarted the CCTV footage and listened with increasing anger to what the two men were plotting. On screen the surroundings were familiar. The men were seated in Curtis's own office. Knowing that Joe, his best friend and business partner, was conspiring with their rival to ditch him came as a bitter shock. By the end of the clip, he knew how complete their plan to destroy him was. Curtis couldn't understand why Joe had taken this course. What had he done to provoke such hatred in a man he trusted so deeply?

It was only when he watched a second recording that the reason became clear. If Curtis recognized the setting for the first clip easily enough, the location of the second was sickeningly familiar. Curtis had known that there was someone when he'd concealed the camera in his own bedroom. Had known his girlfriend was cheating him, but had no idea with whom. As he watched Joe and Marion gyrating on his bed; saw the expression of apparent ecstasy on her face, Curtis realized beyond doubt how completely he had been betrayed.

He waited; his face an expressionless mask as he listened to the couple's post-coital conversation. It was then he realized just how perilous his own existence had become. In similar situations many men would have confronted the couple, possibly even converted their rage into physical violence, but although Curtis had been severely provoked he overcame the urge. Nevertheless, it was a tough battle and for some time he was tempted by the thought of the razor-sharp hatchet he kept in his study to deal with unwanted callers.

Instead of springing into rash action, Curtis continued to stare at the computer long after the screen went blank. Although his body remained motionless, his mind raced as he thought and planned. Eventually, several hours later, he stood up and stretched. His course of action determined, he only had to refine the details of his scheme. In essence it involved the cooperation, whether conscious or otherwise, of several people and organizations; not least of whom were the local police. He smiled at the irony of involving the police in his scheme. Would they, he wondered, become classed as accessories to murder? Curtis rather liked that idea.

The first person to be targeted by Curtis in his scheme was his next-door neighbour. Mrs Brown was a widow who lived alone, and a series of burglaries a couple of years previously had left her highly nervous. The incursions had ceased abruptly after Curtis 'had a word' with a couple of people, but Mrs Brown's fear had not abated to any degree.

It was early evening when he knocked on her door. He got no response, but then he wasn't expecting one – not immediately at least. 'Mrs B' – he called through the letter box – 'it's me. Curtis, from next door.'

After a few minutes, during which he knocked several times and repeated his message, the outside light went on. Curtis blinked, but knew what to do next. He took two paces back and looked up towards the first floor. Mrs Brown would be watching from one of the bedroom windows, and unless she could recognize the caller, she would not open the door.

A moment later the bolts were drawn back and the chain unfastened. Mrs Brown let him inside and Curtis explained the reason for his call.

Two nights later, Curtis parked his hire car a short distance from Mrs Brown's house. He got out, locked the door and walked slowly past the widow's front door, his hands buried deep in the pockets of the hoodie he had bought for this task. He reached his own gate and turned into the drive but then ducked out of sight behind the tall beech hedge. He waited twenty minutes before emerging and retracing his steps. He repeated the manoeuvre three times before returning to the car. As he started the engine, Curtis reflected that before he continued his nocturnal walks he would have to get some warmer clothing. Despite the several layers he was wearing he was shivering with cold. As he drove away he gave thanks to the designers of the heating system fitted to the Mercedes. He knew he would have to repeat tonight's activity until he was sure Mrs Brown had spotted the shadowy figure of the stranger prowling the street. It would be a bonus if she was to mention the Mercedes when she contacted the police; which was exactly what Curtis wanted. Only when he knew that the police were aware of the prowler could he move on to the next phase of the operation.

Scott Harper was content with life. Things were beginning to look up. Harper had taken over ownership of Club Wolfgang, a nightclub in Helmsdale, and had extended and modernized the premises, but had struggled to make a success of the venture. That had been until Curtis's girlfriend, Marion Waters, had been introduced to him in the club. A couple of weeks later she had returned, this time bringing with her a man he recognized as Joe, Curtis's partner. It was from that point that their plan began to take shape. What Scott hadn't been party to, was the conversation that had taken place beforehand.

It was during one of Joe and Marion's prolonged bouts of lovemaking that she made the suggestion. 'Why don't we get shut of Curtis? With him out of the way you can have me all to yourself – whenever you want and as often as you want.'

The idea excited Joe so much that it was some time before they were able to resume the discussion. 'How would we go about it?'

'That's for you to think up. But I've had an idea. We could set Scott Harper up for it. Then, with him doing time for Curtis's murder, we'll have the field to ourselves. And if we took over the running of the club, we'll have the perfect outlet for the gear.'

The plan was a terrific one, Joe had to agree. In fact, everything was going as smoothly as he could have hoped. The only minor irritation had been the break-in at their offices. Nothing had been stolen, or so it appeared, for which Joe was thankful. It meant he wouldn't have to explain the incursion to Curtis, who seemed increasingly moody these days.

*

Sergeant Jack Binns answered the phone and scribbled the details onto a message pad. After replacing the receiver he walked into uniform branch rest room. 'Job for you, Robinson,' he told her. 'Woman in Grange Road reckons there's been a prowler hanging around. Go see Mrs Brown and her next door neighbours. Their names are ...' he struggled to decipher his own handwriting. 'Curtis Smith and Marion Waters. Mrs Brown reckons one of them has seen the prowler as well.'

WPC Anne Robinson had only been transferred to Helmsdale a couple of weeks ago, but had already familiarized herself with the area. She reached Grange Road within a quarter of an hour, and after some difficulty persuaded Mrs Brown to open the door. The complainant was friendly and chatted for some length about the prowler, her nervousness following the earlier burglaries apparent, and gossiped a little about her neighbours. The WPC's reception at the house next door was, by contrast far cooler. When she eventually answered the door, Marion Waters' tone of voice was sharp, her words dismissive as she denied any knowledge of a prowler. Robinson returned to the station, chastened by the thought that the future might hold many such fruitless tasks. It was only as she was entering the station car park that she remembered that Mrs Brown's neighbour had only been wearing a dressing gown and that she had looked hot and flustered, her hair tousled. Was that the reason for her hostile attitude, Anne wondered? Had she unwittingly disturbed the woman as she was indulging in a little afternoon delight? Anne sniffed; hard lines, she thought. If I'm not getting any don't expect me to sympathize with someone who is.

Curtis was about to get into his car when he heard his name being called. He looked round and saw Mrs Brown standing at the end of his drive. She appeared to be somewhat agitated. 'Is something wrong?' he asked.

'He's been here again.'

'Who has?'

'The prowler. The man you told me about. I saw him. He's got a Mercedes.'

So she had seen the car; that was good. 'Oh, him! That's bad news. I'll keep my eyes peeled and if I see him again I'll report it to the police.'

'Don't worry, I've already done that. They sent a policewoman round.' Mrs Brown glanced down at the card in her hand. 'Her name is Constable Anne Robinson. She took all the details I could give her, but I'm no good on car models and it was too dark to see the number plate. I explained that I've seen the prowler at least three times in addition to the time you saw him.'

'Good work, Mrs B. Let's hope they catch him, but in the meantime I'll be on my guard.'

As he drove away, Curtis smiled. Things were coming together nicely. Now he was ready to put the next phase of his plan into action. Instead of driving to the office where he and Joe ran their drug dealership as a sideline under the more respectable guise of a waste disposal business, Curtis headed to the hotel where he had taken a room for the past month. He was looking forward with growing excitement to meeting the girl there. The girl who would replace Marion in his bed.

Later that afternoon, Curtis watched the now familiar scene from his bedroom unfold on the laptop in his hotel room. His companion glanced from the screen to his face. 'Doesn't that bother you?' she asked.

Curtis laughed and began to caress her naked body again. His hands slipped down and cupped her little brown buttocks, pulling her tightly against him. She felt the heat of his arousal as he whispered, 'That doesn't bother me in the slightest. Why should it when I have you? Besides, I've been waiting for this. I wanted it to happen.'

She pulled away and stared at him. 'You wanted it to happen? You wanted him to do your girl?'

'She's not my girl any longer. You're my girl now; my black pearl. And yes, I wanted it to happen, because how else can I do what I have in mind.'

He saw her continued perplexity and explained. Her eyes

widened as he told her his plan. At the end she gasped with astonishment. 'Fuck me!'

He rolled her onto her back. 'Now that is a very good idea.'

Much later, Curtis bade the girl goodbye. 'See you tomorrow.'

'I'll be here.'

'Good, and in the meantime if you want anything there's some stuff in the top drawer. Very best quality gear.'

Her eyes sparkled. 'I might just try some, seeing as you're not here to keep me company.'

Curtis stopped in town and went into the chemist's shop. He hurried back to the car having made his purchase.

Next morning he left his house early. Marion was still asleep, or feigning it. She hadn't spoken to him once. Not when he'd forced himself upon her, or afterwards. He wondered if she'd even noticed that he was wearing a condom. He'd seen the look of fear in her eyes and if he hadn't known what she was planning to do to him, he might even have felt sorry for the ordeal he'd forced upon her.

As soon as she heard the car pull away off the gravel drive, Marion picked up the phone. 'Joe,' she sobbed. 'I need you. Please come here – now.'

Back in the hotel room Curtis watched the live video feed with satisfaction. He'd wondered if Joe and Marion would make love after what had happened the previous night, but they did. Just what he'd hoped for. He glanced across the room at the girl; sleeping now, only the top of her head and one black arm visible; vivid against the snowy-white sheets.

He looked back at the computer and saw that Joe was getting dressed, Marion clinging to him, still in need of consolation. 'Weep, you bitch,' he muttered. 'You won't have to suffer much longer.'

Curtis walked out of the hotel and into the car park. He checked the temporary registration number pasted over the plates on the Mercedes, hoping he didn't encounter any patrol cars en route. The number would be good enough to fool Mrs Brown but he didn't think it would get past police officers.

The phone call came into Helmsdale police station during the early part of the afternoon. Sergeant Jack Binns rang through to the CID suite. 'Mike, I've taken a call from a woman who's near hysterical. She's been on before about a prowler who she reckons has been hanging around a few times at night. Now, she says he's turned up in broad daylight. She reckons he went into the neighbouring house and is still inside.'

'You're sure she's not a crank caller?'

'I don't think so. I sent an officer when she made the complaint a few nights ago and she reckons the woman's kosher.'

'I've nobody available to send. I'll go myself but I'll need a uniform as a backup.'

'How about WPC Robinson, the officer who attended the complaint?'

'Fine, I'll be down in a minute.'

Nash didn't recognize the officer standing by the reception desk. 'You're new, aren't you?' he asked as they walked across the car park.

'Yes, sir, I was posted here only two weeks ago.'

As Nash drove, WPC Robinson filled him in with details of her visit to Mrs Brown.

'Tell me about the neighbour she said had also seen the prowler. Who is he? Did you speak to him?'

'Unfortunately, he wasn't in when I called.' Robinson checked her notebook. 'He lives next door to Mrs Brown, at number seven. His name is Curtis Smith.'

'Is it, indeed? Now that *is* extremely interesting.'

'Why is it interesting?'

'Because we suspect Curtis Smith and his partner Joe Michaels are the major suppliers of Class A drugs into the area.'

As he finished speaking, Nash swung the Range Rover into the street where Mrs Brown lived. 'No sign of a

Mercedes now,' he pointed out after he'd parked.

He followed the WPC across the road, admiring her shapely legs. Not even the uniform or the unflattering shoes could disguise their attractiveness. Mrs Brown was on the doorstep, almost dancing with agitation. 'You've missed him,' she greeted them. 'He went about a quarter of an hour ago. But I've got his registration number.'

'Well done,' Nash smiled reassuringly at her. 'You're sure he went into number seven?'

'Yes, absolutely certain.'

'Is anyone at home, do you know?'

'I'm not sure. Marion, the woman who lives there, might be. But I haven't seen her today.'

'OK, we'd better take a look.' Nash gestured to the WPC to follow him.

'Why do you think this prowler picked number seven? Has he targeted it because Smith lives there, or did he simply pick a house at random?' she asked.

'No idea.' As soon as he knocked on the door Nash knew something was wrong. The door swung open at his first touch. He looked at Robinson. 'I don't like the look of this.'

He called out a couple of times, but got no response. 'We're going in,' he told her, 'better inform the control room.'

She spoke briefly over the radio then followed Nash into the house. Everything seemed normal on the ground floor. The house was almost like a show house, everything neatly ordered and minimal.

'Better try upstairs,' Nash told her.

She followed; her heart beating a little faster at the thought of what they might find on the upper floor. Nash drew a blank with the first doors he tried; an unused spare room, a home office and the house bathroom. The final door was partially open. Nash pushed it wide and took two paces into the room before he stopped suddenly.

Robinson, following hard on his heels, took one look. 'Oh God!' she exclaimed.

Nash remained immobile as he stared at what was

obviously a murder scene. The woman lying on the bed was naked. She had been strangled with her tights; knotted round her throat. Nash noted the bruises on the dead woman's arms, her face and legs and guessed that she might also have been raped. He turned. 'Are you alright?'

'Yes, no problem.'

Nash noted her reaction. 'That suggests you've attended scenes like this before?'

She nodded.

'Never pleasant though. Is that the woman you spoke to before? Marion something-or-other?'

'Marion Waters. Yes, that's her.'

Nash glanced back at the corpse and as he turned his head, he caught a faint aroma. 'Can you smell that?'

Robinson sniffed. 'Yes, some sort of perfume or after-shave, isn't it?'

'Remember that scent. It might be important. Go downstairs and contact Jack Binns. Ask him to get Mexican Pete and SOCO out here. Although I don't think it will take them too long to check this place over.'

For the first time, the WPC looked puzzled. 'Mexican who?'

Nash smiled slightly. 'You are new, aren't you? Mexican Pete, our pathologist. Proper name, Professor Ramirez. And while you're on, ask Jack to try and track down Curtis Smith. I'll contact Superintendent Fleming; tell her what's going on.'

He turned back for another look at the victim and the room. It looked like a classic rape and murder. But did it perhaps look just a little too perfect? Nothing appeared disturbed. Almost as if it had been staged? Nash wondered if he was getting too fanciful, but even hours later, when the SOCO team had turned the crime scene over to CID, the doubt remained.

Twenty-four hours later, Scott Harper was checking the figures from the previous nights' takings when he heard his office door open. He looked up, his frown of annoyance at being disturbed turning to one of amazement as he saw the intruder; recognizing him immediately. 'How did you get in here?'

The question was more than important, it was crucial. Given the amount of cash held on the premises from day to day, security was of the utmost importance. The insurance premiums were high enough already without the possibility of a robbery sending them through the roof. Only Scott and his bar manager had keys to the club, and only Scott had access to the office. The intruder held up a gloved hand and Scott stared, like a hypnotist's victim, transfixed by the bunch of skeleton keys. 'What do you want?' he demanded.

'Amongst other things, I've come here to tell you a little story. Not a very edifying one, I grant you. It's all about cheating. Cheating and betrayal. One in which the betrayer can end up being the betrayed. You should enjoy it, because you're part of it. Not in a starring role, sadly. And not one where you get to see the happy ending, but a vital part as far as the plot's concerned.'

'What are you rambling on about?'

'Sorry, was the analogy too obscure? I'm talking about the nasty little plot you cooked-up with Joe and Marion to get rid of me and take over our highly lucrative enterprise for yourselves.'

'How the fuck did you find that out?'

'It was almost accidental, as it happens. Let's just say I have a nose for intrigue.' Curtis began to laugh and Harper was concerned as to his sanity. After a moment, Curtis became serious again. 'Of course, your problem is that they only told you half a tale.'

'What do you mean?'

'They weren't content to get me out of the business; they were going to have me killed. Not only that, but they were going to see to it that you were framed for my murder. That way they'd have it all. The drugs, the club and each other. A true love story right in front of us,' Curtis sneered. 'Neat though, don't you think?'

'I don't believe you.'

'No? I can show you the footage if you really want. Or I could have done, if I'd either the time or the inclination. You see, I placed a hidden camera; top of the range, voice activated,' he added by way of explanation, 'with a live feed to my computer. Well, two hidden cameras to be exact. One in my office, where I was able to eavesdrop on your sordid little meeting with Joe. And another in the bedroom of my house, where I was a reluctant witness to Joe and Marion's even more sordid encounters, including the one where they discussed setting you up for my murder. That made really good viewing from a potential victim's point of view, I can tell you.'

'The cheating, lying bastards.'

'Quite so, I can understand how you must feel.'

'What are you going to do about it?'

Curtis smiled. He could see the irony of the question, coming from a man who had been plotting to ruin him. He took a couple of paces further into the room and lowered his voice. Even though he was nearer, Scott had to lean forward to hear him. 'The thing is, even though their plan was a good one, it was far from perfect. It relied on the cooperation of too many people. Mine is a whole lot better.'

Almost as a punctuation mark, the bullet entered Scott's brain as Curtis finished speaking. He stared down impassively at the dead man for a few seconds before reaching into his coat pocket and taking out a small bottle. Wearing gloves caused him a little difficulty unscrewing the cap but then he began sprinkling liquid from the bottle around the room, being careful to avoid any touching the corpse. Finally, he picked up the phone on Harper's desk, noting, with more interest than distaste, that the receiver was liberally splattered with cranial fluid. He dialled 999 and spoke as soon as the call was answered. 'I wish to report a murder,' he said, before placing the receiver on the desk alongside the dead man's head.

Curtis left the office and walked out of the building, shivering slightly, not at the enormity of what he'd done, but at the cold wind that blew down the alley alongside the club.

He returned to the hotel; to his room and to the girl. Even as the police arrived at the crime scene, Curtis was lying on the bed, his head thrown back in ecstasy as the girl knelt over him, her soft lips bringing him to frenzied ejaculation. There must be something in this killing lark, he reflected later, as they dropped off to sleep. He couldn't remember being this horny for a long time. Or maybe it was just the girl who seemed pleased to do whatever he demanded of him. He moved closer, and, as she felt his erection hardening against her, she turned over and smiled sleepily. She moved slightly, an erotic invitation. 'Come on, then.'

'What do you reckon, sir?'

'Nash had told her to stop calling him, sir, but WPC Robinson was not quite comfortable using his Christian name. Normally, the absence of formality suited the small team at Helmsdale. Even smaller, with his DS, Clara Mironova, away on holiday and DC Pearce on a course. In their absence, Nash seemed to have co-opted Anne as his assistant. She wondered if this was because she hadn't been fazed by the sight of the murder victim's corpse. If she'd known it was because he liked looking at her legs and her superb figure that even the uniform couldn't quite conceal, she would have been surprised rather than shocked, and possibly a little flattered.

She'd heard a lot about Mike's reputation, but having met him, decided that it was probably more idle gossip than fact. Anyone less like an office Romeo she couldn't imagine. Nash was helpful, polite, friendly and considerate. Had DS Mironova been on hand, she would probably have warned Anne that Mike's charming and polite manner were the traps that had ensnared so many women before her. Whether Anne would have been prepared to listen to that advice is another matter. Besides which, she had her own secrets, and wondered what Nash's reaction would be when he found out about her.

'I'll tell you what I think. I think someone is playing games with us.' Nash replied.

'Why do you say that?'

They were standing in Harper's office. Nash had been impressed by Anne's stoical reaction to the sight of a second corpse, and this time one that had even more sickening signs of violence than the first. Neither the dead man's body, the bullet hole in his forehead or the pool of blood and brain matter on the desk and surrounding carpet seemed to have upset her.

Mexican Pete had just arrived and shook his head at Nash. 'How many more are you going to find for me this week? I do have other work to do. I'm not you personal pathologist you know!' He turned his attention to the body before announcing, 'Yes, he's definitely dead.'

The crime scene investigators had arrived and once their photographers had finished, the pathologist supervised removal of the body.

Nash watched the SOCO team at work. He turned to Anne. 'When we came into this room, did you notice it?'

'Notice what? One look at the dead man and I was too busy trying to keep my lunch where I'd put it to notice much.'

Nash smiled. 'It was the scent I was referring to. It was the same one as at the house yesterday, only in here it's even stronger. You can still smell it.'

Anne sniffed; Nash was right. And unless her nose was deceiving her, it was the same brand. 'It's lingering for some time,' she ventured.

'Good point. I think the killer has been sprinkling it round the room. It certainly wasn't the one Harper was wearing.'

'Was that why you sniffed at his face? I did wonder what you were up to.'

Nash nodded. 'Harper wears ... sorry ... wore a very expensive French brand. The one we can smell now is a far cheaper one; much stronger-scented.'

'You seem to be an expert. How do you know Harper's was an expensive French brand?'

'Because it's the same one that I use; which is how I know it's very expensive. This side of the Channel at least.'

Anne returned to the main question. 'Do you think the killer's doing that to throw us off the scent? Oh!' She realized what she'd said and began to giggle. 'Sorry, I didn't mean it like that.'

Nash grinned. 'I'm glad about that. I'd have been worried had you said it on purpose. No, I think he or she is trying to point us in a particular direction. What that direction is, I can't begin to guess. When we go back to the station let's see if anyone has caught sight of the absentee, Mr Curtis Smith. He's getting to look more and more like the guilty party.'

A week later, Nash and Robinson were in the CID suite when the phone rang. Anne listened to one half of the conversation, trying to gauge who Mike's caller was. Something they had told him had clearly surprised and disturbed the detective. Anne continued to study Nash, confident that he was too preoccupied to notice her scrutiny. It was unusual for anything to surprise him so much, she thought. Nash was more used to dishing out surprises than receiving them, as Anne had discovered. Following their return to the station from the second murder, she had automatically headed towards the uniform branch rest room, until Nash had stopped her.

'Upstairs.' He'd pointed towards the CID suite. 'You have two crime scene reports to write. This isn't like uniform, you know, we put in a full day's work.'

Nash grinned as he saw Jack Binns' upraised finger. Fortunately, Anne missed the obscene gesture. If that hadn't surprised her, Nash's parting comment before they finished for the day certainly did. 'Don't wear your uniform tomorrow, Anne.'

She'd looked at him questioningly. 'You've been seconded to CID for the immediate future. Don't get excited, it isn't a promotion.' Nash had turned to leave, but as an afterthought, asked, 'By the way, can you make a half-decent cup of coffee?'

They had spent the past days studying the door-to-door

responses and trying to establish the whereabouts of Curtis Smith. Nash put the phone down, and for a moment Anne thought he'd caught her watching him, but his mind and thoughts seemed to be elsewhere. He was about to say something when the phone rang once more. This time, Nash's opening remarked identified the caller. 'Yes, Professor, what have you to tell me?'

He listened for a while, and although at times he seemed a little surprised, the information obviously came as far less of a shock than his previous caller's statements. After a while, Nash said, 'That pretty much confirms what SOCO told me. I have one question to ask you, in the light of what you've just said. Can you tell from your test results whether or not the victim was taking a contraceptive pill of any description?'

Nash waited, and even from the other side of his desk, Anne could hear the sound of the pathologist turning papers over at the other end of the phone. Eventually, he spoke, and Nash said, 'Thank you, Professor. That is extremely interesting.'

Anne waited after he put the phone down, and when he didn't speak for a minute, said, 'Anything I can help with?'

Nash smiled at her eagerness. 'The first call was from SOCO. They've matched a lot of fingerprints from the bedroom where we found the first victim to those of Joe Michaels, Curtis Smith's business partner. Michaels served three years when he was twenty-one for drug dealing. He was also charged with attempted murder, but the case was dropped following the mysterious death of the principal witness.'

'Sounds like a nice boy.'

'The second call was from Mexican Pete. He got the lab to do a rush job on a vaginal swab taken from the victim. They tested a semen sample and provisionally matched the DNA to Michaels. The inference we have to draw from that is that Michaels raped and strangled her.'

'But you don't seem convinced. What was the significance of the question about the victim being on the pill?'

'Ramirez told me she had intercourse with someone else during the twenty-four hours before she died. Before she had sex with Michaels, that is. However, he found traces of a lubricant which suggests the unknown male used a condom. Now, we have no evidence to suggest she was on the game, and according to your friend Mrs Brown, the only males to visit the house were her partner, Curtis Smith, and the prowler, who, going from the registration number of the Mercedes, we believe to be Michaels.'

'But surely that makes it an open and shut case, doesn't it?'

'It would do, if the dead woman hadn't been on the pill.'

'I'm sorry, I still don't get it.'

'If the only other person with access to her was Curtis Smith, he was bound to know she was on the pill, why would he use a condom?'

'I understand now. But what does it all mean?'

'I'm not sure, but do you remember what I said when we were in Harper's office?'

'About someone trying to point us in a particular direction, you mean?'

'That's right.'

'And now you're certain of it?'

'No, that's the problem; I'm not at all certain. All I have is a feeling that something's wrong, and I can't act on that. Juries convict on evidence, not a detective's intuition, and all the evidence points to Michaels having committed at least one murder. And if we find he wears a certain brand of after-shave, it would tend to suggest that he's guilty of two.'

'What do you intend to do?'

'Wait for confirmation on the DNA and follow the evidence; arrest Joe Michaels. At least once we get him into an interview room I'll have chance to talk to one of the principals in this case, which will be a novelty. Everyone connected to it seems to be either dead or missing. Which reminds me, any sightings of Curtis Smith yet?'

'Anne shook her head. 'He seems to have vanished

without trace.' She paused, before adding, 'I think it's about time I came clean about myself.'

Nash watched in surprise as she walked across and closed his office door. 'I had to wait for certain facts to be passed to me before I could drop the pretence. My name isn't Anne Robinson, and my rank certainly isn't that of constable. They are both part of the identity that was created for me.' She smiled faintly. 'I'm not even a natural blonde, but in view of the seriousness of what I'm here to investigate, the subterfuge was essential. I am in fact an undercover officer working for the Drugs Intelligence Unit. How much do you know of our current operation?'

'Only what the chief constable told me, that the DIU was already working in the area. I appreciate the need for secrecy, but why choose the role of a police officer? Surely that defeats the object of the exercise?'

'In normal circumstances I would agree with you. However, I'm afraid we now suspect the reason they've managed to avoid detection is that they are being shielded by a corrupt police officer. For a long time suspicion fell on the officers within your force. That might still be the case, however, we've not turned up anything that proves it one way or the other.'

'You've no idea who it might be?'

'Not yet; all I can say definitely is that we believe you are in the clear.'

'You've been investigating me, going through my financial records?'

Robinson smiled apologetically. 'It's standard procedure in a case like this.'

The girl was surprised when she heard the knock on the hotel room door. She glanced at the clock and frowned. Curtis had been staying with her for nearly a week now and had only been gone ten minutes or so. She wasn't expecting anyone. Had he forgotten something? She opened the door; to find a waiter outside standing behind a trolley. 'I didn't order room service,' she said, before looking at the man. 'Oh, Ryan, it's you!'

She waited for him to push the trolley into the room closing and locking the door. She definitely didn't want to be disturbed; for an hour at least. The waiter had already removed his shirt, tie and waistcoat, and was unfastening his trousers when she hastened to help him.

Almost an hour later, as they were lying side by side on the crumpled bed, trying to recover their breath, she gasped, 'That's taking room service to a new level.'

Ryan smiled. 'How's it going?'

'Much as expected. I managed to catch sight of the password as Curtis typed it into his laptop. After that I had access to the hidden cameras he's sited in his house and Michaels' office.'

'Anything interesting to report?'

'Too right there is. Michaels took a phone call from his supplier with details of a delivery. He called those two goons who work for him and gave them details of when and where to make the pick-up. Because they're so thick he had them repeat it a couple of times, which was handy because it gave me chance to write down the details.'

'Handy indeed. What about the other feed? The one from his house?'

'Curtis removed the camera after he strangled the woman, but I recorded the feed of him doing it. I sent it to my phone. I thought it might come in useful one day.'

'Smart work. Did it upset you, watching him strangle her?'

She sat up, and rolled across him, her hand sliding along his thigh. 'Actually, the weird thing is, it made me feel horny. Speaking of which....'

Twenty minutes later she watched him dress, smiling as he struggled into the waistcoat he'd 'borrowed' to complete his uniform. It had obviously been made for someone of far slighter build. 'How much longer?' she asked.

He knew what she meant. 'If you're right we should be out of here tomorrow. Tonight possibly. Why, are you missing me?'

'Something like that.'

She returned his farewell wave, and walked over, locking the door behind him. She wanted to take a shower, and you could never be sure who was going to walk into a hotel room.

Nash had gone through to Netherdale Headquarters to update the superintendent, leaving Anne watching the office. If something were to happen during his absence, he wanted her on hand to take action. Left alone in the CID suite, she sipped her coffee as she stared out of the window. Her thoughts were not on the passers-by in the High Street, however, but on the case – and on Nash. How much truth was there in the rumours about him, she wondered? He was certainly attractive enough, warm and kind, but there was also an expression in his eyes from time to time that awoke a disturbing response inside her.

Jack Binns was walking past the CID suite when he saw their newest officer staring vacantly out of the window. He paused. 'A word of advice, Anne,' he told her gently.

She turned and looked at Binns, her gaze only half-focused. 'What's that, Sarge?'

'If you're wondering about Mike, don't get your hopes up too high. He would never get involved with someone from within the same force. Mike may have the morals of a prowling tom cat, but that's one thing he would never do.'

'Is it that obvious?'

Binns smiled. 'Not really, it's only because I've had chance to see the way you look at him that I guessed.'

As he waited for the kettle to boil, Binns congratulated himself on having saved Robinson from unnecessary heartache. He reckoned without Anne's determination and had forgotten the old maxim, 'never say never'.

Michaels was late. How typical of him, Curtis thought. He wondered what the rigid prison regime would do to him. Perhaps, in a few years time when he eventually emerged, Michaels might have learned the art of punctuality. Curtis stood by the window, watching the snowflakes drifting lazily past until he saw the long, sleek lines of Michaels' Mercedes enter the car park. Curtis walked across to the desk and took a seat alongside it. He waited and listed to the sound of footsteps on the stairs. Joe was going to get quite a shock when he found him sitting in his office. By no means the last surprise Curtis had in mind for his partner. He smiled grimly as the door opened, issuing in the final phase of his plan.

'Curtis? Where have you been? What are you doing here? Haven't you heard the news? About Marion, I mean?'

'Of course I have; that's why I'm here. Why did you do it, Joe?'

'Do it? Do what? You don't think I killed Marion, surely?'

'What happened, Joe? Did she refuse you? Is that why you raped her and strangled her with her own tights? Or did she threaten to tell me that you'd been hitting on her? I can understand why you shot Harper if he was threatening to cut in on our business, but why did you have to kill Marion?'

'I didn't shoot Harper, and I didn't strangle Marion.' Michaels sank into the chair behind the desk. 'You must believe me, Curtis. I wouldn't do that. It's ridiculous even to suggest it.'

'Of course it is, Joe. And I would like to believe you. But I have to be honest; my belief in what my friends tell me has taken quite a knock recently. You asked me to believe that you didn't kill them, and you seemed to imply that it would be simple for me to accept your word. The question I ask myself is, would it be easier for me to believe that statement, rather than, for instance, that you had been sleeping with Marion and were plotting to have me murdered and frame Harper for it?'

Curtis paused, seeing the shock beginning to affect Michaels. 'I can see the practical advantages in the idea. You would get rid of all potential competition at a stroke, and you and Marion would be free to live the highlife together. Not only would you have the drugs money, but you could take over the club. The pair of you could do what you wanted together, without having to sneak around hoping I wouldn't find out. Oh yes, I can see great advantages for you in me being in Helmsdale Cemetery, and Harper inside Felling Prison.'

Michaels' agitation was growing with every word; which suited Curtis perfectly. 'So that was my dilemma, Joe, not knowing for certain which unlikely story to believe. So rather than trust to my own judgement, I decided to look for evidence. And what a shock it was when I found it.'

As he was speaking, Curtis strolled across to the window. The snow was much heavier now, but he was just able to make out the vivid blue and yellow of a police car parked along the road.

Michaels managed to speak. 'You did it! You did it all. You strangled Marion. You shot Harper.'

'Of course I did, Joe. But sadly for you there isn't a shred of evidence to prove it. Your DNA will prove that you had sex with Marion before she was strangled. When I raped her the night before, I used a condom, so there's no evidence against me. Harper was shot with your pistol; the one you bought in America and had smuggled into this country. It has your prints on it; no one else's. Added to that, there's the receipt from the gun shop in your drawer. By now you must be the police's prime suspect.'

Curtis saw Michaels' eyes dart to the wall safe where the gun was usually kept. He laughed. 'It isn't there, Joe. I hid it somewhere else in this room. Did you think I'd leave something as important as that to chance? You won't have time to dispose of it; the police will be here in a few minutes. However, they will have time to find the gun and match the ballistics to the bullet that killed Harper.'

Curtis glanced down at the car park, but there was still no sign of police activity. 'Speaking of time,' he continued, 'you're going to have plenty of time to reflect on the price of betrayal. In your case, I guess that will be somewhere around twenty-five years.'

'How did you find out? About me and Marion?'

Curtis laughed. 'Your after-shave, Joe. I smelt it in my

bedroom weeks ago.' He walked back to the desk. 'That was when I installed a camera and found out that you and Marion weren't just frolicking, you were planning murder.' He leaned forward and lowered his voice. 'A word of advice for you. I'd change that after-shave, if I was you. Especially in view of where you're going. Either that or have your arse sewn up.'

He returned to the window and saw the police car move off and pull to a halt behind Michaels' Mercedes. Another police car headed into the car park, together with a Range Rover. 'I have to be going now,' he glanced back at Michaels as he opened the fire escape door. Joe's face was as white as the snow outside, his hands trembled uncontrollably, and his face had developed a muscular spasm. 'I'll leave you with this thought to console you. It doesn't matter whether anyone believes you or not. The police won't – and that's what counts.'

Michaels heard the note of triumph in Curtis's voice.

'Time I wasn't here. Bye, Joe.'

Michaels remained seated. He was still seated when the police entered. He didn't reply, or even acknowledge that he'd heard DI Nash when he introduced himself and showed his warrant card and served the search warrant for the premises. He didn't reply when he was cautioned and told that he was being arrested on suspicion of the murders of Marion Waters and Scott Harper. Nor did he respond immediately when he was asked if he wished to say anything. When Nash repeated the question, Michaels looked at him, his eyes devoid of any expression. 'Would you believe me if I did?'

'Probably not,' Nash conceded, 'but it really doesn't matter whether I believe you or not. It's the twelve members of the jury you have to convince.'

Nash gestured to two of the waiting officers. 'Cuff him and keep him there while we have a quick look round.'

Anne looked in the filing cabinets and found the gun at the back of the bottom drawer hidden in an old cigar box.

'That will do for starters. Take him away. I want one of

you on the door downstairs and one of you in the corridor here.'

Two officers led Michaels from the room and headed for the stairs.

'Did you smell his after-shave?' Nash asked.

Anne nodded. 'It's the same one, isn't it?'

'Definitely, but fortunately we don't have to rely on that alone.'

'What about your doubts about whether Michaels is guilty?'

Nash shrugged. 'I'm still not one-hundred per cent sure. It all seems too easy.'

'Do you prefer a challenge?'

Nash looked at her. 'Are we still talking about work?'

She blushed a little. 'I suppose so,' she replied weakly.

'Stick around and you might find out.'

His reply confused her even further. She changed the subject. 'We're going to need to search these premises thoroughly, plus his home for evidence of the drugs. I've a specialist team waiting to conduct that search. When should I call them?'

'Do it now.'

Anne took out her mobile, pressed a short code number and waited a second. 'We're in business,' she said. She gave the address before ringing off. 'They'll be here in half an hour.'

Curtis waited outside. What was taking so long, he wondered? The snow was so heavy he'd been forced to shelter in a shop doorway. Having been inside the offices for so long, he hadn't appreciated how much the weather had deteriorated. Now, as he anticipated the final act in the drama he had created, scripted and choreographed, Curtis was able to dispel the piercing cold by thinking of the girl who awaited him at the hotel.

Meeting her had been the best thing that had happened to him in a long time. It wasn't simply the sex, although that was terrific; far better than he remembered it ever having been with Marion. It was the knowledge that she was his alone, and that now he had a woman he could trust and rely on completely. Total loyalty; that was a price worth all the effort. She lit up his whole being. Even her name had a warming ring to it.

Curtis saw the police officers emerge from the building with Michaels handcuffed to one of them. His smile broadened into a grin of triumph as Michaels was bundled into the back of a police car and driven away, the police car slipping slightly on the road surface. His revenge was complete, and total. Now it was time for him to leave. Time for him to go forward, into the future with Amber.

Curtis smiled again. He walked across the pavement, his hands buried in his pockets, the hood of the anorak pulled tight against the snow. Snow that was now falling heavier than ever. Snow that was now more than three inches deep.

He reached the edge of the pavement. Snow deadens sound. He was still smiling when the snowplough hit him. The smile on his face had faded though, by the time one of the officers examined him and told Nash that the man was dead.

When Nash had completed the formalities and Michaels was taken away to the cells, he returned to the CID suite. Robinson was waiting there, her expression gloomy. 'Something wrong?' Nash asked.

'I've had word from our specialists. No trace of drugs at any of the premises. Which means we've missed out again. Not only in nailing the drugs dealers, but also in catching the corrupt officer.'

'If there is one,' Nash commented. 'And if we got it right about Smith and Michaels being involved in the drugs trade.'

'I don't see how we're going to get anywhere now, barring a miracle.'

Nash smiled. 'It'll soon be Christmas. And my DS, Clara, is always saying that's the time for miracles.'

Next morning, it seemed their luck had changed. A phone call from the manager of the Fleece Hotel sent Nash and

Robinson hurrying across the cobbled market place.

'I've a customer who's done a runner,' the man told them. 'He checked in as Curtis Smith, and when the chambermaid went to change the linen in the room this morning, he'd vanished. Not only that, but his belongings have gone too. I immediately ran his credit card through our machine, but it seems to have been stopped for some reason.'

'I think they do that automatically when a customer dies,' Nash told him. 'Curtis Smith was killed in a road accident yesterday. Did the chambermaid clean the room?'

The manager shook his head. 'No, she came straight to me and told me. After I tried his credit card I rang you immediately.'

'We'd like to see it, please.'

Their search of Smith's room revealed nothing of interest, at least to begin with. However, the manager, who had accompanied them as far as the threshold, told them that Smith had been provided with the password for the hotel's free Wi-Fi service. This, in view of the fact that there was no computer in the room, intrigued Nash. Robinson was more disappointed by their failure to find any drugs. 'Did Smith have any visitors during his stay?' Nash asked.

The manager smiled. 'Not visitors, but when he checked in, he was accompanied by a young woman he said was his wife. A very attractive young woman, with a dark complexion,' he ended with some delicacy.

'You mean she was coloured?' Robinson asked.

'Not coloured as such,' the manager looked flustered. 'Oh dear, it's so difficult to say things like that nowadays, knowing what's right and what might cause offence. I'd say she was probably of mixed race parentage. How does that sound?'

'Politically correct, I'd say.' Nash smiled. 'When you said Smith signed the woman in as his wife, you seemed to imply that you didn't believe that to be correct, or was I imagining that?'

'No, I got the impression they weren't married. She

wasn't wearing a wedding ring, or an engagement ring. I know that isn't always a tell-tale sign, but they didn't act like a married couple. You get to be quite expert at spotting such things.'

'And you didn't see her leave?'

'No, I'm sorry. None of my staff saw her go. But she could have left at anytime during the night, I suppose.'

'When they checked in, did they have much luggage?'

The manager looked puzzled. 'The usual, a suitcase each, I believe. And of course he was carrying a laptop bag.'

'So his lady friend empties the room, and manages to carry everything out quietly in the middle of the night?' Nash raised his eyebrows.

'Oh, yes, I take your point' the manager conceded.

Nash had ordered a SOCO team, and when they did a sweep of the room, more information came to light. The leader visited Nash in the CID suite next day. 'We found minute traces of cocaine in one of the dressing table drawers,' he told them, 'but the amount is so small it could have been for personal use. And of course, there's no way of telling how long it's been there, so it may have nothing to do with Smith.'

'Did you find anything that could prove useful?'

'Useful, possibly not, but intriguing, certainly' – the forensic man grinned – 'if only to shed light on Smith's personal life. There is considerable evidence of bodily secretions on the bedding. That and quite a few hair samples, mostly pubic, from the sheets and pillowcases. Those plus a variety of fingerprints.'

'We know Smith was accompanied by a woman,' Nash agreed. 'So that's hardly surprising.'

'No, but when we tested the samples, we found there were three contributors, two male and one female. One of them was Smith, as were a lot of the fingerprints.'

'Any luck with the other prints?'

'That's where it gets really interesting. The other two sets could be in the system, but I've no way of knowing.'

'Why's that?'

'When we ran them for a match, we got an odd message on the screen. It said the information we requested was "restricted access only". Further than that, I can't help you.'

After the forensic officer left, Nash asked Anne, 'What do you make of that?'

'I've no idea. I thought it only applied with suspected terrorists. I certainly wouldn't put either Smith or Michaels in that category, or their associates, for that matter.'

'Where does that leave your enquiry?'

'At a bit of a loose end, I reckon. I'll have a word with my boss later and see what he wants me to do.'

Anne made the call as soon as she returned to the B & B where she was staying. After talking it through with her boss she sat for a long time, staring at the water colour print on the wall, without taking in the detail of the painting. Her thoughts were on Nash. She stirred, restlessly; an idea was forming in her mind. He was a free agent, just as she was. She found him really attractive and was fairly sure he was attracted to her. It had been a long time since she'd been near a man; a long time since she'd been prepared to trust someone, even on a short-term basis. Dare she take the risk? Dare she put her emotions on the line again? Or would it end in heartbreak as it had before? Don't be silly, she told herself, this isn't some great romance. All you're thinking about is two people indulging their physical needs. And apart from that, it would be great fun, wouldn't it? She conjured up a mental image of Nash, the laughter never far from his eyes, and her resistance crumbled. She packed her bag and paid for the room. She got into the car and headed for Wintersett village.

Nash was at home, reading, when he heard the doorbell chime. He went through and opened the door to the storm porch, to find Anne standing on the doorstep, one hand behind her back. He glanced past her, to see her car parked alongside his. 'I've been recalled,' she told him. 'I came to say goodbye.'

He invited her inside. As she passed him, she handed him

35

the bottle she had been concealing. 'I hope you like it, it's my favourite. One of my few vices.'

What were the others? Nash wondered as he thanked her. 'When do you leave?' he asked.

'I've already checked out of the boarding house, although to be fair, I would have done that, even had I been staying longer. It was a bit of a dump.'

She looked round the lounge. 'This is a nice room. You are lucky living out here. I bet the view's spectacular.'

'Pretty good,' Nash agreed.

'Anyway, the bottle was to say thank you. We may not have got the drugs racket sewn-up, but at least we've got two of the principals out of the way, and I've been able to give the Helmsdale force the all-clear.'

'Is that what you came all this way to tell me?' Nash was standing close enough to hear her sharp intake of breath, slight though the sound was.

She looked at him for the first time and Nash was aware of her heightened colour. 'Not quite,' she said, and her voice faltered slightly. 'I ... there was ... I wanted to say something else.'

Nash put his hand on her arm and drew her close to him. He kissed her, but after a few seconds released her. 'I'm sorry, that was taking an unfair advantage. It's just that I've wanted to do that ever since I met you. Even wearing that extremely unflattering uniform. That was the real reason I asked you to come into work in plain clothes.'

Anne smiled. 'I guessed that, or rather I hoped that might have been the reason. And you've nothing to apologize for. I wanted you to kiss me. And of course you're right. That wasn't the only reason I came here. All that wine isn't for you. It's for us to share.'

'Isn't that a bit risky? If you've to drive, I mean?'

Anne smiled. 'Mike, open the bottle please.'

They sat on the sofa, Nash's arm around her waist, sipping the wine. 'Jack Binns told me you'd never get involved with me, because I was working alongside you. Now we've finished the assignment, that changes slightly, don't you think?'

'I suppose so, if that's what you want?'

'It's all I could hope for. We're ships passing in the night, I suppose. That doesn't mean we can't enjoy the passage, does it? Does it, Mike? Does it?'

As she spoke, Anne slipped her hand towards his groin, caressing his thigh. Her eyes looked into his, smoky with desire, seeing the need in his.

In the early hours of the morning, as they were lying in drowsy content, Anne stirred. 'If that's your only hobby,' she told him with a rich chuckle, 'you're extremely good at it. In fact I'd go so far as to say....' her voice tailed off into silence.

'What is it? What have you thought of?'

'Hobbies,' she repeated the word, but her voice made it clear her thoughts were far away. Nash waited. After a moment she sat upright, the duvet falling away to reveal her shapely breasts. He resisted the temptation to caress them.

Anne turned to him. 'Would you say Curtis Smith was a keen gardener?'

Nash thought for a moment. 'Not especially. The garden at his house was neat enough, but nothing special, although at this time of the year, it's not easy to tell.'

'That's exactly what I thought. However, when I first interviewed Mrs Brown, his next-door neighbour, I asked her who else had seen the prowler. She told me it was Smith who had seen him first. I asked how reliable Smith was, and she said he was extremely reliable. She knew that because he rented her greenhouse. Apparently, her late husband had been a very keen gardener and he got a specialist company in to build a huge luxury greenhouse with sophisticated heating system which was installed at the bottom of their massive back garden. Now, why do you think Smith might have wanted the use of that greenhouse?'

'Because by the sound of it, that would be an ideal place to grow cannabis plants.'

'Exactly, and that means my work here hasn't finished

after all.'

'But you've checked out of your boarding house.'

'I know. So that means I'll need somewhere to stay. Got any ideas?'

'Oh yes.' Nash pulled her close to him and began to kiss her. His voice was muffled by her hair as he whispered, 'My idea is that if we're going to continue working together, we ought to start liaising right now.'

Part Two

Amber

It was one of those mornings. The heavy overnight snow made the barber wonder why he'd bothered opening up. After an hour, during which the shop bell didn't ring once, he was beginning to think it would have been better had he stayed in bed.

He'd passed part of the time clearing snow from the pavement in front of the shop and sprinkling grit salt to avoid pedestrians injuring themselves. During this task, he paused to exchange a few words of commiseration with the greengrocer next door, who was also bemoaning the futility of opening that day.

All well and good he thought, after the greengrocer went back inside, but there was a good chance that someone would require vegetables before the day was out. Far less likely, that anyone would venture forth specifically for a haircut. Not for the first time, he debated the wisdom of his chosen occupation. When he took over the lease on the shop and kitted the premises out soon after moving to Helmsdale, he named it Damian's. For him to open up a barber's shop using his surname, Todd, would, he knew invite the sort of humour the locals had made their speciality.

Despite his precaution, word soon got out, and before he's been in business six months, the shop became known locally as Sweeney's. Curiously, this had a beneficial effect on trade rather than otherwise, except on mornings such as this.

Damian had read all the papers provided for the benefit of waiting customers and was attempting the crossword when the tinkling of the shop bell surprised him. He looked up and greeted the client with a welcoming smile. He didn't recognize the young man, but was already rehearsing some topics of conversation as he placed the smock around the customer's shoulders. The customer's instructions, however, rendered Damian speechless and the haircut was completed in silence. Long after the man had paid him and left the shop, Damian, with no further clients to engage his attention, pondered the possible reason for the client's request to have his hair cut in a style that suggested he had just been released from prison.

The proprietor of Helm Autos; company motto 'The finest quality cars in the dale at truly affordable prices' emblazoned above the showroom window, stared gloomily at the deserted street outside. He was also pondering the advisability of opening that morning. The month of December was traditionally the worst part of the year for car sales, with customers as rare as – well, flies in December. Added to the normal dearth of sales were the less than encouraging weather and the effects of the recession. If he hadn't opened he wouldn't have incurred the overheads of heating and lighting. On the other hand, he wouldn't have escaped the nagging he would undoubtedly have had to suffer at home.

The problem was his wife would have been certain to ask about a subject that was particularly sore at the moment. That subject was money – or more correctly, the lack of it. She was planning a shopping expedition for the coming weekend; her objective being to buy the children's Christmas presents. Barring a miracle, when she asked him for the money to buy these, his answer would have to be no. He baulked at having to explain to her, or to the children, that the stark choice was between their presents and a Christmas dinner. Delivering that message was going to make him about as unpopular as a bad smell in a crowded room.

When the postman had arrived, a couple of hours earlier, he had brought a bank statement that heightened his dilemma and deepened his gloom.

The car dealer looked at the stock inside the showroom with an air of repressed desperation. If all else failed, as seemed increasingly likely, he could always send a couple of vehicles to the auction. He winced at the idea. At this time of the year they would fetch prices that were a long way short of what they stood on his books. Taking a loss of that size went against the grain, but the amount raised would ease his cash flow until the New Year, which would hopefully bring better trading conditions. It might also prevent him from being locked out of his own home, he thought ruefully.

The question was which cars to send? Obviously they would have to be the ones that commanded the best prices; or those that would incur the smallest loss. As he was pondering the issue, the showroom door opened. He looked across at the man who had entered and was now inspecting the half dozen vehicles on display. The dealer began one of the trade's favourite games, guessing which of the cars had attracted the punter's interest. The man was possibly in his early-thirties, clean-shaven and with extremely short hair. He was neatly dressed, but nothing about him signalled affluence. Not the 'star buy', then, more likely the Kia, the Hyundai or possibly even the Citroen.

To his surprise, the customer headed straight for the middle of the showroom. There, the top of the range, most expensive model on show had been placed under the group of spotlights that made the metallic paintwork glisten and sparkle, enhancing the magical effect of the sleek lines created by the BMW design team. Given the lack of obvious wealth, this man was probably only a looker, the dealer deduced. Nevertheless, talking to him would stave off the boredom and drive away the gloom for a short while. He got up from behind the sales desk in the corner of the room and walked over to the potential customer, who had opened the driver's door and was now seated behind the steering wheel. As he approached the car, he was rehearsing his sales patter, but to his surprise, the punter took matters out of his hands by greeting him with the words, 'How much for a cash sale, with no part-exchange?'

The dealer thought quickly, a necessary attribute in his job. He had marked the price of the BMW up to give him a margin of well over a thousand pounds. If he knocked that down by half, he would still wipe out his overdraft, be able to give his wife enough to buy the kids' presents and have sufficient left over for the housekeeping she would need to provide Christmas dinner. Best not to appear too keen though; it was easy to scare customers away by over eagerness. 'Well, I don't know....'he began, seemingly considering the matter carefully. 'I had to pay over the odds to get it. This model is in great demand. Still, for a cash sale, with no part-ex, I suppose I could come down a bit. How about if I was to knock four-hundred off the price on the screen?'

If the worst came to the worst, he would have been prepared to forego all his profit, even take a small loss, although that went against the grain for the BMW, but to his astonishment, the customer said, 'That seems fair enough. If you want to prepare the paperwork now, I'll bring you a bankers draft when I collect the car. Can you have it ready for me tomorrow?'

'I could, although it would be better the following day. I ought to have it serviced first.'

'Don't worry about that. I need the car as soon as possible. I can always bring it back after Christmas for the service.'

'OK, let's get the paperwork sorted out, then.'

As he wrote the customer's details down, it was all the dealer could do to stop his hand from trembling. A bankers draft was as good as cash. Once issued, it could not be revoked. And with the funds from the sale he could do all he needed and still have sufficient left to buy his wife the necklace she had admired in the jeweller's window the previous week. The season looked as if it was going to be festive after all.

The car that pulled up was noticeable, in that it was a model rarely seen on the Westlea estate. There were BMWs around, true enough, but latest model, Series 7s with all the accessories, were way out of the reach of the residents. The sole occupant emerged from the car and carefully locked it before setting off down the crumbling concrete path towards a block containing four flats. Whatever the architect had in mind had long since been corrupted by years of neglect and abuse from a wide variety of residents, none of whom took the slightest pride in the state of their surroundings.

The BMW driver paused in the entrance hall, sniffing with distaste the aroma that assailed his nostrils. Obviously one or more of the residents, their visitors, or possibly some stray cats and dogs, of which there were a large number around the estate, had not been able to contain their need to urinate until they were in a more suitable location.

He examined the faded, scrawled surnames on the doors to the two ground floor flats and seeing the one he wanted, searched in vain for a doorbell. Instead, he knocked loudly on the cracked and peeling paintwork of the upper panel. Getting no response, he tried again, this time longer and harder. This produced two results, a slight bruising to the knuckles on his right hand, accompanied by a small shower of paint flakes that fluttered to the ground.

Abandoning the direct approach, the visitor took a small knife from a sheath on his belt and used the handle to tap loudly and continuously on the door, watching with interest as more paint fell away. After several minutes, he heard the sound of bolts being drawn back, and a key turned. The door opened fractionally, only sufficiently for one eye to peer suspiciously out at the disturber of the peace. 'Yes?'

As a greeting, it was less than effusive, but the visitor was not deterred. 'Are you Jared?' he asked the owner of the eye.

'Who the fuck are you?' There was little, if any dilution in the level of suspicion.

'My name's Ryan. I've been sent because of what's happened to Joe. I take it you have heard about Joe Michaels?'

The eye neither admitted nor denied knowledge of Michaels, or what had happened to him. 'Sent? Who sent you?'

'The Albanians. I work for them.'

If the door opened wider on receipt of this information, the change was too infinitesimal to be noticed. 'If you do work for them, you'll know what happens next,' the eye suggested.

'If you mean the password, which I take it you do, the answer is, Tirana.'

Real progress, the man who had introduced himself as Ryan thought, as the door swung open a further six inches, allowing the rest of the eye's face to appear. 'That it, then?' Jared, if it truly was Jared, asked.

Ryan smiled. 'Of course not, and I admire your security. Now you have to give me the correct reply.'

'Scanderbeg,' Jared muttered, so quietly that Ryan had to ask him to repeat it. 'Good, now we've got that out of the way.'

'What do they want?' Jared asked.

'Are you going to let me inside, or do I stand here and discuss the instructions I have for you so the rest of the estate can hear?'

Whether Ryan's sarcasm was noted or went over Jared's head, his face still registered no emotion other than the level of suspicion and hostility as when he'd first opened the door. Whatever his feelings, he allowed Ryan to pass into the dingy hallway before slamming the door, locking it and sliding the bolts home. Ryan inspected his surroundings swiftly before turning back to look at his reluctant host. His eyes widened slightly at the sight of the pistol in the man's right hand, but he made no comment. Obviously, complete trust had not yet been achieved. 'That way.' Jared gestured with the pistol.

Ryan went through into the lounge which smelt faintly of cooked cabbage, and far more strongly of cannabis. The source of the latter was undoubtedly the man slumped in one of the armchairs watching a dreary daytime TV show. A roll-up smouldered between the fingers of one hand, but Ryan guessed that little of the content had originated in the tobacco fields of Virginia. 'You must be Greg.' He smiled pleasantly at the man.

'Who the fuck are you?'

Ryan wondered if this was the traditional greeting on the estate. Before he could reply, Jared, who seemed to have appointed himself as the visitor's spokesman, said, 'Told me his name's Ryan. Reckons the Albanians have sent him 'cos of what happened to Joe.'

'How do we know he's who he says he is?'

'Well we can't ask Joe, and we can't ask the Albanians, but he's got the passwords off. Thought I'd best get him inside before we ask him any other questions. Don't want any busybodies overhearing us, especially if we've to persuade him.'

That wasn't quite how Ryan remembered the doorstep conversation, but he let it ride. 'What else do you need to know?' he asked.

'Why the Albanians sent you. That'll do for starters.'

'Who else is there to send? Joe's been unavoidably detained, and Curtis can't talk to you anymore – except maybe via an Ouija board. I've been sent to run things for the time being.'

'Why do we need you? What if Joe gets off?'

'You think that's likely? Go buy a lottery ticket for Saturday night's draw. You'll have more chance of winning than Joe has of avoiding a life stretch. The message I've got for you is that from now on you take orders from me. And when I say "now" I mean immediately, which includes Sunday.'

Ryan saw the startled glance exchanged between Joe's henchmen and knew that the statement and the inferred knowledge of their plans had gone a long way to convincing them that he was genuine. He pressed home his advantage. 'Yes, I know all about Sunday. Did you think they'd send me here with only half a tale? I know the time, the place and the delivery method. Tell me, have you bought the rucksack yet?'

His final sentence convinced them, as Ryan knew it

would. 'I take it from the silence the answer's no? Not to worry, there will be plenty of time for that. When you do, remember to put something inside to weigh it down. If it's too light, someone might notice. There must be absolutely nothing to arouse suspicion. The other thing is, make sure you're wearing suitable clothing. Remember, we're supposed to be on a hiking expedition. Yes' – he interpreted Jared's look of surprise – 'I shall be coming with you. I've been given specific instructions to that effect. They want me to ensure everything runs smoothly. There have been enough cock-ups recently without you adding to them. I hardly need remind you both of the value of the gear we're going to collect, do I? Or to explain in detail what would happen to the pair of you should that consignment fall into the wrong hands? The Albanians aren't exactly renowned for their forgiving nature, believe me.

'What's more, we'll be staying out overnight at a hostel. That way, if anyone did get to hear of the transaction, they'd be looking for someone coming into Helmsdale on Sunday. When we come back on Monday, the heat will be off. Then you can go ahead with distribution and collecting the money. One more thing, what about transport? How were you proposing to get to the rendezvous?'

After he'd spoken, Ryan wondered if 'rendezvous' was within their vocabulary, but Greg's reply reassured him. 'We got a motor.'

'Yes, I know that, I've seen it outside – and heard it. Sorry, that's out of the question. No way are you using that.'

'Why not?' Jared was hurt. The car was his pride and joy. A bit on the flashy side, but so what? Perfect for the estate – and for pulling birds.

'It's way too conspicuous for one thing. Not only that, it would be totally wrong for the place we're going. The idea is to go unnoticed, not to draw attention to ourselves. Something far more sedate. A recent model estate car, perhaps, maybe one a bit long in the tooth. Yes, old but reliable, that would be perfect. I'll see what I can find.'

Ryan left the flat and walked across the small grassed

area to his car. Before getting into the BMW, he took out his mobile and pressed a short code. The call was answered instantly. 'How's it going?' he asked.

He listened for a few seconds, watching the windows of the flat out of his eye corner. 'Yes,' he said in reply to a question, 'I've just left them. They're staring at me out of the window even as I speak. Yes, they swallowed it hook, line and sinker. They probably think this is me phoning the Albanians to report. Have you found what you were looking for?'

He grinned at the torrent of obscenities that served as a reply to his question. 'Well, you know the saying, no pain, no gain,' he commented provocatively. 'Yes, I'm setting off now.' He ended the call and got into his car.

Had he the chance to overhear the conversation inside the flat, Ryan would have congratulated himself on the accuracy of his guesswork. 'He's on his mobile,' Greg reported. 'Reckon he's talking to the Albanians?'

Jared joined him at the window. 'Maybe, maybe not. He said he was going to sort out a set of wheels for Sunday. He might be on with that. I still don't trust him.'

'There's no way of checking,' Greg pointed out. 'We don't know how to contact the Albanians. Joe took care of all that. And we sure as hell can't contact Joe where he is. Besides which, this Ryan bloke had all the info'. Not only the passwords and that, but the details about Sunday. No way he could have got them if he wasn't right.'

'Yes, I suppose so,' Jared agreed. Any misgivings he still felt were more or less placated by Greg's argument. More or less, but not completely banished.

Mrs Brown, Curtis Smith's next door neighbour, was in talkative mood when the police descended on her house. Nash and Robinson were accompanied by a team of officers. The old lady was taken aback at first by their request to search her greenhouse, but when Nash explained that they were looking for cannabis plants they thought Smith might have been growing there, together with other evidence of drugs, she readily agreed. Anne quelled the widow's fears by explaining that they didn't suspect her of any wrongdoing, her eyes sparkled with repressed excitement.

Leaving the team to carry out the search, Nash and the DIU officer remained in Mrs Brown's kitchen, taking her statement and chatting to her as she made mugs of coffee for all her unexpected visitors. An officer, summoned by Robinson to collect their tray of drinks on which Mrs Brown had placed a plate of biscuits, reported that they had found a large quantity of suspect plants and were bagging them for disposal. When he had returned to the garden, Mrs Brown shook her head sorrowfully. 'I thought they were such a quiet, respectable couple. I never imagined they would get involved in anything like this.'

'That's why Smith remained undetected for so long,' Nash told her. 'A lot of the people we deal with give themselves away in the first instance by their lifestyle. Smith was a bit cleverer than most.'

'It didn't help him in the end, though,' Anne commented. 'Even if he hadn't been killed, there's no doubt he would have been in serious trouble.'

'It only shows, you should never take anyone at face value. One hears such terrible things about conmen, people who come to your door pretending to be all sorts of officials, and once you let them in they steal things and know all about you. That's why I never open my door to anyone I don't know. I wonder who will move into the house next door. Really, I'm quite upset at the thought of it. I believed Mr Smith was nice, and look what a rogue he turned out to be.'

It was over an hour before the team finished their work. As his colleagues removed a collection of black bin liners containing the confiscated plants to the van, their leader returned the tray, now devoid of biscuits to Mrs Brown, thanking her for her hospitality. 'We've seized three dozen mature plants and a tray of seedlings,' he reported to Nash and Robinson.'

'Excellent, was there anything else of interest?'

The officer paused before answering Nash. 'No other

drugs or indication that there had been any, if that's what you're referring to. There was only one other potential piece of evidence, but whether it is of any significance or not, I've no idea.'

'What might that be?'

'This.' He held up a clear plastic evidence bag, which Nash could see contained a small oblong piece of paper. 'What is it?' Robinson asked.

'It's a till receipt from a restaurant. Quite an expensive restaurant too, judging by the prices. Of course,' he turned and smiled at the householder, 'it could belong to Mrs Brown, and have absolutely nothing to do with Curtis Smith.'

Mrs Brown shook her head; her denial emphatic. 'I haven't been out for a meal since before my husband died, four years ago. Even if I had someone to go with, I certainly couldn't justify all that expense, not on my pension.'

'We'll not inconvenience you any further, Mrs Brown.' They thanked her for the coffee and left.

'Is the restaurant name on the receipt?' Nash asked as they headed down the path. 'That might help determine if it was Smith's.'

The officer turned the bag over and peered at the receipt. 'The Bridge Inn, Black Fell Head,' he read aloud.

Nash whistled. 'That's certainly expensive, and well off the beaten track to put it mildly.'

'Where is this place, Black Fell Head,' Anne asked. 'I've never heard of it?'

'Neither have I,' the officer agreed, 'and I thought I knew the area pretty well.'

'Black Fell Head is on the high moors, the far side of Stark Ghyll from here. It's about as far up the dale as you can get without crossing into Cumbria. The Bridge Inn was a shooting lodge that was once the property of the Slingsby-Darrow family. Lord Slingsby-Darrow, the present earl's father, sold it off about fifty years ago to help meet estate duty. The grandfather, old "Slings and Arrows" as he was nicknamed, used to entertain guests for shooting weekends before the war. Fellow aristocrats, minor royalty, all sorts of people stayed there. The rumour is that a number of ladies who were not too particular in their social habits were also brought along for the occasion,' Nash added.

'After the sale, the property was converted into a country hotel, with a restaurant and bars. During the 1970s, I believe. The hotel is very popular with honeymooners, and the restaurant has a terrific reputation. According to what I hear, they charge accordingly. The bar is also a favourite resting place for hikers doing the coast-to-coast walk, and climbers who tackle Black Fell and Stark Ghyll. They hold an annual fell race that starts and finishes in the hotel car park, and that attracts huge crowds.'

'It doesn't sound like the sort of place frequented by someone like Curtis Smith,' Anne suggested.

'No,' Nash agreed. 'In fact I'd say it was the least likely venue for him to choose for a social jaunt. Which makes me wonder if that receipt actually was his.' He turned to the officer. 'Can you get that to forensics for me please; get it checked for fingerprints. And see if the amount tallies with any of his credit cards. By the way, is there a date on it?'

'Yes, it was August 5th of this year.'

'That was a Sunday,' Anne told them.

'How do you know that?'

'That's my birthday.'

On the way back to the station, Anne looked across at Nash. 'Do you think that receipt has any bearing on what we're investigating?'

'I'm not sure. Even if it is significant, we've no idea who or what we should be looking for. And I have to say, it does seem remarkably unlikely, given what I know of the Bridge Inn.'

Saturday morning was bright, clear and cold. The snow the weathermen had predicted would return had not materialized. Alex Osman, the manager of the Bridge Inn looked ruefully out from the reception area at the cloudless blue sky. He wondered if it was possible to sue the Met

Office for loss of trade. Their gloomy prognostications and severe weather warnings for the area had acted as an effective deterrent to potential residents and diners alike. This, despite the fact that by mid-morning the dale was flooded in sunlight that dispelled the biting cold of the overnight frost.

All but one of their room reservations had cancelled; the only bright note being a late booking his assistant had taken the previous day for a double room. It was much the same with the restaurant. In the period leading up to Christmas, there should have been a full complement of diners for both Saturday night dinner and the ever popular Sunday lunch carvery. The sheet for both meals was liberally covered with crossed out names, leaving only a handful of covers that would barely meet their overheads. That was the penalty they paid for being in so inaccessible a location, and one that was only served by winding moorland roads.

The remote situation of the inn, and the magnificent scenery close by were a great attraction when the weather was good, but what brought visitors in huge numbers when conditions were good, also caused them to shun the area when adverse weather threatened.

His mood lightened marginally as he watched a Range Rover pull into the car park. The occupants got out, stretching from the journey, before removing their cases from the boot and heading to the inn door. This would be the late reservation, the manager guessed.

He saw the man was carrying both bags. Despite this, he courteously held the door open for the woman. Not married, then, the manager reflected cynically. He handed the registration card to the man, whose face seemed vaguely familiar, but from where, he couldn't be certain.

As the couple followed his directions to the stairs leading to the first floor, the manager wondered what their relationship was. Part of the relationship, he corrected himself with a private smile; he was fairly certain he could guess the main reason for them being at the inn. Were they the boss with his secretary, he wondered? Or a married couple, but not married to each other? Or was this the start of a new relationship? The man looked like a professional. A doctor, perhaps, or a lawyer? An accountant, even, or a successful businessman? The car and the smart attire were the best clues. If he'd guessed all morning, the manager might not have got the right answer. That was mainly because, in his mind, police officers did not own expensive cars such as a Range Rover.

Upstairs, Nash was seated on the edge of the bed, watching Anne as she changed into clothing more suitable for their promised walk. 'We'll go up Black Fell,' Nash told her. 'There's an easy walking route from this side. The other side, you need climbing gear. It's a stiff climb, but well worth it when you reach the summit. The view from there is spectacular.'

'Anne was standing close to the window. 'It's not a bad view from here.' She pointed to the dale, which stretched out from the inn all the way down to Helmsdale, scarcely visible in the far distance.

'I couldn't agree more.'

Something in the way Nash said it made Anne turned to look at him. He was staring at her, in undisguised admiration. Anne was clad in only bra and pants. It was clear where his attention was concentrated. She blushed, but told him severely, 'Are we going for this walk, or just talking about it? If you don't hurry up and get changed we'll miss the daylight.'

The climb took over two hours. When they reached the summit, Anne gazed with admiration at the stupendous countryside revealed by her unique viewpoint. Even now, in the depth of winter, when the fields and hedgerows were blanketed in white, the scene was breathtaking. She took in the places where the low winter sun had not touched and woods that glistened with the silver touch of frost. 'This view is fantastic,' she exclaimed.

'I told you it would be,' Nash's reply was muffled, indistinct.

Anne tore her gaze from the beauty before her with an effort and glanced back at her companion. Rather than join in her admiration of the wooded fells, the river meandering along the basin and the pretty villages that were strewn along the dale, Nash was staring back the way they had come, his hands cupped to his face.

Anne walked back the few yards that separated them. 'What can you see?' she asked.

He lowered his binoculars. 'Not much, to be honest. The pub's very quiet. There are no vehicles in the car park except ours and a van. Delivering fresh vegetables, by the look of it. There's no activity in the surrounding area either.'

'Isn't that odd? I thought at this time of the year the hillsides would be bristling with gunmen intent on murdering game birds?'

Nash smiled at Anne's interpretation of the rural life, but couldn't resist teasing her. 'Spoken like a real townie,' he mocked. 'The grouse shooting season ends on December 10th and we're too high up for pheasant. They prefer it down there.' He gestured towards the lower end of the dale. 'Go down there and it will be real carnage.'

'I didn't know I was accompanying an expert.' Anne looked towards the inn once more. 'This all seems so wrong. Even in my wildest imagination I couldn't picture a drugs racket being run from here. Not only because the area is so lovely, but it's so out of the way. It's the last place anyone would choose to set up an operation such as the one we're investigating.'

'You think we're wasting our time on a wild goose chase?'

'I reckon so, what do you think?'

Nash lifted the binoculars once more and swept the area. Anne had a point, he conceded. 'Do you want me to cancel tonight's booking? I can make the excuse that we're worried the weather might trap us here. The forecast last night was pretty grim. I feel sure that manager chap will understand.'

'I'm not sure. Now we know that receipt was paid by Curtis Smith, there had to be a reason for him coming out here.'

'How about this? Unless you have a better idea, why don't we see it through? Spend tonight here, go for an early walk before breakfast and then set off back late morning?'

'OK, I guess if we're going to waste a weekend, we might as well spend it together in a beautiful place like this.'

'I think as backhanded compliments go, that's one of the best I've had.'

'It wasn't meant that way,' Anne protested. 'I'd better let my boss know what we're doing though.'

'Pardon?'

Anne blushed. 'I meant tell him we're staying here to check the drugs thing out. I won't tell him we're sharing a room.'

'You'll have to use the phone in the hotel room. No chance of getting a mobile signal out here.'

However, when she tried, Anne got no response. 'I'm not going to leave a voicemail message,' she told Nash. 'I'll try him again in the morning.'

'What's he like; this boss of yours?'

Anne shrugged. 'Macmillan? He's all right, I suppose. I took the job because of the work, not my colleagues. Maybe if I'd met Superintendent Macmillan beforehand I wouldn't have been quite so keen, but he has a good reputation for getting results.'

'I suppose that's where I'm lucky. The officers in Helmsdale get along well together. Possibly that's more important in a small force like ours than a big organization like DIU.'

Nash watched Anne, who was staring out of the window as the short winter afternoon ended in a fiery red sunset. He walked over and stood behind her, putting his arms round her, his hands sliding gently towards her breasts. 'There's a couple of hours before they start serving dinner,' he whispered. 'What do you suggest we do until then?'

Next morning, after going for a more leisurely stroll around the lanes close to the inn, they returned in time for Anne to phone her boss again. Nash listened to the conversation with only marginal interest, his attention focused on Anne. He wondered what it was that drove her fierce ambition. Once, he had been like that, until, homesick for his native county and weary of the high pressure created by working in the Met, he had returned home. When she finished the call, they began packing their overnight bags, taking their time; both feeling a strange reluctance to bring the weekend to a close. They checked out of the room and once Nash had settled the bill, left their cases in reception and went through to test the inn's breakfast menu.

The waiter eyed the couple with approval as he watched them. With few diners, he had ample leisure to take in those who had braved the weather. The man and woman were sitting close together, their attention completely on each other. It had been exactly the same at dinner the previous night. Although they had chosen their meals carefully from the wide variety on the menu, and had done justice to the food put before them, it was obvious their attention was not wholly on what they were eating. They had pulled their chairs close and were conversing in little more than a whisper; words that were clearly designed for themselves alone. The waiter sighed, such romantic behaviour appealed to his warm-blooded Mediterranean nature. He would have been more than a little surprised at the mundane content of their conversation, or how little it had to do with romance.

'If there is anything untoward going on here, it's far too well concealed for me to spot it,' Nash admitted. 'If I had to design a set for a film about an English country hotel, its staff and clientele, I couldn't have come up with anything better than this.'

'I agree. Today has been a waste of time. As was last night.'

'Oh, I don't know. Last night did have its good points, as I remember.'

Anne slapped him affectionately on the back of the hand. 'That wasn't what I was referring to, as you know very well. Stop fishing for compliments.'

They lingered over their coffee in the lounge, not because of any great hopes that they would spot some illegal activity, but because neither of them was keen for their idyll to end. Eventually, they bowed to the inevitable march of time. It was almost lunchtime when they collected their cases from reception and thanked the manager. The weather was becoming overcast as they drove out of the car park. Nash had switched the headlights on, and they soon noticed one or two snowflakes drifting lazily across the beam.

Had they left ten minutes later, they would have witnessed the arrival of an estate car containing three occupants. What the outcome would have been had that happened is a matter for speculation, but events would certainly have taken a very different course.

As they drove carefully, slowly back down the dale towards Wintersett and Nash's home, Anne reflected on the weekend, and what had preceded it. She had accepted the assignment as just another posting, little knowing what was in store for her. An intimate relationship with a colleague from another force had been the last thing on her mind. Her time with Mike had been exciting. His company brought a stimulation to her she couldn't have imagined. She was aware of the dangers; aware that a long-term relationship was out of the question, but for the moment, none of that mattered. For the moment, all she cared about was extracting every ounce of pleasure from being with him, holding him, making love to him. How she would cope when it ended, that was something she wasn't prepared to dwell on. This feeling of joy was something she had not experienced for a long time. Only once before, in fact, and that time it had ended in sadness, sadness, anger and recrimination. That wouldn't happen with Mike. Of that, Anne was sure, and the thought comforted her. Tonight would be their last night together. Forget tomorrow, Anne was determined this night would be one that would light up their memories for a long time to come.

Alex Osman eyed the trio of new arrivals warily. He

watched them crossing the car park and had half a mind to request they go elsewhere. The fact that the bar contained only a few walkers caused him to rethink, but even as they entered the pub, he wondered about them, and whether he was doing the right thing. They were dressed right enough, warm outdoor clothing, hiking boots, all the correct equipment right down to the backpacks, but something about them didn't ring true. If they were there on a walking holiday, he'd have to rethink his ideas about summing people up.

Their appearance suggested that they'd be more at home on an inner city council estate than out here on the moors. That was certainly the case with two of them, at least. They looked as if they'd fit in well on Helmsdale's Westlea estate, or the Carthill in Netherdale. The third member of the party was more the right type for the inn, and for a hiking trip, but going by the company he was keeping you couldn't be sure. He'd been driving the car when they pulled into the car park. Even the car looked out of place amongst the sleek, well polished sporty models preferred by his usual customers partaking of the Sunday lunch in the renowned carvery at the Bridge Inn. The manager wasn't at all surprised when they went into the bar rather than heading for the dining room, and it took some effort to hide his relief.

Their order, two pints of cider and an orange juice came as no surprise either. The manager noticed one of the newcomers place his rucksack at the base of the coat stand outside the door leading to the bar, where several similar ones were already in position.

As the afternoon passed, the two passengers continued to drink, whilst the third, who had stuck to orange juice throughout, ordered a sandwich, which he ate whilst studying the literature placed in a rack by the bar for the benefit of customers. The two drinkers conversed together in low voices, barely above a whisper, as if they were used to not wanting the gist of their discussion overheard. The driver, by contrast, rarely spoke to, or listened into the others' talk. It was late afternoon before they finished drinking. The two passengers went to the gents, whilst the driver fiddled with his mobile phone. As soon as the drinkers re-emerged the trio left the country inn. The manager also watched carefully as one of them collected his rucksack from the coat stand. He was very keen to ensure the dubious guest only took one.

'Why do we have to go in for the rigmarole? Why not head straight back home?' Jared asked as they left the car park.

'We could do that,' Ryan agreed, 'but you know damned well the police will be waiting for us. That was the information we were given. It's only today that we're in danger. Tomorrow the coast will be clear. All we have to do is stay out of sight until then and we'll be fine.'

'How do you know?' Jared was still suspicious.

'Because the Albanians told me, and they've got contacts in the police. High up in the police. In the DIU.' Ryan felt safe in telling the other two this. They wouldn't be able to repeat it.

Greg stared out of the window at the bleak expanse of moorland stretching to the summit of a peak on the far horizon. 'We'll be safe, you reckon? Unless we die of cold out here, you mean. We must be mad to even go ahead with the idea.'

Ryan acknowledged that Greg had a point, but didn't say so. Better to concentrate on what they were carrying. 'Think about the reward, it will be worth the discomfort of a night in a hostel,' he pointed out.

The other two considered what he'd said. Thought of the money they would get for what they were carrying silenced them, which suited their companion ideally. He concentrated on driving. The snow that was now falling quite heavily was making his job more difficult by the minute. By the time they'd reached the middle of the moor, his two companions had been asleep for almost half an hour, having nodded off soon after their conversation on leaving the pub car park. He noticed that they had woken up as they were reaching the most remote part of the wilderness. He felt the need of conversation; even though theirs was usually less than enthralling. As he was doing all the work, it was the least they could do.

'Bloody hell.' Greg listened to the rough note of the engine. 'Will we make it to that hostel; do you think? Have we got far to go?'

'Another twenty miles,' Ryan told him. 'We should be OK as long as this old banger holds out, and the weather doesn't deteriorate.' As he spoke, he remembered the forecast he'd heard that morning, giving warnings of heavy snowfall in the area.

'Why did we have to use this crate? Why not that Beamer of yours?' Jared asked him.

'I told you, the police will be watching for cars like that.' Ryan paused before continuing, 'Did you read the brochure?'

'What brochure?' Greg was still part comatose. Admittedly, Ryan thought, with Greg it wasn't always easy to spot the difference. In fact to be honest, it was never easy.

'The one in the pub,' he explained patiently. 'It was in amongst all those other flyers on the end of the bar. It was all about this area. I thought it might prove useful if anyone asked questions, seeing we're supposed to be on a hiking trip. But I expect the pair of you were too busy drinking to read anything.'

Jared winced at the sarcasm, wondering again why they'd been saddled with Ryan. He wasn't one of them, and had been foisted on them at the last minute. Both he and Greg had been deeply suspicious when Ryan had turned up out of the blue and explained what they were going to do, but he had all the right credentials and knew all the right people. In the end they'd agreed to go along with the scheme, albeit reluctantly. Maybe if they'd known at the outset what was involved it would have been a different story.

'What brochure are you on about?' Greg stirred himself to ask.

'It was advertising local attractions, and telling some of the stories about things that had happened round here. Did you know one of the Civil War battles was fought right where that pub now stands?'

'There are some local attractions?' Jared gestured to the bleak countryside. 'You could have fooled me.'

'Yes, there are some, believe it or not.'

'I've known a few pubs that have battles outside them on a regular basis,' Greg added. 'Usually late on Saturday night.'

'I feel sure you do. The story that interested me was about the ghost of Ghyll Head Moor.'

'What ghost?' Jared asked. His tone was soporific, and it was obvious that he too was only notionally conscious.

'A couple of centuries ago a trio of lads were crossing the moor one snowy night after a heavy drinking session. They came across a young gypsy girl who belonged to a local encampment. All three raped and sodomized the girl; but when they sobered up and realized what they'd done they murdered her and hid her body to get rid of the evidence. The story is that they never made it off the moor and perished in a sudden blizzard. However, it doesn't end there, because every so often her avenging ghost returns and claims a victim; always a young bloke who vanishes, never to be seen again. Apparently, there have been half a dozen unexplained disappearances over the years.'

'Every moor has a ghost story like that.' Greg belched loudly. Greg had but few charms; and those were kept hidden; very well hidden at that. He was also a cynic. The afternoon was cold, and although the threatened heavy snow hadn't arrived, there were ominous banks of cloud forming in the distance and only occasional snowflakes dancing in the headlamps. Inside the car, however, it was warm and comfortable, proof that at least the heating system was operating efficiently, even though the engine did sound ropy. 'I bet the landlord sat up one night and made these stories up in order to make his pub seem more interesting.' Ryan heard the derisive tone in Greg's voice. He could do a mean sneer when he tried, could Greg.

'There were references to local history books and articles

in the brochure,' Ryan protested.

'Well I don't believe a fucking word of it,' Greg muttered. 'It sounds like an episode from that TV programme they used to show on one of the satellite channels. Tales of the something or other. I'll be glad when we reach that hostel. Not because of any gippos or ghosts or even ghostly gippos, but I don't fancy being stranded out here in this dead-and-alive hole in a snowstorm.'

Jared shuddered. 'Don't even think it. Tempting fate, that's what you're doing.'

It soon seemed as if Jared was right. The weather changes quickly on the moors; particularly in winter. Almost as soon as the sun dipped below the horizon the bank of cloud that had appeared, obliterated the remaining brightness as it filled the darkening sky, driven by a strong north-easterly wind. Soon it was snowing; snow that flickered horizontally across the car's headlights in an ever thickening curtain. Ryan swung the car to the left at a fork in the road, a junction that was without signposts, glancing in his rear-view mirror as he did so, and observing with satisfaction that both his passengers were fast asleep once more. After they had travelled a couple of miles Ryan seemed to realize that he had taken the wrong turning, and pulled to a halt alongside a gate that marked a break in the dry stone wall alongside the narrow ribbon of tarmac that was fast being obliterated in a carpet of white.

'Damn!' he exclaimed, loudly enough for the occupants of the back seat to stir.

'What is it?'

'I reckon I should have taken the other road at that last junction. There was no sign, and now I think we're lost.'

'Oh, that's bloody brilliant. That's all we need. Lost in a fucking snowstorm in an old banger that could conk out any minute,' Jared complained in a whining tone of voice that was beginning to get on Ryan's nerves.

'Well, you two are no fucking help. All you've done to contribute to the day is get pissed and fall asleep. If I didn't need you I'd turf the pair of you out right now.'

Even Greg was silent after that. Ryan started to drive again, inching slowly forward as he looked for a place to turn round. After a few minutes, the dry stone wall ended, and the slight protection it provided against the driving snow went with it.

'Can't we turn back now?' Greg asked.

'We should have turned in that gateway,' Jared chimed in.

'Do you want to drive?' Ryan asked curtly. 'But you can't, can you? Not in the state you're both in! So whilst I'm in charge of the car, I make the decisions, right? As for turning here – no thanks; there wasn't room. I may not know exactly where we are, but one thing I do know, is that this area is notorious for its peat bogs, and I don't fancy finishing up in one of them. This car might not be much of a loss, but I certainly don't want to be inside when it sinks into one of those.'

A few minutes later the car engine coughed; then fell silent. Ryan glanced round at the others as he brought the car coasting to a standstill. 'What's up now?' Jared asked.

'This fucking car's about had it, that's what's up. The garage didn't warn me this might happen. I asked them for something reliable, even if it was old. What a fucking place to breakdown; lost in the middle of a moor, during a blizzard.'

'Can't we ring for help?'

'What with, Jared? Mobiles won't work out here; there's no signal. We'll just have to wait it out.'

Jared and Greg had downed five pints of cider apiece at lunchtime. This was nothing out of the ordinary, they did that quite regularly. Nevertheless, the effect was beginning to be felt, first of all by Greg.

'Still snowing.' Jared had wound his window down an inch.

'I need a pee,' Greg declared.

The amount they'd put away, Ryan was surprised they'd lasted this long. Greg got out of the back of the car. 'Watch out for the peat bogs,' Jared called out. 'And be careful that gypsy woman doesn't get hold of you,' he added with a laugh.

The open door allowed an Arctic blast inside. Greg slammed the door shut and vanished into the driving snow.

'I still don't see the need for all this messing about,' Jared muttered in a sulky tone.

'No, but then you're not running this operation, the Albanians are.'

Minutes passed in what could only be described as an angry silence. Ryan was wondering if he'd got it right.

Jared was still sulking. 'Greg's been gone a while,' he said eventually.

'He'd a lot to get rid of,' Ryan suggested in a bored tone. 'Either that, or he's fallen into a snowdrift. I suppose one of us ought to look for him,' his voice conveyed his reluctance.

'I'll go,' Jared offered. 'I need a pee too.'

He got out; lowering the temperature further. The sole remaining occupant of the car waited, listening carefully in the silence of the snow. At one point he thought he'd heard a muffled sound, almost like a gunshot; but he could have been mistaken. He waited patiently. Twenty minutes after Jared had gone in search of Greg and relief, Ryan saw the lights of an approaching vehicle in his rear-view mirror. It pulled to a halt behind him and the driver got out. Seconds later the passenger door alongside Ryan opened.

'It's bloody cold out there. For fuck's sake, start the engine and get the heater working.'

Ryan turned the ignition switch. The engine started first time. 'Job done?' he asked, his casual tone masking his excitement.

'No problem; did you get it?'

Ryan gestured over his shoulder. 'What did you do with them?'

'They're waiting beside a peat bog. I thought if we put them inside this old crate we can dispose of the lot in one go. They'll never be found.'

'They'll not be missed either. Pair of useless tossers. I bet they were scared witless when you appeared out of the blizzard?'

'One of them certainly pissed himself when I held the gun to his head. He was muttering a right load of gibberish, something about a ghost. What the hell did you tell them?'

'I told them a ghost story.' Ryan started to laugh.

'A what?'

'A story about the ghost of Ghyll Head Moor.'

'Sounds like fun. What was it? It certainly got the two of them wound up.'

The passenger listened to the tale of the gypsy girl, and the revenge she sought against young men. 'And they believed you? They actually believed that nonsense?'

'Amber,' Ryan told her, 'some men will believe anything in the right circumstances. Alone, in the middle of a remote moor during a snowstorm, then a lovely young woman appears from nowhere. No wonder they pissed themselves. I'm surprised that's all they did.'

'So now there's just you and me.' As she spoke, Amber took her gloved hand from the pocket of her heavy coat, the dull grey metal of the pistol she was holding gleaming slightly in the reflected light of the blizzard. 'You and me, alone out here on the moor. And you're the only witness to what I've done.'

'And the snow, don't forget the snow, Amber.'

'How could I forget the snow?' She laughed, and waved her hand. 'Stop the engine,' she ordered. Her tone was backed up by the pistol she was pointing at him. Ryan didn't argue.

The snow that had fallen concealed the grass that grew up the middle of the tarmac strip, emphasizing how little traffic passed that way. It could be days, weeks even before another vehicle went along that road. Ryan felt a sudden chill, as he realized the vulnerability of his position. Could he really trust her? In spite of what they'd been to one another he was no longer sure? Nor was his concern eased by Amber's next words.

'Get in the back.' She waved the pistol in his direction. She'd already killed two men that night; Ryan didn't want to be the third. He scrambled over the seat into the back of the car. 'Now take your clothes off.'

His eyes widened, either with alarm or anticipation. 'What are you going to do?' he asked, half fearing the reply

Sometime later, Amber returned to the front seat of the car. 'That was brilliant, absolutely great.' Her eyes sparkled with excitement, and the sensuality of the moment. She patted Ryan's groin as he zipped his trousers up. 'I've never fucked anyone on a bed of snow before. It warmed me up too,' Amber looked back as he started the engine. 'I only hope it's all right.'

'It will be,' he reassured her. 'I'm sure it'll be fine, although I wasn't wearing a condom.'

·'I don't mean that, you idiot.' She slapped him gently. 'I'll go put the stuff in the Beamer.'

A couple of minutes later she was back.

'Where do I go?' Ryan asked.

She pointed to the left. 'There's a little cart track there. I found out they used it for wagons in the old days when they cut peat to use instead of coal. That'll take you round to where I left the bodies.'

It was almost half an hour later when they returned to the BMW. By that time, the blizzard was raging with full fury. They got back into the car, sighing with relief as they shook the snow from their hair, dusted it from their clothing and waited for the heater to warm their shivering limbs.

'Will anyone report them missing, do you think?' Amber asked.

'I doubt it. Only their customers are likely to even notice they've disappeared, I can't see them ringing the police. And anyway, we're not going to be around to bother about whether anyone's twigged that they're no longer about or not, are we? We're going to be on a beach somewhere living the high life.'

Amber shivered, despite the warmth of the car. 'One thing I won't miss is this fucking weather; that I can be sure of.'

Ryan started the engine and they drove off; content in

their own little world, the world they had created by the crimes they had committed. Neither of them felt the least bit guilty about the taking of two human lives, worthless though those might have been. They weren't the type to worry about something they considered as irrelevant as remorse. For them, the only things that mattered were themselves. Just Amber and Ryan, and of course the snow. The snow they'd made love on. Packets of pure cocaine worth over £5 million.

The previous summer had been one of the worst for years for the farming industry. Winter feed and bedding straw were already scarce and commanding ridiculously high prices. The farmer whose property was on the outskirts of Drover's Halt had been lucky. He'd been tipped off about a farm at Bishop's Cross that was going out of the dairy business and the farmer had agreed to sell him a trailer-load of bedding straw without him having to pay too high a premium. The only downside had been that he'd had to forego his Sunday lunch in order to collect the load.

It was late-afternoon before he got all the bales onto the trailer and roped the load securely. At those prices, he wasn't prepared to risk losing one along the winding lanes around Drover's Halt. As he set off back home, the weather was already showing signs of the threatened snowstorm. He was anxious to get the trailer into the shelter of his barn before the straw got too wet. However, the weather overtook him, and he was soon crawling along, through near-blizzard conditions. He was confident of making it home, although the road was already white over. The tractor was about the best possible vehicle in such conditions, and the fully laden trailer added to its road-holding capability rather than detracting from it.

The wind had picked up and was driving the snow horizontally across the road. Unknown to the farmer, whose whole concentration was on picking out the road ahead, the side of his trailer was covered in snow, rendering it all but invisible from side on.

The narrow country lanes towards the top of the dale can be tricky at the best of times for those not familiar with their cunning twists and turns. Add in a near-whiteout and they go from tricky to highly treacherous. The snow had already covered the road sign giving warning of the T junction ahead. The stop notice painted on the tarmac had long since been masked by the lying snow.

Deceived by the lack of warning, Ryan didn't see the junction until far too late. Even then, the couple might have got away with it, but as he stamped on the foot brake in panic, the BMW wheels locked and the car lost traction. As he fought to control the steering wheel, which bucked and twisted in his hand, Ryan saw to his fresh horror the tractor lights passing immediately in front of them, seemingly no more than feet away.

He had almost got the BMW back on a straight line, but now, with only a split second to spare, he needed to turn to their right to avoid the tractor. As he did so the BMW went into a fresh skid, and with the wheels locked and all traction lost, they slid across the junction, missing the tractor by no more than two feet. Neither Ryan nor Amber could see the trailer, and were oblivious to the fresh danger until the impact of their collision.

The farmer had seen the BMW snaking towards him, knew the car was out of control and realized the inevitable that was about to happen. All this passed through his mind in no more than a split second, giving him no time to do more than brace himself for the collision.

Suddenly, it was no longer Ryan, but the farmer who was fighting for control, as he attempted to prevent the heavy bulk of the trailer from tipping onto its side, taking the tractor with it. It was touch-and-go for a few seconds; hours to the farmer. Eventually, he managed to bring the tractor under control and pulled to a halt, breathing an enormous sigh of relief. Having ensured his own safety, the farmer's next concern was for the occupant or occupants of the car. He leapt from the cab of his tractor and made his way, as swiftly as the treacherous surface would allow, towards the vehicle.

The BMW was lodged securely between the front and rear axles of the trailer, the back of the car protruding like some malignant growth. The farmer reached the passenger side of the vehicle, clinging on to the trailer to prevent himself falling over on the icebound surface. He peered in through the window, and could see there were two people trapped inside, both slumped forward. A stray thought crossed the farmer's mind. Why had the airbags not inflated? He was not to know that the vehicle had not been serviced, and that there was a major fault in the electrical system, which had prevented the life-saving mechanism from operating.

He tried to wrench the passenger door open, to no avail. He reached through the smashed window and checked for a pulse, first on the female passenger who moaned slightly at his touch, and then the driver who failed to respond at all. Both were alive, which was a huge bonus. How bad their injuries were was another matter, one the farmer was not qualified to tackle. He needed expert assistance, and he needed it quickly. He switched off the car's ignition. Concern for the safety of the injured occupants formed only part of his desire to avoid a possible conflagration. He was aware that if the vehicle caught fire, it wouldn't take much for the fire to spread to the contents of the trailer. The prospect of the load of straw bales catching fire was a risk he was desperate to avoid – especially at the price he'd paid for it. He hurried back to the tractor and snatched his mobile from its cradle, praying that the signal, which could be less than perfect, wouldn't let him down. He breathed a sigh of relief when his 999 call brought a ringing tone in response, and he was able to alert the emergency services.

The ambulance was first to arrive, followed by a fire engine. They concentrated their efforts on trying to extract the couple from the BMW; a tricky procedure as they were uncertain as to the extent of their injuries. They were in the process of evaluating the potential damage that might result from moving the passenger when the first police car arrived on the scene.

'We're going to have to take the roof off,' Doug Curran, the fire officer told the police driver. 'The difficulty is; the paramedics reckon if we move them we might be doing more harm than good.'

'Can't you get a doctor to assess them?'

The senior paramedic replied. 'We asked, but there's no one available. The one who was supposed to be on duty is stuck in Leeds. Apparently, the weather's much worse in the West Riding. They had to pull another medic in, but he's on site at an RTA on the York ring road. He wouldn't be able to get here for hours – and if this lot gets any worse, he might not get here at all. By all accounts the worst of the snow hasn't got here yet, but it's heading our way. We could all finish up stuck out here, and that wouldn't do them any good. I've sent for another crew to help transport them.'

A second police car arrived, and the officers were detailed to take a statement from the farmer, whilst the others assisted in lifting the woman out of the passenger seat onto a spinal board, securing her head and neck with a restraint, and then onto a protective stretcher. As they were completing the last stage of this complicated procedure, one of the police officers saw something fall from the woman's pocket and land heavily on his foot. Once the paramedics had lifted her into the ambulance, he bent and picked up the object, staring at it in astonishment He called to his colleague. 'I think you'd better come and have a look at this. What the hell she's doing carrying that, I've no idea.'

Together, they examined the pistol, which at first they thought was a replica. After a moment, one of them sniffed at the barrel. 'This is no replica,' he exclaimed. 'And what's more, it's been fired – and quite recently unless I'm mistaken. I think we'd better alert the control room. I feel sure CID will want to know about it.'

'Let's help these lads get the driver out first, and then they can get on their way. This weather's getting worse by the minute, and we shouldn't delay any longer than we have to.'

Once the driver had been extracted, they watched the flashing lights of the ambulance s as they headed off towards Netherdale General Hospital. Within minutes, another set of lights signalled the approach of the police recovery vehicle, which would remove the BMW to their garage for examination by traffic division. As they waited, the officer who had found the pistol returned to the BMW and shone his torch into the back of the car. Seconds later, he called to the other officers. 'I think I can guess why that woman was packing a gun,' he told them.

They all stared into the vehicle, and as the torch beam reached the back seat, saw the collection of packets stacked there, the contents as white as the driving snow outside. 'I think we'll have to delay removing the car. Get onto the control room. CID will definitely want to know about this. Best find out who's on call at Helmsdale.'

Nash and Robinson had reached Smelt Mill Cottage and were seated in front of a roaring log fire in the lounge. The combination of fresh air, exercise and the late lunch Nash had prepared, had induced a state of drowsy content. Anne put all thoughts of her imminent departure firmly out of her mind and was determined to extract every ounce of pleasure from her remaining time with Mike. 'Don't you get lonely out her, when your son's away at school?'

'Not really, he gets lots of good long holidays, and I go to visit him regularly during term time. There always seems to be plenty to do. Even without unexpected visitors,' he added slyly.

Their romantic idyll was rudely interrupted by the strident insistence of the telephone. Nash muttered something extremely rude and reached across for the handset. 'Yes, Jack?'

Anne knew at once that the caller was Sergeant Binns. What emergency had caused him to phone at this hour on a Sunday, she wondered? The thought that it might have anything to do with the case they were investigating never crossed her mind. She watched Nash, and saw his expression change from surprise to concern, to incredulity, then acceptance, and finally into decisiveness.

'Right, Jack, we'll be on our way out there as soon as we can. Yes, she's here with me. We were ... er ...going through the case notes. No, I think the Range Rover will cope OK, as long as I take it steady.'

He rang off and looked across the room at Anne. 'Sorry. I think I've just done your reputation no good. Jack knows you're here with me and he's bound to think the worst.'

'Do you think for one minute I care whether people know I've been sleeping with you or not?'

Nash smiled briefly, but said, 'Anyway, you'd better get your coat. We've work to do.'

'Why, what's happened?'

Nash explained what Binns had told him, and added, 'The car was travelling towards Helmsdale on the stretch of road leading to Drover's Halt. That's the road we came down. It's by far the most direct route from the Bridge Inn. Anyone who works with me will tell you that I don't believe in coincidence – certainly not that sort of coincidence.'

They were about to leave the house when Nash stopped and pulled his mobile from his pocket. 'I'd better get Jack to order a SOCO team to the crash site. They're going to love me for dragging them out at this time on a Sunday, and in this weather.'

'Poor them,' Anne retorted. 'Anyone would think that's what they're paid for.'

'You're a very hard woman.'

The forensic team had obviously responded quickly to the call out, whatever their feelings might have been, for they were already at work when Nash and Robinson arrived. Their leader briefed the detectives. 'We've taken the pistol from the uniform lads. They were quite correct; it has been fired very recently. We've also tested the contents of one of the packets. It's cocaine, right enough.'

'That leads me to wondering what or who the woman was

shooting at? Have you run the vehicle through ANPR?'

'Yes, but the last recorded owner lives in Leeds, and there's a change of ownership pending on the computer, which suggests it was bought by Helm Car Sales, so we believe our information might be out of date. I was going to suggest contacting them, what do you think?'

'Please do that. Anything else we should know?'

'Not until we get the car to the garage and give it a thorough examination.'

'In that case we'll head off to Netherdale and see how the occupants are doing.'

They greeted the uniformed officers who were standing guard over the cubicles in A & E where the two suspects were being treated, and got an update from the sister in charge of the department. 'The woman has regained consciousness,' she told them. 'We're waiting on the radiologist so we can send her for X Ray, both for suspected broken ribs and the head injury. You can see her, but only for a few minutes.'

'What about the driver?'

'Still unconscious, I'm afraid, but at this stage we don't believe his injuries are life-threatening. Again, we're waiting on the radiologist.'

The detectives followed the sister, who drew back the curtain affording privacy to the cubicle's sole occupant. They stared at the woman, who, as if conscious of their presence, opened her eyes. Nash saw her expression change to one of shock and fear as Robinson spoke. 'Hello, Amber. I think you've got a bit of explaining to do.'

The fact that she'd been recognized seemed to have rendered the woman speechless, so after several unanswered questions, Nash signalled to Robinson, and they left the cubicle. Once outside, he asked. 'It's obvious you know her, and that she knows you. Who is she?'

'Her name is Amber Gabriel, and she was a case officer with DIU until just over a year ago, when she was allowed to resign. I say allowed to resign, because there wasn't sufficient evidence against her to bring a case for corruption and misconduct. She was suspected of active involvement in a drug importing scheme, but it couldn't be proved. Now, perhaps it can. The problem we had is that although we couldn't be sure, we believe someone else at DIU was working with her and feeding her information that enabled her to avoid getting caught. I don't know any more about the case because everyone at the unit is very tight-lipped about it, and for some reason or other, I was kept out of the enquiry.'

'OK, let's have a look at the driver. Who knows,' Nash was half-joking, 'you might know him as well.'

If recognition had shocked Amber, the sight of the unconscious man on the hospital bed had a devastating effect on Anne. Nash took one look at the patient and then turned towards Robinson, in time to see her face whiten with shock. She stuffed her hand against her mouth. Nash thought she was going to faint and put a supporting hand under her elbow, feeling her arm tremble violently. He guided her out of the cubicle and signalled to the uniformed officer to pull the curtain across. Anne pointed towards the toilets, and Nash paced up and down for several minutes before she returned. She still looked pale and it was obvious she had been crying.

She looked at Nash, her expression one of abject misery. 'I'm sorry, Mike, but you'll have to continue with this investigation on your own, or contact Macmillan if you need help.'

'Why? I thought you were keen to see it through?'

'I would have been, under normal circumstances. But I'm afraid, no matter how much I might want to, it isn't possible.'

'You can't simply leave it at that. You'll have to explain.'

'Put it this way; regulations wouldn't allow me to continue my involvement. That's because the man in that cubicle is called Ryan Collins. He's a serving DIU officer. Not only that, but until eighteen months ago, he was my husband.'

*

Anne had gone when Nash reached home that evening. He read the note she had left for him with real regret. Not only for the end of their relationship, but the emotional stress she would be going through. His conversation earlier with her boss had given some clue as to the storm that awaited her when she returned to DIU. Macmillan had already indicated that she would be put on suspension because of her relationship with Collins, even though the marriage had ended.

Next morning, when Nash reached Helmsdale, there was a message for him to contact the forensic team in Netherdale. He called their office and identified himself. 'You wanted to speak to me?'

'Ah, yes,' the SOCO chief coughed slightly. 'It's to do with the BMW we brought in from that RTA. First of all we confirmed the contents of the packages as cocaine. Pure stuff, with a street value somewhere in the region of £5 million.'

'That's a hell of a lot for a small area like this,' Nash observed. 'I hope you've got it securely locked away?'

'Don't say things like that, even as a joke. Anyway, I don't suppose all of it was intended to stay round here, do you?'

'No, I suppose not, which throws open the question of who was handling the distribution. Possibly something we'll never know. These characters tend to be able to disappear easily because they can afford the money to cover their tracks. Anything else of interest in the car?'

'Yes, and I apologize that we didn't find it earlier. We recovered a mobile phone from beneath the front seat. We checked with the phone provider and it belongs to the woman, Amber Gabriel. When we examined it, we found some very interesting information on there. I've documented it but I suggest you come over and take a look at the video clips.'

Nash thanked him and went downstairs to reception, chatting to Jack Binns as he passed through.

'I had a call whilst you were on the phone,' Binns told him. 'Viv will be back tomorrow. The course finished a day early.'

'Thank goodness for that,' Nash sighed with relief. The return of his DC, Viv Pearce, was good news. 'I was beginning to feel like the captain of the Marie Celeste up there.'

Once he had watched the video clips and read the text messages, he informed the SOCO chief, 'I'm going out to the Bridge Inn, providing the roads are passable, and depending on what the people there tell me, I might want a search team in the area. I think we may have a clue as to the recently fired gun.'

'Yes, I somehow thought that's what you would say. What do you think of that video clip of the Waters woman being murdered?'

'Very unpleasant, but I'll act on that later. The info' from this text has to be our number one priority. It won't do Joe Michaels any harm to stay under lock and key for a few more days.'

Fortunately for Nash the snow had relented overnight and the Range Rover made easy work even of the ice-bound roads. He was even able to enjoy some magnificent views of the stunning scenery, topped by the glistening white peak of Stark Ghyll.

The interview with the manager took place in the man's office. Once he got over the shock that one of his guests at the weekend had been a police officer, and that he had been working, he soon provided Nash with the confirmation he required.

Nash asked to use the manager's phone, and gave instructions to the search team to join him. As he waited for confirmation of their departure, he chatted to the manager. Noticing a slightly strange inflexion in the man's voice, Nash enquired as to his origins.

'I am from Albania originally. Both my brother, who manages the restaurant, and I came to this country over twenty years ago, when such things were far more difficult than now. We have worked in the hotel business ever since then. Not many people notice my slight accent, but I suppose in your job you have to be more observant than most. Our surname was Osmani, but we simply knocked the 'i' off and became the Osman brothers. The only difference is there are only two of us, and we can't sing.'

Nash smiled at the humour. 'Do you employ many of your fellow countrymen?' Nash's question sounded like idle curiosity, which it certainly wasn't.

'Most definitely not,' the manager's tone was emphatic, and the expression that went with it was one of disdain. 'Many of those who come to this country now, far from seeking political asylum or wanting a better standard of living, merely look for a quick and dishonest way to make huge amounts of money. I prefer to stay well clear of them. This is not the sort of establishment that can afford anything but the highest standards.'

They chatted a while longer about the difficulties and challenges of the hotel industry. 'One of the secrets,' Osman told him, 'is to get a good chef – and keep him. I have one of the best, and have so far been lucky enough to beat off any opposition for his services; although it means paying him more than I would like. It's worth it though for the trade he brings in, and as long as I can put up with his foibles. They're all prima donnas,' Osman added. 'You should have witnessed some of the ones I've had to put up with, especially in London. This one's nothing compared to them.'

'What's his peculiarity?' Nash was interested, despite his keenness to get on with the search.

'He can't stand aubergines, or eggplants, whatever you like to call them. Won't have one on the premises.' Osman shrugged. 'That would be more of a problem elsewhere, here, few people ask for anything that exotic anyway.'

When he met up with the search team, Nash explained what they were looking for. 'Somewhere between here and the moor top you should find an old Ford Mondeo estate, which, unless I am very much mistaken, will contain the bodies of two young men. They were seen leaving the inn along with Ryan Collins, who was driving. The manager happened to see them leave and confirmed the direction they took. As you know, when we examined the BMW, we found a pistol that had recently fired two shots. I think you're bright enough to guess the rest.'

A few days later, Ryan Collins and Amber Gabriel were transferred from hospital to the less comfortable accommodation reserved for them at Netherdale police station. Nash, accompanied by DC Pearce, interviewed them in the presence of their legal representative.

Both interviews began in much the same way. 'I have bad news for you,' Nash said with a bright smile. 'I'm afraid your luck was most definitely out on Sunday. I'm not referring to your accident, or the huge quantity of cocaine found in your possession. I'm talking about your attempt to dispose of the Mondeo and the bodies of the two men you shot. Unfortunately for you, the car didn't sink into the marsh as you intended. Well, it did, but not very far. Apparently, there's a large outcrop of rock, which of course you wouldn't have seen during the snowstorm. It only sank up to the level of the windows so we were able to recover it, and to also match the bullets in the bodies to the gun found in the BMW.'

Having outlined the strength of the case against them, Nash and Pearce left them to discuss their position with the solicitor who was representing both of them, and who had been looking more and more miserable as Nash was speaking. As they waited in the corridor, Nash filled DC Pearce in on the remaining facts of the case. He had just finished when a constable hailed him with a message. 'SOCO want to speak to you, when you've a minute, sir.'

'Another day, another mobile,' the SOCO chief told him. 'This one belongs to Jared Savage. He and his brother Greg were the two stiffs in the iced Mondeo. There's a couple of missed calls on it. I think you're going to be extremely interested in the caller ID. I've documented it all for you.'

'I'll get Viv Pearce to come up now and collect it, seeing

as we're on site,' Nash replied.

Minutes later, they were examining the call log from the phone when the prisoners' solicitor emerged from the interview rooms and confirmed that his clients were ready to make statements.

After they had taken these, Nash and Pearce went along to the canteen for a coffee. 'This is a sorry mess,' Viv said. 'What do you plan to do about it, Mike?'

'I'm not sure there is anything I can do about it, as I'm personally involved.'

Viv stared at him. 'You mean you and this Anne Robinson woman? You were...?'

'Exactly, which makes my position very difficult.'

'You could be in real trouble.'

'I know. Which is why I intend to do nothing until the chief comes back. I'll tell her exactly what's happened, place all the evidence in front of her and let her decide what action to take.

Nash's interview with the chief constable was an uncomfortable experience, one he didn't want to repeat. Although the chief was extremely fond of Nash and regarded him as one of the most astute detectives she had ever worked with, she was not blind to his weakness as far as women were concerned.

Thus far, that hadn't posed a problem. Now, however, if the statements of the two witnesses were to be believed, Nash had become involved in a sexual relationship with a fellow officer who was now suspected of running a drug trafficking operation. Both Amber and Ryan had stated that they knew Anne Robinson was behind the drugs operation, running the supply chain whilst sheltering behind her post at DIU. Their decision to hijack the shipment was as much to get clear of her influence as for the money itself, they claimed. Although they hadn't provided concrete evidence, the insinuation was obvious.

Towards the end of Nash's explanation, when he mentioned the discovery of Jared Savage's phone, the chief constable's eyes widened with shock. 'You're absolutely certain about this, Mike?'

'There can be no doubt,' Nash told her. He laid the phone log on the desk. 'See for yourself. The missed call and the missed text are both listed there. Both with Anne Robinson's caller ID. Warning Jared about Collins and that there was a police presence at the inn.'

Once she had studied the transcript, making a careful note of the exact wording of the text and the times of the message and the missed call, the chief knew what her only course of action could be. 'I'll take over now,' she instructed Nash. 'You are on leave as of now. Don't attempt to contact Robinson, and if she contacts you, hang up. Go home, collect Daniel and stay home for Christmas. I shall have to order an internal enquiry, as I think you know.'

'I agree, ma'am, and I believe someone ought to take my statement immediately. The reason I say that is because there is one fact I haven't mentioned yet. I was saving it until last,' he added with a smile.

Nash explained, and the chief's eyes widened with shock. 'Now I see what you mean,' she agreed. 'Is that everything?'

'Apart from the video clip on Amber's phone. It clearly shows Curtis Smith murdering Marian Waters. Much as it goes against the grain, I think we'll have to release Joe Michaels.'

Part Three

Daddy's Little Angel

It was nearly twelve months later and in the CID suite of Helmsdale police station, the sole occupant, Detective Sergeant Clara Mironova, was reading a case file that had been prepared for submission to the Crown Prosecution Service. The offence was one of burglary, and the facts were beyond dispute, as the three teenage offenders had been arrested within the premises they had entered illegally.

Mironova initialled the report and closed the file before placing it in the tray for collection prior to being forwarded to Netherdale in their internal mailbag. She sat back, her thoughts a long way from the commonplace file she had been studying. She was still seated there when the door opened and the station's uniformed sergeant, Jack Binns entered, bearing a mug of coffee.

'Thanks, Jack,' Mironova smiled.

'Something wrong, Clara? You looked deep in thought.'

'I was merely dwelling on what a strange year it's been.'

'Strange? In what way?'

'Well, you have to admit it's been unusual. The year started with the DIU scandal and Mike all but suspended from duty. Then there was the misconduct enquiry—' Clara broke off as she saw Binns smiling. 'What's so funny?' she demanded, although she thought she knew.

'I was recalling the evidence you gave on Mike's behalf.'

She blushed slightly. 'Oh, that.'

Binns wasn't going to be denied his bit of fun. 'I particularly enjoyed hearing the part when the chairman asked you if you thought it was unusual for Mike to have formed an intimate relationship with the Robinson woman after so short a time, and you said that was quite normal for Mike.'

'Yes, Jack. I was there, remember.'

Binns pressed on unheeding her protest. 'And then when he asked if Mike was attracted to anyone wearing a skirt, you told him that as far as you were aware, Mike had never fucked a Scotsman.'

'I didn't say fucked,' Clara protested. 'I said slept with.'

'Same difference,' Binns pointed out. 'In Mike's case certainly. Is that all you were worried about?'

'I wasn't worrying. And it wasn't the enquiry I was thinking about, not really. OK, Mike got off with only a mild rebuke for his conduct, but as far as I'm aware, although Ryan Collins and Amber Gabriel have been convicted of murder, the rest of the case still hasn't been resolved.'

'You mean the Robinson woman?'

'Yes, as far as I know, she's still suspended, and there seems to be no sign of her being charged yet.'

'I thought that was down to lack of evidence?'

'That might well be true. Although Collins and Gabriel made statements accusing Robinson of running the drugs racket, they could offer no more by way of proof than those phone messages. Quite obviously CPS didn't believe they had sufficient to bring about a successful prosecution. Even though Macmillan and the rest of the DIU mob made several visits here to try and establish a link between her and the dealers.'

'It makes you wonder how long they'll continue paying her full salary and keeping her suspended, before they bite the bullet and kick her out. After all, it's almost a year now.'

'That's another oddity. Why haven't they done something by now? What is it they're waiting for?'

'Is that all? Or are there more weird things going through your mind.'

'There are lots of things I find puzzling. Mike's been acting strangely. Normally he's very open and tells me everything he's doing – well, almost everything,' Clara added delicately. 'But this year he's kept a lot of things close to his chest, which is unlike him. He's taken leave three times, always at short notice, and when that happens, he's been vague about how long he'll be absent for.'

'Could that have something to do with Daniel, perhaps?'

'I don't think so. In fact, I know they're not. For one thing, they all occurred when Daniel was at school, and on one occasion, when Daniel couldn't get hold of his father he rang me to ask if I knew where Mike was. Another strange part of it is that Mike's absences always seem to have coincided with the DIU lot descending on Helmsdale.'

'You think he could be avoiding them? It could be pure coincidence.'

Clara shook her head. 'I don't know. And how many times have you heard Mike say he doesn't believe in coincidence?'

Binns laughed. 'I take your point. Taken individually these facts don't seem to add up to much, but when you string them altogether, it does seem a bit odd.'

'Added to that, he's now gone on leave again, with only two weeks before Daniel breaks up for Christmas. You'd think Mike would want to save all the leave he could so he could spend it with his son, wouldn't you?'

'And you've no clue what he's up to?'

'No, although I phoned him at home after I spoke to Daniel and he had someone there with him; more than one person, by the sound of it. And I'm almost sure I recognized one of the voices, although she didn't say enough for me to be absolutely certain.'

'Let me guess, one of Mike's girlfriends?'

Mironova smiled. 'I certainly hope not, Jack. Unless I'm mistaken, it was the chief constable I heard. Although why she would be visiting Mike at home when he's supposed to be on leave, I've no idea.'

'Yes, I take your point. That would be going a bit too far, even for Mike.'

'On top of everything else, this is the first occasion since Mike took over here when we have an unsolved murder on the books.'

'Joe Michaels, you mean? He's not exactly much of a loss.'

'That's beside the point, Jack. Whether the man was a saint or a sinner, no one had the right to gun him down so callously immediately following his release from the remand centre.'

'Are there any clues as to who might have done it?'

'Not really. There's a long list of suspects, but an equally long list of unbreakable alibis to rule each and every one of them out. We've looked at Michaels' drugs connection, his personal life, friends of his late and unlamented partner Curtis Smith, but without success.'

'Never mind, Clara, Christmas is coming, a time for miracles, so you often say, and perhaps your miracle will be in the shape of answers to all your questions.'

Mironova smiled at Binns' optimism, but, as she recalled later, as predictions go, it was probably one of the most accurate of all time.

'What's the message? What did the boss say?'

'He said we're gonna have to do something about Benny. Teach him a lesson, like.'

'What do you mean?'

'He needs to learn respect. Needs to know we're not to be messed with.'

Kyle looked at his older brother. 'How we gonna do that, Nathan?'

Nathan leaned forward. 'Who was it took over the supply after the others got wasted? Who was it the boss trusted with the gear on the estate and in the rest of town?'

'We did ... er ... we were.'

'Yeah, and who lays out the folding for all the gear that comes into town?'

'We do.'

'Yeah, and when Benny comes to us crying the poor tale and begging for a share of the action, do we tell him to get stuffed? No way, because we're soft-hearted – or soft in the head. We let him run the gear to the punters for us. He gets a nice cut of the profits, thank you very much, and at the same time gets to know all the users. Am I right?'

'Yeah, dead right, Nathan.'

'And how does he repay us? By setting up his own operation and flogging coke and crystal on his own. Not only that, but undercutting us into the bargain. Now that's not right, that's not nice, is it?'

'No way, Nathan. So what we gonna do about it?'

'The boss found out Benny's got a big drop coming on Friday; a shipment he bought from that Turkish bloke in Leeds. He told me where and when it's happening. We've to wait till Benny's paid for the gear, rough him up a bit and take the stuff.'

'That won't be easy. Benny's a big bloke and he's put one or two in hospital in his time.'

Nathan smiled coldly. He pulled a pistol from his pocket and held it up. 'This should stop him.'

Kyle shivered; this was all getting a bit heavy. 'Where did you get that?'

'The boss gave me it. Told me to bring it along to the meet on Friday. The boss is sending a bloke along to help with the job.'

Friday was cold and bright. As the time for the meeting approached, Kyle and Nathan waited at the end of the footpath that led between the houses on the Westlea. Behind them, as the full moon rose, the open fields gleamed with frost. The temperature hadn't been above freezing for two days and the first snowfall of winter was forecast for the weekend. They had been there about ten minutes when another figure approached. 'Nathan, Kyle?' the man asked.

'Who wants to know?'

'Who do you think? The Albanian sent me to meet you here.'

The brothers relaxed. 'Right,' Nathan told him. 'I'm Nathan, this here is Kyle.'

'Did you bring it?' The man held his hand out.

'Course I did.' Nathan glanced round before removing the pistol from his coat and passing it to the man, butt first just like they did on CSI.

'Look, there's Benny,' Kyle whispered. 'Now all we have to do is wait for the hand over.'

Minutes later, a second man appeared in the distance and greeted Benny. The watchers saw two packages being exchanged, then Benny's supplier turned and walked out of the alley. As Benny followed, Kyle, Nathan and the stranger closed in on him.

What followed was brief, but brutal. The intended beating didn't materialize; Benny was too big, too powerful, even for two of them. Having lost the element of surprise, the contest was unequal. Recognizing they'd lost the initiative, Nathan glanced round for help. The stranger pulled the pistol from his coat.

Maybe his intention was only to frighten Benny, or to wound him. Only he knew which, but in the event the single bullet hit the big man in the chest. As Benny slumped, dying, on the uneven paving stones, the killers looked at one another. Kyle's expression was one of horror; whilst Nathan's was much the same. Only the stranger showed savage, gloating satisfaction.

'Let's get out of here,' Kyle urged.

'Hang on,' the stranger intervened, 'we haven't got what we came for.'

It took a few moments to find the package that Benny had dropped in the scuffle. As Nathan bent to retrieve the drugs, Kyle noticed movement out of his eye corner. He looked to the end of the alley and saw a figure only a dozen yards from where they were standing. The full moon was now high in the sky and Kyle knew all three of them must be clearly visible to the witness, whose face was in shadow.

'Someone saw us,' he whispered.

Nathan and the stranger looked down the alley, but the figure had gone. 'You're imagining it,' Nathan told his brother.

'I wasn't,' Kyle protested. 'There was somebody standing there.'

'They've gone now. Anyway, if it was someone from round here they'll keep their trap shut, if they know what's good for them.'

The stranger spoke. 'Now listen, and listen good, you two. This isn't some schoolyard game. This is business; big business. That means no chances taken, got it. Find out the name and address of that witness and make sure they're silenced.' He prodded Benny's corpse with his foot. 'Just the same as this one's silenced. Get me? Now, this shipment is free, right. It's free because we've taken action. It remains free so long as I hear that you've found that witness, whoever they are, and dealt with them before they have chance to squeal to the cops. Is that clear? Or will I have to come looking for you the same way I had to come looking for him?' He kicked Benny's corpse again.

Angela Phillips let herself into the house. Once inside, she locked the door, put the chain on and slid the bolts across. Moving to the kitchen, she did the same with the back door. She leaned against it, panting for breath. She had been running, but it was fear that caused her breathlessness.

Angela had seen everything that happened in the alley. Not only that, but she had recognized two of the killers. It was the knowledge that they might have seen her, and the thought that she might have been recognized that prompted Angela's fear.

She should have been home earlier; would have been if the netball practice session after school hadn't gone on so late. At the age of fourteen, Angela was already one of the top players in the county. Academically, she was bright, rarely finishing outside the top three in her year.

Her mother was proud of her, and so too was her headmaster. He had worried that things might have been different on that day, three years earlier, when he had the unenviable to task of being the one to tell her that her father had been killed. His concern that Angela would react badly, take a wrong course in life had been unfounded. There had been savage irony in the way Sergeant Phillips had died. Having served in Iraq and completed two tours of Afghanistan unscathed, his death in a training accident was brutally poignant.

Angela went up to her bedroom. She drew the curtains before daring to switch her bedside light on. In the soft glow of the lamp, the young girl sat on the edge of the bed, staring at the photograph of her father on her dresser. Tears formed in the corners of her eyes and spilled over, coursing down her cheeks. 'I miss you, Daddy,' she sobbed.

In the silence of her room, and in the loneliness of her fear, Angela imagined she could almost hear his voice saying, as he had said so many times, 'What's wrong, my little angel?'

He always called her that; had done ever since she could remember, especially when he knew she was upset and in need of comfort.

She had been so proud of him. She saw none of the savage irony her headmaster noted about the manner of his death. To Angela it made no difference whether the cause was a Taliban bullet or a fall from a rope whilst crossing a swollen river. All she cared about was that he had died doing his duty. And now, in spite of her desperate fear, Angela knew that she would have to do hers, terrified though she might be at the prospect and the possible consequences.

Her biggest quandary was whether or not to tell her mother what had happened. Tina had to work in order to supplement her widow's pension. In fact she had two jobs, and Angela knew that more often than not her mother went to bed weary, and dragged herself up next morning almost as tired. Both jobs were physically demanding, and one involved anti-social hours. She worked as an office cleaner from late afternoon to early evening, and from there often went straight to work behind the bar of the Coach and Horses. Normally, Angela would try not to burden her mother with her problems. But this was as far from normal as you could get. More than ever, Angela needed her father to help and advise her. That wasn't possible, so, unfair though it might be, Angela knew that at some stage she would have to tell her mother what she had seen. That was one decision out of the way. Now all that remained was to discover if she was able to pluck up enough courage to do the right thing. To do her duty.

The news of Benny's death spread rapidly round the Westlea. Within minutes of the murder, most of the residents knew someone had been shot. By the time the incident tape had cordoned the crime scene, almost as many of them knew the identity of the victim. Only an hour or so later, the names of two of the killers and their motive were being widely rumoured.

None of this reached Angela until her mother returned home. Friday was one of Tina Phillips' double shift days, which meant going straight from the offices to the pub, grabbing a snack en route. She was surprised to find the door both bolted and chained, and had to ring the bell for Angela to let her in. 'I guess you've heard about the murder?' she asked.

'No, Mum, I've been home all night. But you keep telling me to lock up properly, and tonight I remembered.'

Tina related the story, and was mildly surprised by Angela's seeming lack of interest. Soon afterwards, Angela told her she was tired and, after kissing her goodnight, went upstairs. Tina walked into the kitchen to make coffee. As she waited for the kettle to boil she noticed there was no crockery in the sink or the dishwasher. She checked the kitchen bin for signs of a takeaway, but again found nothing. Obviously, Angela hadn't eaten anything. She remembered Angela's lack of interest in the exciting news of the murder, and wondered if the child was coming down with something. Tina made a mental note to talk to her in the morning.

Although Angela was quiet all weekend, when Tina asked her if anything was wrong, or if she was feeling poorly, she denied that she was either unwell or upset. Guessing the cause of the problem is never easy for a parent, and in this case, when Angela did admit to having an upset stomach, Tina, deduced that the root of the problem was hormonal. For once, however, her mother's instinct was way off target.

Bill Kitson

Angela had been in a torment of indecision. Being trapped indoors by the snow that had started to fall on the Saturday morning was actually a blessing in disguise. It provided Angela with a perfect excuse for not venturing from the house. In fact, she was afraid to go out; unsure whether the killers had recognized her as easily as she had identified them. She was trapped inside by an irrational fear; almost as if there was a large sign on her forehead stating that she was witness to a murder.

Angela knew well enough what her duty was. Her father had instilled that in her from an early age, almost before she could walk. 'Why do you have to go away, Daddy?' she had protested, every time he packed for another tour.

'I have to, my little angel,' he would tell her. 'I don't want to leave you and Mummy, but it is my duty to protect you. For Queen and Country. That's the promise I made when I signed up. That means protecting all of you.'

And with that, Angela had to be content, until, as she grew older, she learned to appreciate all that duty involved and what terrible dangers her daddy faced. Knowing he did so willingly, somehow made it worse, but now that the baton of duty had been passed to her, as Angela saw it, she knew she could not shirk it for fear of letting her daddy's memory down.

Knowing her duty was one thing, overcoming the fear that went with it, quite another. After hours of agonizing over the weekend, Angela rationalized her fears. If her daddy could overcome fear to do his duty, then so could she.

By Sunday morning, Angela's mind was made up. She went into the kitchen, where Tina was preparing lunch. 'Mum, I need to talk to you.'

Tina looked up from the carrots she was peeling. Seeing her daughter's troubled expression, and remembering how moody Angela had been all weekend, Tina's heart lurched, afraid that she was to be confronted by one of a mother's worst nightmares. Then common sense prevailed. Angela wasn't that sort of girl. 'What is it, honey? What's wrong?'

Angela hesitated; even the act of recalling what she'd

seen brought the horror of it all flooding back. 'That murder on Friday. I saw it.'

'What?'

'I saw it happen. I was passing the end of the alley. I saw the men in there. They were fighting. Well, three of them were; the other one just stood and watched. Then he took a gun out and shot one of the men. I saw the flash, heard the bang and then the man who'd been shot fell to the ground. I ran away as fast as I could.'

Angela burst into tears, in part from relief at having unburdened herself of the dreadful secret she had carried. Tina reached out and took Angela in her arms, rocking and cradling her, murmuring soothing words of comfort. 'Have you told anyone about it?' she asked after a few minutes.

'No, Mum, I was too scared,' Angela's voice was muffled as she buried her head in her mother's shoulder.

Tina stroked her hair. 'Did you recognize the men?'

'Yes, I'd seen the dead man lots of times. He used to hang around the school gates sometimes, and on the estate. He sells drugs. So do the other two. Nathan and Kyle Drummond, I think they're called.'

'Oh yes, I know those two,' Tina agreed. 'They're a nasty pair of thugs. What about the other man; the one who fired the shot? Did you know him? Is he local? Off the estate, I mean?'

'No, definitely not. I've never seen him before. I got a good look too, because he was in direct line of the street lamp. I'll never forget his face.' Angela shuddered, and Tina held her tighter.

'My poor darling, you've been keeping all this to yourself ever since Friday night. Why didn't you tell me earlier?'

'You were working yesterday, and when you came in you looked so tired, I couldn't worry you with it then. I wish I didn't have to now, but I didn't have anyone else to turn to.'

'Don't be silly, that's what I'm here for. Now, let's be practical. Do you think they saw you?'

'I'm not sure. They might have done, I suppose. I wasn't very far away.'

'Would they have recognized you? Nathan and Kyle, I mean?'

'They might have done, but I can't be sure. The light was behind me, and they were fighting until the shot was fired. One of them, Kyle I think it was, looked up, but I was already running, so possibly they didn't even see me.'

'OK, so let's not panic, or jump to the worst possible conclusion. By the sound of it, I think it's very unlikely that they either saw or recognized you. That means they're not going to come knocking on our door as long as we don't tell anyone. Not for the time being, at least.'

Angela straightened up and freed herself from her mother's grasp. 'I will have to tell someone, Mum,' she said firmly. 'I will have to tell the police. I simply must. Daddy would have wanted me to, wouldn't he? And if I don't, I'll be letting him down.'

In the face of Angela's determination, Tina knew she would be wasting her breath arguing. Her heart flinched at the thought of the consequences; even as she admired her daughter's courage and resolve. There was little else she could do but provide support and encouragement.

Later, after they had eaten a lunch that neither of them had much appetite for, Tina broached the subject once more. 'One thing we can't do is phone the police. If the killers did recognize you, they'll be watching. And if the police came to the house it would be a sure sign that you were talking to them. The only alternative, as I see it, and it's going to be very tricky, is to go to the police station and tell them there. The problem is how to get there without anyone noticing.'

'I had an idea about that, Mum. I have a free lesson tomorrow afternoon. I could go then, and nobody would notice.'

'What if they're hanging around the school gates watching for you? It's too dangerous.'

'Not if I ask one of the teachers to give me a lift into town. She's done it before. If I tell everyone I've got a dentist's appointment, then if Nathan and Kyle ask anybody, they'll think I'm having a filling or something.'

Tina stared at her daughter with astonished pride. Was there no end to Angela's courage and resourcefulness, she wondered? 'In that case, if I walk with you to school in the morning, the same as I often do, and if you phone me the minute you get in from having been to the police, I'll come straight home once I've finished the cleaning job. Will that be all right?'

Their walk to Helmsdale Grammar School next morning passed off without incident, but Tina breathed a huge sigh of relief once she saw Angela vanish inside the main entrance. That relief would only be temporary, she knew, and she would continue to worry until she got the phone call. During the afternoon, Tina checked her mobile three times, not because she thought there might be a message or a missed call, but simply to make sure the battery was fully charged. She also checked her watch every fifteen minutes or so, convinced on more than one occasion that it had stopped.

The teacher willingly agreed to drop Angela by the dental surgery. Driving out of the school gates, Angela checked to see that there were no suspicious characters lurking about. After thanking her chauffeuse for the lift, Angela paused at the door of the surgery before turning around and heading for the police station. Outside the building, she stopped once more and took a deep breath, before entering via the double glass door. The middle-aged man behind the reception counter had sergeant's stripes on his sleeve, reminding Angela of her daddy. He smiled at the teenager. 'Hello, I'm Sergeant Binns. How can I help you?'

Angela's reply was so quiet that he had to bend forward to catch what she said. 'I've come about ... I want to talk to somebody ... it's about the murder. I saw who did it.'

'I see. What's your name?'

Angela gave it, her voice little more than a whisper.

'OK, Angela. I'm going to get a nice lady detective to come and talk to you. Her name's Clara. You'll like her. Would you like to have a seat while you wait?'

Angela would have preferred to stand up, or walk around,

anything to soothe her agitation, but the seat Sergeant Binns
had indicated was to the side of the reception area, screened
from the outside by a reeded-glass panel. Angela opted for
the protection from view the bench offered.

Upstairs, in the CID suite, Detective Sergeant Mironova was
seated in her boss's office reading the murder scene crime
reports. Her expression was sombre. Given the past history
of the victim, she had little doubt the crime was drugs-
related, and could even compile a list of likely suspects.
Proving it, however, was likely to be extremely difficult,
unless they got lucky.

The murder had been committed in the middle of the
Westlea, and despite exhaustive house-to-house enquiries in
the area around the crime scene, nobody admitted to having
seen or heard anything. If that didn't change, and they were
unable to recover the murder weapon and link it to the killer,
the case would remain unsolved. Clara was annoyed. With
DI Mike Nash away on leave, she was the senior officer.
Mironova was keen to clear the murder up; to prove that she
could handle a case such as this without Nash looking over
her shoulder. Her phone rang. She picked it up, still
concentrating on the photos of the dead man. 'Yes, Jack,'
she said.

Seconds later, the photos were forgotten as she
concentrated on what Binns was saying. She put the phone
down and went out into the main office. DC Pearce looked
up, saw the excited expression on her face. 'What's up?'

'Come on, Viv. We've got ourselves an eyewitness. At
least that's what Jack thinks.'

It was a further two hours before Angela left the station.
Sergeant Binns had been right. The lady detective, Clara,
had been nice, as had the handsome coloured DC who told
her his name was Viv. They had even talked a little about
Angela's father, which had helped, and it was obvious that
Clara understood what Angela meant. Clara's statement that
her fiancé was also a soldier explained that.

Viv had suggested they should provide officers to protect

Angela. Clara saw the look of horror on the girl's face and smiled reassuringly. 'I don't think so. If we did that on the Westlea, we might as well stick a two-foot high sign on the roof saying, "murder witness lives here". What we can do is get extra patrols to drive by on a regular basis, keep an eye on Angela's house.' She smiled at the girl. 'How does that sound.'

'Much better,' Angela agreed.

As Pearce went back upstairs to prepare arrest warrants for the two alleged killers Angela had identified, Clara walked Angela towards the reception area. As they reached the end of the corridor, the girl's pace slowed. Clara looked at her, and saw the doubt in Angela's face. 'Something wrong?' she asked, keeping her tone casual.

Angela looked round. 'Is there another way out?'

'You're worried someone might recognize you and put two and two together?' She saw Angela nod. 'I don't think that's very likely,' Clara reassured her. 'I think the last place those two thugs would want to hang around at the moment is outside a police station, don't you?'

'I suppose so,' Angela was still unconvinced. 'I was thinking more of their friends.'

'You've got a point,' Clara conceded. 'Although I don't think it's all that likely. I'm not sure Nathan and Kyle have the brains to work that out. However, if it makes things easier for you, how would it be if you weren't to leave the police station at all?'

'I can't stay here,' Angela protested.

Clara smiled at the notion that the child might have thought she was suggesting locking her up. 'That wasn't quite what I had in mind.' She pointed towards the end of the corridor. 'That's a connecting door. It leads to the ambulance depot. There's another at the far end giving access to the fire station, and from there, I can let you out of the back door, which takes you into the rear of the car park. Even in the unlikely event that someone saw you leave from there, they wouldn't have any idea that you'd been in this end of the building.'

Mironova escorted Angela through the ambulance depot and across the inside of the fire station, both of which were deserted, much to Angela's relief. Before opening the outer door, Clara put a hand on Angela's arm, reassuring her. 'Don't worry, we'll make sure neither you nor your mother come to any harm because of these thugs and what you saw. What you've done today is a very brave thing. You're obviously afraid, but that hasn't stopped you doing what's right. Your father would be really proud of you.'

The thought buoyed Angela as she stepped out into the cold of the December dusk. She glanced to the right and then to the left, relaxing slightly as she saw that the car park was deserted apart from a few cars parked a long distance away. She walked quickly towards the entrance, but her courage faltered as she saw the lights of a car swing off the main road towards where she was standing. She only relaxed once it passed her and continued to the far end of the open space in front of the building.

As the car halted, a motion sensitive security light came on, flooding the front of the car park in time to catch the driver as he climbed out of the car. The scene was reminiscent of Friday night, and within seconds, Angela was running; running as fast as she could towards the market place, then out onto Netherdale Road, turning left and then right as she dashed into the Westlea estate, and with one final sprint reaching the front door of her house.

She let herself in, slid the bolts home and fumbled the chain into position. It took her several minutes to get her breath back sufficiently to call her mother. The message caused Tina to plead with her supervisor that her daughter had been taken ill, and that she needed to go home immediately.

Back at the police station, once she'd seen Angela safely from the premises, DS Mironova went upstairs to the CID suite. She phoned through to their Netherdale headquarters, only to be told that the chief constable was attending a meeting in Manchester, and wouldn't be available until the following day. She put the phone down and looked across at

Pearce, who had just taken a call from Jack Binns on reception. 'We've a visitor,' Viv told her. 'At least you can tell somebody the good news.'

'Who is it?'

'Macmillan, from DIU. Jack says he's waiting in reception.'

'I report to the chief, the super, or Mike, nobody else,' Clara told him abruptly. There was no logical reason for Mironova not to share the information with the DIU chief that two of the killers had been identified, but Clara felt reluctant to act without consulting her superiors. Maybe, she thought wryly, that was a sign that she wasn't yet ready for promotion.

Quite how the news got out, nobody could say, but by Monday evening, rumour was rife on the Westlea. The police had suspects for Benny's murder. An eyewitness had seen the killing. Not only that; but the eyewitness, who lived on the estate had been able to identify them. Arrests were expected at any time. By the time Angela, who was ignorant of the rumours, left for school on the Tuesday, the names of the suspects were being bandied about. At the newsagents, the greengrocers, convenience store and even at the bus stop as those waiting for a bus into town shivered in the sub-zero temperature; there was only one topic of conversation.

The confirmation of the names of the suspects was probably due to the occupants of neighbouring houses being woken at dawn by the sound of an armed police unit under the guidance of DS Mironova breaking down the door of the house where Nathan and Kyle's family lived. Although the raid was abortive, those with sufficient curiosity to brave the cold and crawl from under their duvet to see what was causing the racket were easily able to put two and two together.

The lack of success was down to the fact that the brothers had heard the rumour and, anticipating the police raid, had moved out the previous night. Not that they'd moved far. If they'd been the type to rise early, they could have watched the raid. Their temporary accommodation came courtesy of Nathan's new girlfriend. Any reluctance she might have had about harbouring wanted men was overcome when Nathan presented her with a sizeable quantity of their stock-in-trade, for she was also one of his customers.

The relationship was mutually rewarding. Nathan got a willing partner for his amateur amatory advances, and she got sufficient drugs to dull her appreciation of how poor his performance in bed was. Kyle, who was consigned to the spare room, had some difficulty sleeping. This had little to do with conscience over his part in Benny's murder, or fear of the consequences of their action; more from the unmistakeable sounds of copulation that carried clearly through the dividing wall.

After the abortive raid on Nathan and Kyle Drummond's family home, Mironova told Pearce to return to Helmsdale station. 'If Macmillan comes snooping around again, tell him where I am and nothing more. I'm going to talk to the chief.'

Her meeting with Gloria O'Donnell lasted longer than Mironova anticipated. When she left, the chief's final comments had her at once intrigued and puzzled. 'I think you can anticipate a call from Nash sometime today,' she'd told Clara. 'It's time you were brought up to speed with developments. He'll probably need your help anyway. In the meantime, don't tell anyone else more than you feel you have to, especially with regard to what we've been discussing.'

She watched Mironova leave and then picked up her phone. 'Mike,' she said when her call was answered, 'I've some news for you. Big news. I think we're getting near to the end-game at long last. Listen to what Clara's just told me.'

Late that afternoon, Clara received a text message on her mobile. It simply read, 'Smelt Mill Cottage, straight from work. Tell no one, M.'

Why, Clara wondered, was Mike being so secretive? Not only Mike, but the chief constable, who obviously knew what was going on. As did everyone else, it seemed. Perhaps tonight, Clara might join that club.

She reached Wintersett village just as the pub was switching its outside lights on in the hope of catching some trade from those thirsty after a day's toil. Once through the village, she soon reached Nash's house. Nash was in residence, and by the look of it, not alone. Two other cars were on the drive in addition to his Range Rover. The outside lights were on, so Mike was obviously expecting her. This was proved as he opened the house door even before she had got out of her car. 'Hello, Mike, what's going on?' she greeted him. 'I thought you'd be skiing in the Alps or something.'

Nash smiled. 'Sorry for all the subterfuge and secrecy; and for being unable to tell you anything. But it wasn't my decision. In fact none of what's been happening has been my doing; I've simply been following orders.'

He ushered Clara into the lounge, where she was surprised to find three other occupants, only one of whom she recognized. 'Ma'am,' she exclaimed in surprise, as the chief constable acknowledged her, only just stopping herself from adding, 'what are you doing here?'

It was when Nash introduced his other guests that Mironova's surprise turned to bewildered astonishment. Her curiosity lasted for some time as all three told her parts of a story that took her from South America to Europe and back into their own area. At the end of it, Nash said, 'Thanks to you and this brave young girl, we now have chance to finish this once and for all. The reason I wanted you to come here tonight is that, in addition to putting you in the picture, there are a few things I want you to do for me. I need you to make a phone call, for one. Nash outlined the rest of what he needed, and finished by saying, 'The situation is now critical. We already know from the text message we intercepted that these two scum bags, Nathan and Kyle Drummond, have been instructed to kill the witness. We even know how they plan to do it. That means we have to set up protection for her and her mother. At the same time we need to flush the whole gang out, not just the foot soldiers but the generals as well and rid ourselves of the problem for good. As long as we're all in agreement, I think you can call a meeting tomorrow, Clara. Bring Lisa Andrews over from HQ and get her, Viv and Jack involved. Jack can spend a day or two in civvies. Ask Tom Pratt to come over as well. He can fill in for Jack on reception until this is over.' He glanced round, saw the others looking approvingly at him. 'These are people I'd trust with my life,' he assured those who didn't know the personnel he'd mentioned. 'I know they will keep the matter top secret, and I'm confident they can keep Angela Phillips safe until we're in a position to make the arrests.'

Nash turned to Clara. 'Now, will you make that phone call, and let me speak to them please?'

Angela kissed her mother goodbye before letting herself out of the front door. 'Don't worry about me, Mum, I'll be fine.'

'You're not nervous, are you?'

Angela shook her head. 'I was, until last night when we got that phone call. That helped a lot.'

She walked slowly and carefully down the path, conscious of the places where their footsteps had trodden the covering of snow into hard-packed ice.

Tina watched her daughter leave, and, before closing the door, noticed a coloured man with a holdall walking up the garden path a few doors further along the street. There had been several such men canvassing the estate over the past few months – ex offenders on a rehabilitation programme, or so they claimed. Tina smiled at the irony; given the less than unblemished record of some of the estate's inhabitants.

Sure enough, several minutes later the doorbell rang. Tina opened the door as far as the chain would allow. The coloured man began his sales pitch, his accent rough, his eyes hidden behind large sunglasses that gave him a sinister look. That wouldn't do much for customer confidence, Tina thought. She was in the middle of telling him she didn't require anything when his voice changed, became low and urgent as he urged her to check the ID card he was holding out.

Tina's eyes opened wide with surprise, but she removed the chain and swung the door back to allow him into the hallway, remarking in a loud voice, 'You'd better come in and show me some of what you've got. I'm always prepared to give someone a second chance, provided they're willing to work.'

Once she had closed the door, the vendor removed his sunglasses and smiled apologetically. 'Sorry for the subterfuge, but Inspector Nash thought it was necessary. I'm DC Pearce, and I've brought some photos for you and Angela to see. There is one set each, for you to keep. These are the people who will be acting as your protection detail. One or other of them will be within yards of you, day or night until this is over. Mike, Inspector Nash, that is, has information that it should be all sorted out by the weekend. That's his photo there. One of them is shadowing Angela to school as we speak.'

After Pearce had left, handing her a couple of dusters and a mop-head before she opened the door, and thanking her effusively as he stood on the path, Tina spent some minutes examining the photographs, on the back of which someone, she assumed Nash, had inscribed their names. It was surprising, she thought, how easily comforted someone could be, simply by being handed a set of photos. She remembered what Pearce had said about somebody always being within yards of both her and Angela. Tina stared out of the window and after several moments noticed someone seated in a car parked some distance down the road. She could not be sure, but she thought the driver looked like the woman in one of the photos. She relaxed, feeling even more positive that this would have a satisfactory outcome.

One of the most difficult parts of the whole operation, as Nash conceded later in his report to the internal inquiry, was the time-consuming surveillance of the Bridge Inn, from where they were certain the drugs distribution was being controlled. They had been forced to wait several months before the opportunity to set up CCTV cameras with sophisticated transmission equipment to send images to remote monitors could be installed without the suspects being alerted. Permission to use the equipment and other similarly hi-tech gadgetry had been difficult to obtain, and it was only when the Chief Constable had used the authority of her rank to plead the case with the Home Secretary that sanction was obtained on a strictly limited basis.

Their chance to install the CCTV cameras came because of the drugs syndicate's decision to close down the local distribution network following the previous year's scare caused by Ryan Collins and Amber Gabriel. For a long time, the detectives believed their efforts had been in vain and that the closure was to be permanent, but work carried out by undercover officers in Europe eventually assured them that the suspension was temporary. All they needed to know was when and how the drugs got from the port to the various inland outlets, principally those in North and West Yorkshire, Teesside and Tyne and Wear.

At around the time that Tina Phillips was ushering DC Pearce in his guise as an ex-offender into her home, teams of officers throughout the north east of England were watching CCTV images of a succession of deliveries they suspected contained illegal substances. Nash, who had a live feed to his computer at Smelt Mill Cottage, was viewing footage supplied by fibre optic hidden cameras placed within the Bridge Inn and the surrounding area. He and his companion watched as a van pulled into the car park and came to a halt close to the delivery door alongside the kitchens.

Nash's companion sat back, relaxing in the easy chair. 'Fruit and vegetables. Nothing for us.'

Nash stared at the screen as the driver lifted a box from the rear of the van and carried it towards the inn door. 'Hang on,' Nash said, 'Go back a few frames and enhance the image. Let's see what's in that box.'

After a moment scrutinizing the frame, his companion said, 'They look like aubergines to me.'

'That's what I thought,' Nash agreed. 'But I'll bet you a month's pay they're not. That's where the drugs are being hidden. That's how they're getting them here without anyone suspecting anything.'

'How do you know?'

'Because when I was talking to the manager of the inn last year, he told me their chef hates aubergines and won't let them onto the premises. If that's the case why is the greengrocer delivering a full box of them; and why isn't the sous-chef sending them back? I think this is our cue to raid the inn. I'd better make the phone call and find out what the others want to do about it.'

The conference call took longer than expected, and with frustration as the only outcome for Nash. He pleaded that with the identification of the man involved at the inn, plus what Angela Phillips had told him, they now had sufficient to arrest all the guilty parties and close the drugs network down. However, the others outvoted him, and along with their superior number, their rank gave them the final say. 'Stick to the original plan,' he was told. 'Wait for one of them to make a move.'

The brothers had remained inside the flat for days. The copious supply of drugs Nathan had brought with him had kept his girlfriend comatose for much of that time. That didn't worry her lover, who had more important things to worry about. The downside to this was that they had to fend for themselves, something they were unused to, and particularly poor at.

Saturday morning brought a crisis meeting. 'We can't go on like this,' Kyle complained. 'It's not so bad for you; you're getting your leg over every night. I'm stuck in that freezing cold box shivering my bollocks off and listening to her moaning and groaning as you get your end away.'

'What do you suggest we do? Go out and get ourselves arrested? Why don't we make their job easier by walking into Helmsdale nick and giving ourselves up?'

'We gotta do something,' Kyle insisted.

Nathan sighed, but he knew Kyle was right. The problem was, Nathan was used to being in charge and, as things stood, he didn't even have a plan. It was at that point that Kyle had an idea. This was something that didn't happen often, but the more he thought about it, the better it seemed. He pointed to the bedroom. 'Why don't we get her to go and find out what the score is? You can tell her who to talk to; people we can trust to give her the news without splitting on us.'

Nathan looked at his brother with something approaching respect. Getting an idea from Kyle was like being stung by a wasp. It happened so rarely it came as a huge shock. Getting one that was sensible was even rarer, but the more he thought about it, the more Nathan realized it was a good idea. He managed to get the girl up and dressed, poured a couple of mugs of coffee down her throat, and explained the problem. After she repeated his instructions enough times to satisfy him she would act on them, he peeled off several notes from a large wad he carried and instructed her to do some shopping. Before letting her out of the flat Nathan made her repeat the names of the people who would bring her up to speed on events.

Following her departure, the brothers spent a tense few hours awaiting her return, whilst at the same time watching the street and surrounding area for signs of police activity. When they eventually let her back into the flat, she brought both good news and bad. 'There's warrants out for both of you,' she told them. 'Your house was raided Tuesday morning at dawn. Four vans full of coppers, all armed to the teeth and wearing flak jackets.'

There had actually only been two vans, and only one of those contained an Armed Response Unit, but such is the way with rumours. 'Who fingered us; did you find that out?' Nathan asked the question that was at the forefront of both their minds.

'Yeah, rumour is it was the Phillips' kid. She lives on the other side of the estate with her mum. Her dad was that soldier who got killed. It was in all the papers, and they took up a collection for the widow and kid.'

Later that day, Nathan sent a text to inform their boss of the development, and the identity of the witness, and to ask for advice on how to handle the situation. The message didn't read like that, but given Nathan's limited command of his native language, the meaning was clear enough. He didn't wait for an instant response, as always he knew there would be no reply until the early hours of the morning, at the earliest. Nathan had no idea why this was, and not being of an enquiring mind, merely accepted this as normal.

Sure enough, next morning when he checked his phone, the reply was there, the command stark and uncompromising. 'You had your instructions. Take kid out,' he read. 'Make it look accidental. Stolen car hit & run best. Back-up will be there. Send text to following number when ready.'

Nathan stared at the mobile number for a long time. He swallowed, considering the task he and Kyle had been given, wondering if they would have the bottle to go ahead with it. Then reality kicked in. If the kid got on the witness stand, he and Kyle would go down for a long time. Worse still, if they didn't do as instructed, they risked upsetting their masters. And Nathan had all too vivid memories of what happened to someone who crossed them. Later that morning, he told Kyle the plan, presenting it as his own, which failed to deceive his younger brother.

'You remember what the man said. I had a text from the boss as well. He says we gotta get shut of the girl. She's the only thing they've got on us.'

'You mean kill her? But she's only a kid.'

'So what? She's old enough to put us inside for life.'

'Hang on though, if we do her in, the filth are going to know it was us. Even if they don't find the gun.'

'They would do, if we had the gun. But we don't have it, do we? The bloke took it with him, remember. So if we ain't got it, they can't prove Benny's shooting had anything to do with us – providing we silence the kid. And if the girl's death isn't murder, they can't lay the blame for that on us either; can they?'

'How do you mean?'

'If it's a tragic accident. A hit and run, say? They can't pin that on us. First off we gotta get ourselves a motor. By that I mean we gotta nick one.'

'There's plenty around here to choose from.'

Nathan looked at his brother scornfully. 'Not likely, dummy. That would be like shitting on our own doorstep. Besides, they'd know it was us, even if some nosey bastard didn't see us.'

'Where from, then?'

'I know the perfect spot. We go into town, and get to the station. The long stay car park there, that's the place to nick one.'

'Why there?'

'For one thing, there's no CCTV on that car park. For another, lots of cars get parked there from Monday to Friday. People working in London and places like that,' Nathan explained. 'They have a special permit section. We nick one of them, it'll likely not be missed until Friday night, by which time we'll have done what we need to do with it, hopefully, and torched the motor.'

Kyle thought over what Nathan had told him. He had to admit the plan was a good one. He couldn't see any way it could go wrong.

On Monday morning, as Angela was preparing to leave for school, Tina asked, 'Can you fend for yourself tonight? As far as food goes, I mean. I haven't had chance to prepare anything and I've an extra shift at the pub this lunchtime.'

'Sure, Mum, I'll get a takeaway.'

Tina laughed. 'How did I guess you'd do that? Angela's liking for Chinese food was something she had inherited from her father. That liking had been enhanced earlier in the year, when the fish and chip shop nearby had closed down. The lease on the premises had been acquired by the proprietor of Helmsdale's only Chinese restaurant, the Fu Manchu, nicknamed 'Few Men Chew' by locals. Not wishing to dilute the brand, the owner had opened the takeaway on the estate under the title 'Fu Manchu Two'.

Although the owner knew the premises needed some work, he was prepared to put up with the deficiencies until the business was up and running. He wasn't prepared to put money into renovating a leasehold property until he was sure the investment would show a satisfactory return. Early signs were encouraging enough for him to contemplate starting some of these jobs in the New Year – the English one; that is. One of the first items on the agenda was definitely going to be having the extractor fan serviced, overhauled or replaced. The extreme heat in the tiny kitchen made it an essential piece of equipment, but at the present, the fan motor gave off some eerie, almost unearthly screeching sounds; that set the teeth of staff and customers alike on edge; reminding them of souls in torment. The scary noises emitted by the motor worried the proprietor, who was concerned that the equipment might not last until he could get the engineers in to fix it.

To begin with everything did go according to Nathan's plan. They waited until the afternoon hoping they would get a better choice of long-stay vehicles. The car they opted for was a Ford S-Max, big and powerful enough to do what they had in mind for it, and not showy enough to attract attention in the way that a Merc or a BMW would. It also had blacked out windows, ideal for their purpose.

It was beginning to snow again as they drove out of the car park. Nathan, who had got behind the wheel immediately he'd hot-wired the car, told Kyle, 'We gotta go to the allotments next.'

'What for?'

'We need petrol. Lots of it.'

'Why?'

Nathan shook his head and sighed. 'To torch the car, dickhead.'

'Oh, yeah. But why the allotments?'

'The old man who does gardening for people, he keeps a

load of cans of petrol there. He uses it for strimmers, lawnmowers, hedge trimmers, all sorts of gear.'

'You're planning to break into his shed?'

'Of course I am. We can hardly drive onto a garage forecourt and buy half a dozen cans of unleaded, can we? Even if the attendant didn't recognize us, or think there was something dodgy in the amount we were buying, they do have CCTV there; that I do know.'

Breaking into the hut on the allotment proved no problem, and soon they had loaded the boot of the S-Max with half a dozen two-litre cans full of petrol. Darkness was falling as they parked the car at the end of the street that contained Angela's house. Once he had stopped the engine, Nathan ordered Kyle to put his seat back into the recline position and lie down.

'Why?'

'If a cop car cruises past, they'll have been warned to be on the lookout for a couple of blokes, possibly in a car. If they see a car with only one bloke inside, they'll think nothing of it.'

Kyle had to admit that Nathan seemed to have thought of everything. The brothers settled down to watch and wait.

Had they risked stealing the car from the railway station a little earlier, or if they had been a bit quicker getting the cans from the allotment, they would have been in time to see Angela arrive home. It was only after she had removed her outer coat and taken her school bag upstairs that Angela remembered what her mother had said about tea. She glanced at the clock; it was far too early, the takeaway wouldn't be open yet. Besides, Angela had a lot of homework to do. She wondered briefly why teachers seemed to delight in giving out extra work as the end of term got nearer. She sighed and switched her laptop on. She had several projects to complete, and at least two of them required a lot of research. Much of the necessary information could be obtained from the internet.

She moved methodically from topic to topic, writing

copious notes on each subject ready to insert them into the essays she planned to write. Immersed in her work, she barely noticed the passage of time, until eventually, she realized she felt hungry.

Before leaving the house, she sent a text message to the number she had been given, stating her planned movement. That, she knew, would enable Inspector Nash to warn her protectors and give them chance to get in position. Her concentration had been so total that she had not only failed to realize what time it was, but hadn't noticed the rapid deterioration in the weather. It was only after she put her coat and beret on and headed for the door, that Angela realized it was snowing heavily, and had obviously been doing so for some considerable time.

She opened the front door, but hesitated on the threshold, shocked somewhat by the whiteout facing her. She was undecided whether to risk going out as she was, or whether to change her shoes for the heavy winter boots in her bedroom wardrobe. It was only a short walk to the takeaway, however, so Angela decided to risk it. She had forgotten that the shoes she was wearing were in urgent need of re-soling.

As she paused in the doorway, the light from the hallway was clearly visible to the couple in the car, even through the curtain of falling snow. 'Kyle, we're in luck. She's just come out of the house.'

Kyle sat upright. 'How do you know it's her?'

'Didn't you listen to what we were told? The mother has a cleaning job at this time every day. It has to be the kid. Better send that text to the backup, we're in business.'

It took Nathan a few minutes to restart the engine, by which time the girl had vanished into the snow. They moved slowly forward, peering through the windscreen, but could see no sign of her. Towards the far end of the street, the houses on the left hand side gave way to a parade of shops. There was a dry cleaning business, a bakery, and a greengrocery, all of which had closed some time earlier. The only premises illuminated were those of the Chinese takeaway, and as they reached it, Kyle spotted the solitary customer inside. 'She's there, in the Chinky,' he exclaimed.

Nathan stopped the car and looked into the takeaway. Having confirmed Kyle's sighting, he reversed the car slowly, feeling a certain amount of wheel-slip as the S-Max struggled for traction on the icy road. Once in position, Nathan parked on the left and they waited, engine running but with no lights showing.

The delivery driver was annoyed, but knew there was nothing he could do. When he pulled into the yard behind Good Buys supermarket in Netherdale, he knew at a glance that he was going to be delayed. His brief conversation with the warehouse foreman did little to lighten his mood. 'We've three trucks to offload before we get to yours,' the foreman told him. 'All of them full loads.'

The driver did a rapid calculation. The delay was going to set him back nearly two hours, and he still had one more delivery to make, at the Chinese takeaway in Helmsdale. He considered going to that drop first, and even went to the extent of trying their number from his mobile, but the call went straight to voicemail. His other problem was going to be the risk that he would run out of tachograph hours. He switched on the radio and waited. The local radio station didn't do much to cheer him up. In addition to his other problems, the news bulletin ended with the weather forecast. He listened and groaned. 'Just what I need,' he muttered.

By the time he offloaded and started out for Helmsdale, the threatened snow was already beginning to fall, lightly at first, but as he neared his destination, it was already settling on the road, the tarmac turning first light grey, then steadily whiter and whiter, until the road markings had vanished altogether. The driver thought about the delivery point at the takeaway. Reversing down the alley at the end of the terrace was not going to be fun in these conditions. The trickiest part of the manoeuvre was the turn into the narrow entrance. It would be far better if he could do a straight reverse.

Then he remembered that the alley had a wider counterpart across the road. If he drove into that, his truck would be positioned perfectly for a straight run back towards the delivery point. He relaxed slightly, then glanced at the clock. His tension racked up again. If he got a trouble-free delivery and was able to get on the road again quickly, and if the weather didn't cause any further hold-ups, he might just get back to his depot before his time ran out. Otherwise, he would have to find a place to stop overnight. And around Helmsdale, they were about as common as rocking horse manure.

Nathan and Kyle had been concentrating on the takeaway, waiting for the girl to emerge. They knew she would have to cross the road; knew, that when she did so it would give them their chance. Their attention was distracted momentarily when they saw the wagon drive cautiously round the corner at the far end of the street. They watched as the driver swung the large vehicle across the road, concerned that his manoeuvre would ruin their carefully made plans. Both of them relaxed as the vehicle inched its way slowly into a side street, the gleaming red tail light vanishing from view.

Seconds later, Nathan saw the takeaway door open. 'We're on,' he shouted, as he began revving the engine. He slammed his foot on the accelerator and as the powerful car moved forward, he felt the steering wheel light in his hands. Nathan was too inexperienced a driver in snow to grasp the significance of this.

Inside the takeaway, Angela had been chatting to the owner's wife as she waited for her order. When this was passed across the counter, she turned to leave. Behind her, in the kitchen, the proprietor mopped his brow. The small kitchen was already stifling. He moved across to the wall and switched the extractor fan on, before joining his wife in the front of the shop. 'Nice kid,' he gestured to their customer.

'Yes,' his wife agreed, 'very polite and friendly.'

Angela walked carefully along the pavement. Despite her

caution she slipped a couple of times and wished she had changed into her boots. As she reached the kerb, the extractor fan started up. She wasn't aware that the noise came from the fan. She looked round, startled, her face drained of all colour until her complexion matched that of the snow. Had she heard it? Or, were her ears deceiving her? She shook her head, she was imagining it. She took a step into the road, and as she did so the sound came again. 'Angel, Angel.' It was her father's voice calling to her.

She swung round, and as she did so, saw a man running directly at her, his arms outstretched. She opened her mouth to scream, but he reached her, pushing her violently on to her back, sending her skidding across the pavement. A split second later the air was expelled from her lungs as a large body fell on top of her. She gasped and pushed, but to no avail.

'Fuck! Missed her,' Nathan screamed. He hit the brakes hard, desperate to go back and finish the job. The wheels locked as traction was lost and the car went into a skid. In his panic, Nathan turned the wheel – the wrong way.

The truck driver, having lined the approach up like a golfer with a vital putt, began to reverse, slowly at first, but then with increasing speed. He glanced both ways, but saw no approaching lights, so began to cross the road, his eyes darting in turn from one to the other of his wing mirrors.

The extractor fan muffled the sound of the truck's engine, muffled the sound of the reversing alarm as the Ford, totally out of control, spun in a crazy elliptical semi-circle along the street, both occupants screaming with fear. The sound of their screams ended abruptly as the car, still travelling at well in excess of 50 MPH, hit the back end of the truck.

Angela heard the crashing sound of the collision. There was a long moment of silence; then a huge explosion, followed by a blinding flash of light. The man rolled to one side. Angela felt his hands grasp her under the shoulders as he hauled her to her feet. 'Are you OK, Angela? Didn't you hear me call you?'

Angela rubbed her head, and looked round, puzzled.

What had happened? She stared incredulously at the inferno. She saw the truck driver, reeling from the shock of the collision, emerge from his cab and run towards the back of his trailer, before retreating from the fireball that was consuming the car, its occupants and the rear of his vehicle.

Seconds later, the takeaway owner and his wife came running out of the shop and joined the driver. As they surveyed the inferno, the driver, still in shock looked at them and asked, 'Did you order the fried rice?'

Almost as if the collision was a signal, several cars pulled up and as the drivers emerged, Angela thought she could recognize some of them from the photos DC Pearce had provided. The promise had been fulfilled. Angela's bodyguards were all around her. She was aware that the man holding her was awaiting her answer. He repeated the question, and it was then Angela recognized her saviour from his photo. It was Mr Nash. 'Yes, I think so, but I thought....' she answered slowly.

She realized he was still holding her, support and protection all in one. She blushed inwardly at her boldness, but leaned her head against his shoulder. 'Was that...? Was that them?' She gestured towards the burning vehicle.

'Yes, I think it was,' Nash said. 'But we won't be sure until we get them out of the car – if we can.'

Angela could see the drivers, she'd assumed were police officers, tackling the blaze with extinguishers from their vehicles, and as she watched, the owner of the Fu Manchu emerged from the restaurant carrying two larger extinguishers from the takeaway's kitchen. She began to tremble, as shock and the realization of how narrowly she had escaped death hit her. Nash felt her reaction and tightened his hold on her. 'It's all right, Angela,' he told her, his voice calm, the word slow and deliberate to allow her to grasp them fully. 'It's all over now. Those two thugs and the people they work for can't threaten or harm you anymore. We've already arrested the other members of the gang. They'll all be going to prison for a long, long time.'

Nash didn't tell the girl how close her escape had been,

he felt sure she already knew that. Nor did he tell her that an even more potent threat to her safety had been arrested only minutes before, around the time she was preparing to go out, and that the arrest had been made within a stone's throw of her front door.

The flat was a small, one-bedroom apartment, built as part of the Westlea estate at the council's insistence that some facility be provided for single occupancy. It had long been let to a tenant who did little more than sleep there. The man had a job with live-in accommodation, which he declined, preferring to return to the estate that had been his home for his whole life rather than live in at the place of his work.

At about the time that Angela was preparing to go out, the tenant had answered his flat door, and stared in astonishment at his visitor. 'What are you doing here?' he'd demanded.

The visitor walked past him into the flat. 'I came because of the text you sent me. What's the problem?

'Problem? There is no problem. What makes you think there's a problem? And I didn't send you a text.'

'Of course you did. I have it here on my mobile. It has your number and caller ID....' The visitor's voice tailed off into silence, a silence that was rudely broken as the door was forced open by a door enforcer, known to the users as the big red key.

Before either of them could react, the room was filled with men in bullet-proof vests shouting, 'Armed police. Do not move.'

Seconds later they had been handcuffed, despite the visitor's protestation. 'I am a police officer, with the Drugs Intelligence Unit. My warrant card is in my pocket.'

At first it seemed the words were going to pass unchallenged, but then a figure emerged from behind the wall of armed officers. 'Yes, we know that,' Nash replied. 'But I also have to tell you that you are under arrest for the murder of Benny Wood.'

At that moment, two mobiles bleeped almost

simultaneously. Nash stared at the message on his screen before removing a second mobile from the visitor's pocket. He read the message on that phone; then turned and spoke to the leader of the Armed Response Unit. 'Those two little scrotes are going to try and kill our witness. I have to go. Take these two to the station and slap them in cells.' He paused. 'Don't stand any nonsense from them, particularly Superintendent Macmillan.'

Two days later, there was a meeting in the Helmsdale CID suite; one that Nash thought of as a sort of semi-official debrief. In attendance were the chief constable, Superintendent Fleming, who had arrived back that day following secondment to a counter narcotics squad operating in Europe, Detective Inspector Anne Robinson, still called this as they were not privy to her true identity, the Helmsdale team and DC Andrews from Netherdale. Jack Binns had left reception duties to Tom Pratt to be in on the meeting, but that was natural. Little happened in Helmsdale that Jack didn't get to hear of first.

'To start with some good news.' O'Donnell looked round approvingly. 'I had confirmation from our ballistics expert yesterday afternoon that the gun found in Macmillan's car was definitely the one used to kill both Benny Wood and Joe Michaels. That last piece of evidence seals what I think has been a highly successful operation in which all of you should take pride in your involvement.'

'I have to apologize,' Mironova told Robinson. 'I've spent all year thinking of you as a rogue cop, corrupt and dealing drugs.'

'That was deliberate.' Anne looked across at Nash and smiled, making the chief constable wince slightly. 'Everyone was led to believe that was the case so I could continue working undercover to expose the real villains. If people thought I was suspended, they wouldn't bother to find out where I was. That left me free to join Superintendent Fleming in the hunt for one of the biggest cocaine rings this country has ever seen. The Helmsdale part of the operation was only a small piece in the jigsaw. The trail has taken us across Europe, parts of Asia, and several countries in South America. It's a shame we didn't qualify for air miles,' she ended with a rueful smile.

'But what about the evidence against you?' Lisa Andrews was frowning in puzzlement. 'I saw those warning messages sent to Jared Savage on the day he was killed. They definitely came from your phone.'

'That's correct, Lisa,' the chief constable agreed, 'but fortunately for Anne, Mike spotted the time they were sent. He knew Anne could not have sent them, because she was with him at the time – and in a place where there was no mobile coverage. Neither of them has seen fit to give me a convincing explanation of what they were doing at that moment,' the chief ended dryly, 'and come to think of it, I'm not sure I'm all that keen to know.'

Clara saw Anne was scarlet with embarrassment, and even Nash's face looked a little pinker than normal. 'How did they pass the phone off as Anne's?' she asked.

'It's called cloning,' Nash explained. The IT boys told me exactly how it's done. I understood about one word in ten of what they were saying. However, once we knew that was what had happened, we felt sure it had to be someone close to Anne, to enable them to steal her identity.'

'All the DIU phones are issued from our head office,' Anne added, 'so the most likely source of the villainy had to be within that office. The fact that a couple of villains had been or were current DIU officers added further circumstantial evidence. Chief Constable O'Donnell gave me the choice, I could either clear my name then and there, or help crack the whole rotten mess.'

'How did you know it was Macmillan who was behind it?' Pearce asked.

'We didn't, until quite recently,' Anne admitted. 'However, once we examined all the personnel files of everyone who could possibly be involved, we discovered lots of interesting fact about Superintendent Macmillan. Because he began his career in Teesside, we assumed that he came from there, but in fact he's local to Helmsdale. His mother was the daughter of one of the tenants of the Slingsby-Darrow estate. We don't know who his father was. The birth certificate simply says "unknown", which from what we later found out about the mother is hardly surprising. She later took up with another man, one in a long line, apparently, and gave birth to another son, Macmillan's stepbrother, who became sous-chef at the Bridge Inn. As you know, he was the man arrested along with Macmillan.'

'And of course, because of his connection with the area, Macmillan knew of the inn,' Nash took up the story. 'Then we found out that Macmillan's wife is a director and majority shareholder of a property company, amongst whose assets is the Bridge Inn. Quite where she got the money to buy such an expensive piece of real estate is something we will be investigating.'

'So this story about the Albanians? I take it they had no connection to the drugs racket?' Pearce asked.

'No, they were simply convenient scapegoats, like Anne. Something Macmillan was very clever at – until we copied his tactics.' Nash smiled ruefully.

'When we checked his career records,' Anne continued, 'we found that one of his early arrests was a man who later became a wholesale supplier of fruit and vegetables, delivering to the Bridge Inn. We believe Macmillan might have been corrupt, even back then, and may possibly have already become involved in the drugs trade when he was stationed in Teesside.'

'We had a lot of trouble getting permission for all the covert surveillance,' Nash told them. 'It took the chief's considerable persuasive powers to overcome the official nervousness about invasion of privacy. In the end, I took a gamble by approaching the manager of the inn and getting his written permission to the CCTV set-up. He agreed, once I assured him that neither he nor his brother would suffer in consequence. Of course, although we knew we could put together a convincing case against Macmillan for the drug racket, the shooting of Benny Wood was a different matter.

Then we had a stroke of good fortune. When Angela Phillips saw the shooting, and came to tell her story to Clara, the poor kid got the fright of her young life, because she saw the man who'd shot Benny outside the police station. She was terrified she'd signed her own death warrant by coming to us. When I spoke to her on the phone she was in a dreadful state.'

'That's why you phoned me to check what visitors we'd had on Monday,' Binns interrupted.

'Yes, I needed to be sure the killer hadn't been some low life brought in for the job by Nathan and Kyle Drummond. But when Angela described the man she'd seen to me, I felt sure it had to be Macmillan.'

'And of course, that's why you stepped up the protection detail for Angela and her mother,' Clara suggested. She turned to the chief constable. 'And why you told me to keep the news about Angela's witnessing the shooting to myself.'

'Correct,' O'Donnell replied. 'At that point we needed the last piece of evidence, and we were trying to buy time to get it. Luckily, that proof was forthcoming at just the right time.'

'Luck has played a big part in this whole case from start to finish,' Nash commented. 'It's almost as if we'd a guardian angel looking after us.'

'A snow angel perhaps,' Pearce suggested.

'Is that a reference to the weather – or the cocaine?' Nash asked.

That evening, as Anne was dining with Mike at Smelt Mill Cottage, she reflected with some sadness that this would be their last weekend together. It had been a great adventure, and although she knew it was time for them both to move on, she had some regrets, and felt sure Mike did too. She smiled, and Nash asked, 'What's amusing you?'

'Something O'Donnell said before she left your office. Her exact words were, "I understand you have to report for duty back at DIU on Monday. Please leave my best detective in a fit state for work".'

Nash grinned. 'What was your reply?'

'I told her that it takes two to tango, so if she finds you asleep behind your desk, she shouldn't put all the blame on me.'

'If that's the case, we'd better get an early night.'

Six months later, Angela was waiting to give evidence at the trial of Macmillan. Clara Mironova chatted to her mother in the corridor outside the courtroom. 'Angela looks to have survived her ordeal well.'

'She has.' Tina smiled fondly. 'She hero-worshipped her father, and the chance to do something she regarded as her duty has been good for her. Speaking of hero-worship, though, Angela has a new pin-up on her bedroom wall. She took a photo she cut out from the *Netherdale Gazette* and had it blown up to poster size.'

'A photo? What of?'

'Not what – who?' Tina laughed at Clara's puzzled expression. 'Inspector Nash of course. He's Angela's pin-up. She has a real crush on him. Collects all the press cuttings she can find and pastes them into a scrapbook. I'm rather pleased, because I think that's far healthier than having an obsession with some overpaid footballer or pop star.'

Clara saw Tina's expression change; saw a dreamy look in her eyes, as she added, 'And you can't really blame her, can you? After all, he so pleasant, so friendly, and really handsome, don't you think? He isn't married, is he?'

For a long time afterwards, Tina wondered why Clara had rolled her eyes and muttered, 'Not another one.'

****

False Witness

Bill Kitson

INTRODUCTION

*They say that I'm mad; criminally insane – and that I should have been locked away in a mental institution not a prison. But **they** don't know me.*

*They say that I killed six women; slaughtered them in a brutal manner. But **they** don't know the half of it.*

*They say the reason they know I killed six women is because of the MO. Do **they** really believe I would be dumb enough to stick to the same MO?*

*They say that women will be safe now that I'm under lock and key. Little do **they** know.*

Chapter One

The fight had been over a girl. What else, at the age of sixteen? Not just any girl, but Victoria Lindsay – only the prettiest girl in the school. And she knew it. Knew that both of them were trying their hardest to get her horizontal. Not only knew it, but enjoying their rivalry, playing them off against each other, fanning their fierce jealousy until eventually, with no other course open to her, and sparked by her own hyperactive hormones, she had made her choice.

By the time matters came to a head they were both so desperate they'd probably have jogged naked round the playing field seven times just for a feel of her breasts.

It all kicked off when he saw Vicky, his Vicky, strolling round the corner of the science block with his rival. His arm was round her waist, drawing her closer as his hand slipped lower and rested against her buttocks.

And Vicky, what was she doing? Not only tolerating the intimate contact, but obviously enjoying it. That much he could tell by the way she was staring adoringly into his rival's eyes. Nobody could touch her there, feel her that way unless they'd had her. As he tasted the bitterness of failure, rage overcame him.

That was when the fight started. As bouts go, it was hardly world heavyweight championship class. But it ended with humiliation piled on humiliation for him. Not only forced to admit his rival's conquest of Vicky, but being beaten half-senseless by the boy who'd taken her from him, all the while having to listen to Vicky shouting for his opponent, cheering every punch.

They say he who laughs last; laughs longest. Years later, Vicky Lindsay would become his first victim.

It was a slow night for trade. In fact it had been a slow month. Holidays were the cause. Whenever schools were out, trade dropped. Many of her customers would be spending their time with their wives and families, pretending to enjoy the role of devoted husband and father. Of course, once the holidays were over, the kids back at school and the wives occupied with running the home, the punters would return, swapping the devoted husband role for the great lover they imagined themselves to be.

Marnie leaned against the wall in her usual place, bored rigid. She would welcome a punter, not purely for the money, although that would be welcome, but for something to do. Or someone, she corrected herself with a grin.

She decided she'd give it until nine o'clock, then she'd pack it in for the night. Marnie glanced at her watch; fifteen minutes to go. Then a car turned the corner. Would it speed up or slow down? It slowed, and with the instinct born of years of experience, Marnie knew this would be a john. She walked across the pavement and waited at the kerb.

The car came to a halt alongside her, the driver's window already down. 'Looking for a date?' She used her standard opening line.

'Hop in,' the driver replied.

Marnie got into the passenger seat and clipped her seat belt on. As they set off, heading for the edge of town, she wondered if he was a talker. Some punters were – most hardly spoke at all. After the two hours of boredom she'd just passed she'd welcome a bit more in the way of conversation than the usual grunts and moans.

'What's your name?' he asked after a while.

'Marnie,' she replied. It wasn't; except professionally. She'd read or heard it somewhere and decided she liked it. 'What's yours?'

He told her, and in response to her further questions, said he wasn't married – didn't even have a girlfriend. 'My job doesn't help,' he explained. 'I'm a long-distance lorry driver. I spend almost all week on the road. I even sleep in my cab. I'm what they call a tramper.'

Marnie laughed. 'A tramper and a tramp,' she suggested.

'Yes, seems kind of appropriate,' he agreed.

They reached open countryside and he pulled the car into

a lay-by alongside woodland. He was in the act of unzipping his pants when Marnie stopped him. 'Money first,' she held her hand out. 'This isn't true love. I'm a working girl with rent to pay.'

'Of course.' He laughed. 'How much?'

She told him, and watched him count out the notes, seeing him go past the figure she'd quoted. Did that mean extras, she wondered. Or something unusual? In Marnie's profession there was no such thing as perversion, just a sliding scale of fees.

He handed the money over and Marnie tucked it into the pocket of her denim coat. By then he was across on her side of the car, the safety belt unclipped and the seat in the reclining position. Marnie relaxed and decided to let him enjoy it for as long as he could manage. Anyway, it wasn't as if punters were causing a traffic jam trying to get to her pitch, and he had paid over the odds.

Eventually, he climaxed. She stroked his hair briefly. 'I hope that was worth the money?' she whispered.

He smiled and reached behind her to the back seat of the car. He picked up a short length of fine nylon cord and slipped it over her neck in a noose. Then he strangled her. As she stopped thrashing and went limp, he took the cord from around her neck, reached into her jacket and removed the money he'd paid. 'There are some things,' he told the dead woman, 'that money simply cannot buy. Anyway, you don't need to worry about the rent anymore.'

He pulled the four rings from her fingers, removed her necklace, took the bangles from her wrist and ripped her hooped earrings off without bothering to unfasten them; tearing her lobes. She wasn't going to feel the pain, so it didn't matter.

He opened the glove compartment and took out a clear plastic food bag bearing the name of a large supermarket chain. In the space reserved for the date and contents he wrote her name, using a felt-tipped marker pen. He put the bag back into the glovebox and climbed over the dead woman to get out of the passenger door. The night air was cool, but as he felt a draught below his waist, he realized he'd forgotten to zip his flies up. He corrected the omission, then reached into the back of the car for a torch. He hoisted the woman's corpse onto his shoulder in a fireman's lift and turned to head for the woods. He was over a hundred yards into the undergrowth, following the path he'd used when selecting the area, before switching the torch on.

Half an hour later, sweating and close to exhaustion, and with his arms and shoulders aching from carrying the load, he reached the clearing he'd picked for her last resting place. He laid her in the shallow grave before picking up the shovel he'd left there that morning and beginning to cover her with soil.

As he worked, he started humming. Although this was his first working girl, she was actually his third victim, and he was beginning to enjoy the process; more so than he'd ever believed possible. Once you got over the moral scruples, it was all rather straightforward. The trick was to remain in control; not let it take over. That was when you made mistakes, or your luck ran out. He'd read a lot about serial killers and how in most cases it was more by fluke than by any great detective work that they'd been caught. Either that, or their own carelessness. Dennis Nilsen using the sewer for disposal was a prime example, or Peter Sutcliffe and the false number plates. Sloppy, that's what it was. All he had to remember was to keep a lid on his desires and let a decent interval pass between kills; that was the key to success.

Not that the waiting time would be wasted. He could use it to select another suitable burial site. He had thought about using the same woods for all of them, but decided against it. What if in burying one, he actually disturbed another. That would be too bad. Besides, the more spread out they were, the harder they would be for the police to find, if they ever got round to looking.

The middle-aged man stared about him for a long time, turning first one way, then the other before he had to face the fact that he was lost. Completely and utterly lost. The small clearing he was in was at the end of a narrow, badly overgrown path. He'd been faced with a choice of two paths at the junction in the woods and had selected this one. The wrong one, as he now knew to his cost. When he'd paused, indecisive, this had looked the more promising of the two, and it seemed to lead in vaguely the right direction for where he was headed.

He wasn't sufficiently experienced, either in woodcraft or as a hiker to know that the path he'd followed was actually a deer trail, and that deer can get through gaps and into places that human's are unable to reach. It had been at his doctor's advice that he'd begun hiking. The medic had told him that walking would be the best form of exercise. It would strengthen his muscles, enable him to lose weight and get fit following his recent operation.

As with everything else he tackled, once his mind was made up, he plunged into the venture wholeheartedly – or headfirst. He'd bought an expensive pair of walking boots, complete with special socks, waterproof clothing, a small rucksack, and a long stick with an ornate handle, in preference to the poles used by many. Nowhere in the advice his doctor had given, or in the many books and periodicals on hiking that he'd studied, did he find mention of becoming lost in a remote forest as having beneficial health effects.

The clearing had no discernible exit, and as he stared from bush to shrub to tree to briar, neither could he make out the point at which he'd entered it. His dismay was complete, but standing there dwelling on his stupidity or misfortune wasn't going to put matters right. He stepped forward, towards where he thought the path might be and as he did so he stumbled, his foot catching some protruding object. He glanced down, expecting to see a tree root, or a briar tendril that had snagged his ankle. Instead, with mounting horror and distaste, he recognized the skeletal remains of a foot. A human foot.

In all the careful preparation he'd made prior to setting out on his hiking expedition, he'd made one sensible decision. After several moments staring in shock and growing nausea at the place where the disturbed earth had obviously been removed to dig a grave, the hiker slipped the rucksack from off his back and took out his mobile phone. He pressed 999 and waited, hoping against hope that there would be a signal out here. His relief when the emergency operator answered was so great that he failed to respond to the operator's question and had to be asked a second time which service he required.

'I was hiking in Bridewell Woods. I think I've found a body. A dead body. A human body.'

The explicit headline was scrawled on placards throughout the region, bringing additional circulation to the local newspaper. The killer picked up a copy at the supermarket and began reading the article.

BRIDEWELL WOODS BODY IDENTIFIED

The skeletal remains of the woman found by a hiker in Bridewell Woods two months ago have been identified as those of Madeleine (Marnie) Padgett, the prostitute reported missing in August last year. A police spokesman confirmed that the cause of death was strangulation and it was believed that the body had lain in the shallow grave since shortly after her death.

How had the hiker found her, the killer wondered? Had he been careless? Had he failed to cover the body completely perhaps? Admittedly it had been dark, but that was no excuse. It was the sort of sloppiness that he found inexcusable in others. The sort that could get you found out. He'd have to make sure with the next one. Thinking of which, perhaps it was time for another. He'd been feeling sort of restless recently, and that was probably the reason. Before he did anything, though, he'd have to check something out first. Or do the best he could. It wasn't the sort of question you could simply go along and ask. He smiled as he pictured the horrified reaction that would follow if he told them why he wanted the information. It would need to be planned and carried out with extreme care, but he was rather good at that.

Thinking of which, the news article had given him an idea. Perhaps it would make sense to tell the police where the others were buried. After all, if nobody knew about them, how could they appreciate his skill? How would he gain the recognition his greatness deserved? It would have to be done gradually, of course, after sufficient time had elapsed for there to be no evidence linking them to him. That was the case with Marnie, and would be with the other two. That was the reason he'd removed their clothing before burying them. Well, one of the reasons, anyway.

The phone call came in almost two years to the day after Marnie was reported missing. The police station where the message was received was over a hundred miles from where Marnie had lived – and died. At first, the telephonist who answered the phone was uncertain whether the call was a hoax or not. The fact that the caller's voice was heavily disguised didn't help. Detectives who analyzed the tape later guessed that the caller might have recorded the message and played it back at the wrong speed, alternating the pace to make the delivery switch from falsetto to double bass.

What was unmistakeable was the grim information given by the caller – if the call was genuine. 'You're looking for a missing woman. That prossie who vanished last year. You ought to try Cadogan Woods, up towards the north end. That's where I buried her.'

Sure enough, two days later, a police search team found the naked body of the missing prostitute in a shallow grave exactly where the caller had predicted. Like Marnie, she had been strangled, her clothing and jewellery removed and she had lain interred in the grave for almost a year.

During the three years that followed, three more police stations spread across England received similar calls. In each case the caller pointed to the location of the bodies. In each case the search team found the victims. All had been prostitutes, all had been strangled and all jewellery had been removed from their corpses. In each case, the body had been buried for a sufficiently long time for any evidence that might have existed to have either vanished completely or be sufficiently corrupted to be of no use to an investigation. The Woodland Strangler, as one enterprising reporter nicknamed the killer, was beginning to establish his reputation.

It was Friday afternoon, and there was a lull in activity at the West Midlands police station. This was a welcome break before the night shift came on duty and began bringing in their usual crop of regular visitors and first time offenders who had celebrated the end of the working week a little too strenuously.

The reception sergeant was using the quiet spell to catch up on filing a small mountain of paperwork that was threatening to bury his desk from sight for all eternity. He looked up as the door to the street opened and gave a silent groan. It wasn't that he actively disliked the reporter from the local newspaper, but spending half an hour answering or fending off the man's questions wasn't going to help reduce his filing stack.

The visitor approached the sergeant and asked, 'Is Jessie about?'

The fixed smile on the sergeant's face was replaced by the more genuine article. If the reporter wanted to speak to Detective Sergeant James, that meant he would have chance to continue with his filing. 'I'll buzz through to CID and see if he's got time to speak to you. Can I tell him what it's about?'

The reporter gestured to the missing person poster on the notice board to the sergeant's right. 'Say it's about her, I have some information, although how useful it is, I'm not sure.'

The sergeant glanced across. The blurred photograph of the missing prostitute Kitty Prentice hardly did the girl justice, but it was the best image they had. Kitty had been reported missing over a week earlier, and if the reporter did have some information, they couldn't afford to ignore it. The sergeant knew that there was already some speculation in CID as to whether the missing woman might have fallen victim to the most notorious serial killer of recent times. He picked up the phone. 'Jessie? I've got Big Mac here to see you. He reckons he might have some news about Kitty Prentice.' He listened for a while, then said, 'I don't know. He wouldn't say.'

The sergeant lowered the handset and asked, 'Jessie wants to know what sort of information you have.'

'Tell him I think Kitty might be another Woodland Strangler victim.'

DS James, known from the day he joined the force as Jessie, watched the reporter as the man poured three teaspoons of sugar into his coffee. He didn't find anything unusual in Big Mac's action. The canteen's coffee was generally acknowledged to be the worst available for many miles. Some wag from the night shift had even slipped into canteen during the early hours of one morning and stuck one of those hazardous chemical warning stickers on the machine, the ones depicting a skull and crossbones. When the canteen manager had complained, seventeen people from the rank of DI downwards had confessed to the crime. James waited patiently as the reporter stirred the noxious liquid, watched him take a sip and waited for the inevitable grimace. He wasn't disappointed. Big Mac gestured to the mug. If your DI drinks that, it goes a long way to explaining his sour disposition.'

He glanced round, as if looking to see if anyone could overhear what he was about to say. They were alone in the canteen, which made the action more of a habitual reflex one than from any real discomfort. Big Mac, whose nickname stemmed from both his surname, MacDowell, and his liking for the enormously popular fast food that he devoured on a regular basis, shuffled his chair closer and leaned forward.

'My editor put me on the Kitty Prentice story as soon as

the news broke that she was missing. He seemed to think right from the start that she might have been a strangler victim. So I started asking around the working girls. One of them told me something that makes me think my editor had it dead right. I believe Kitty was abducted and killed by the Woodland Strangler.'

'What makes you so convinced of that? He's never operated in this area before.'

'Ah, but that's the thing with him. It's part of his signature, his MO, call it what you like. He does one, moves onto a different area and then when the local force have all but given up on finding the missing woman, he rings up and tells them where to find her. Am I right?'

'OK, so it is just possible that Kitty was abducted by the strangler,' James conceded. 'Equally, she could have had enough of life here and legged-it to Birmingham or London where the pickings are greater.'

'Oh yes? You really think so? You think she just upped and went without taking even a change of clothes or any personal belongings? I talked to her landlord. Remember, he was the one reported her missing. He told me he went into her room when he hadn't seen her for a couple of days and it was as if she'd just stepped out to go to the corner shop for a packet of fags. No, either she's a strangler victim, or she was done in by her pimp, who is a really nasty little turd, or she could have fallen foul of a strangler copycat. Of the three, I'm inclined to think this was the genuine article. A Woodland Strangler case on your doorstep.'

'What makes you so convinced? What is it you know that we don't? Or are you simply trying to make a story where there isn't one? Are you fishing, or do you really have some useful facts to support the theory?'

The reporter looked round once more, although nobody had entered the canteen whilst they had been talking. 'OK,' he said; his voice little more than a whisper. 'Here's what I know. But before I tell you, I need assurances.'

'What sort of assurances?'

'First, that you won't try to get me to name my source,

because if so, all bets are off. Second, that I get an exclusive if this goes the way I expect.'

'I can't give you a promise about an exclusive, that's not in my remit, as you know. The other depends on who the source is.'

'It's another of the prossies.'

'Another working girl?' James frowned. 'Who is she? Why didn't she come forward with this information?'

'Don't be naive, Jessie. Can you honestly see one of those girls walking into a police station of their own accord? You'd be more likely to see them attending Sunday morning service at the local Methodist chapel.'

'What sort of information does she have?'

'Look, before I tell you, I want your promise not to go looking for her. This girl's scared shitless. She made me swear I wouldn't reveal her name, either in the paper, or to your lot. I had to give my word or I wouldn't have got the story. If you go sniffing round her, she'll think I betrayed her confidence.'

'OK,' James relented, 'so let's forget her identity. What's her story and why do you think it's so important?'

'Because she was attacked the night that Kitty disappeared. Only she got lucky and escaped.'

'What exactly happened?'

'She was picked up by a john. She'd not seen him before, but she said he seemed OK to begin with. Then after he'd shot his load he tried to strangle her with a piece of rope. That's the Woodland Strangler's MO, isn't it? Luckily this girl had taken a self-defence course organized by the Collective of English Prostitutes and she managed to fight him off. She got out of the car and ran all the way back to town. She was afraid he would follow her and was bricking it until she got to her room and bolted the door. Even then she wouldn't go out at night for a few days. Then she heard about Kitty and put two and two together. By the time I came along she was gagging for someone to confide in. She was so terrified she even left the money he paid her behind. I had to reimburse that before she'd say a word,' Big Mac ended gloomily, 'and I didn't even get my end away.'

'My heart bleeds for you,' James retorted. 'It certainly sounds as if the girl had a lucky escape, but I still don't see why you automatically think it was the Woodland Strangler at work. God knows there are plenty of perverts out there who get their rocks off from attacking women. They seem to think sex workers are fair game.'

'Ah, but what I haven't told you is where he took the girl. When I said she's to run back into town, I meant all the way from Henning Wood. That's a hell of a way. Even driving. There are plenty of secluded locations much nearer town where you can go to play hide the sausage without being disturbed. On the other hand, a remote stretch of woodland and the use of the rope seem to fit the Strangler's MO perfectly. And, having failed with her, it seems a logical assumption that he might have gone back, picked up Kitty, who wasn't as lucky, and finished her off.'

'You seem to have got it all pretty well worked out, so why are you bothering to tell me? I thought you would have kept it for your paper. Your editor seems to delight in running special articles criticizing us for inefficiency.'

Big Mac winced, for there was more than a grain of truth in what the detective had said. 'I told you, I want an exclusive if, and when, Kitty's body is found, and another if there's a chance of catching the killer.'

'And like I said at the beginning, you know I can't give you that.'

'No, but you can persuade that surly DI of yours to give me one.' Big Mac paused and grinned. 'In the more polite interpretation of that phrase, of course,' he added.

James took the story to his DI, who reluctantly gave the thumbs-up to the request for exclusive first access to any police activity on the Kitty Prentice investigation. Two days later, when a search team discovered a freshly dug mound of earth in a remote part of Henning Wood, it looked as if that would soon become a murder inquiry.

After careful excavation of the sight, forensic officers uncovered the body of Kitty Prentice, the Woodland

Strangler's sixth victim. This time, however, the corpse had not been in the ground long enough for decomposition to remove evidence of the killer's activity. A vaginal swab revealed semen and the sample meant that police had a DNA profile of the last man to have intercourse with the dead woman. This news was revealed to the public in the first of Big Mac's exclusives, under the headline, THE WOODLAND STRANGLER, IS THE NET CLOSING?

Three weeks later, the second exclusive, headlined, WOODLAND STRANGLER SUSPECT DETAINED, resulted in sales of that edition of the paper to exceed even those of the issue that contained the special sixteen-page pull-out of the Diamond Jubilee.

Chapter Two

The trial was a straightforward one; the verdict as close to a foregone conclusion as is possible in the complex minefield of the British legal system. This, despite the strenuous efforts of defence counsel to persuade the jury that their client's version of events was the correct one. The defendant's claim, which he delivered in a vehement statement, that he admitted picking up Kitty Prentice, and admitted paying her for sex, but that they had done it in the cab of his truck, not in or near Henning Wood as the prosecution suggested, was obviously more damaging than he or his legal adviser intended. When he was cross-examined, the prosecutor simply asked him to explain how he expected the jury to believe his innocence when he was the last person to have sex with the dead woman, his DNA was on her and inside her, and that rope, of a similar type to that used to strangle her, had been found in his cab. Rope, the counsel pointed out, in the distinctive blue and yellow livery of the company that he worked for, as had been explained to them by the pathologist during his evidence.

When the prosecutor rose to make his closing remarks, few within the court believed there would be anything other than a guilty verdict. He pointed out to the jury that the defence had come up with no evidence to suggest that their client was innocent, and that his admission of having sex with her in the hours leading up to her death plus the discovery of rope similar to that used to garrotte her in his possession amounted to overwhelming proof of his guilt. He went on to point out that West Midlands Police had checked Bryant's work schedules, and all the murders had taken place either when Bryant was on leave, or working close to where the women were killed. The jury lived up to everyone's expectation and with little more than the time taken to run through the facts of the case, returned to the courtroom to deliver their guilty verdict. The judge congratulated them for the wisdom of their decision before turning to address the defendant.

'I have no doubt in my mind that this verdict is correct. This murder was one of the most brutally savage within my long experience, and I am firmly of the opinion that you are an evil menace to society, and that women would never be safe whilst you remain free. Although the prosecution saw fit to bring only this case before the court, I have no doubt in my mind that the other crimes attributed to the so-called Woodland Strangler can now also be considered closed.'

The judge ended by sentencing Paul Bryant to life imprisonment, adding a recommendation to the effect that he should serve a minimum of twenty-five years before being considered for parole. 'By my calculation you will be almost seventy years of age at that time, should you survive, and it is my hope that your physical condition will have deteriorated to such an extent that you no longer pose a threat to those weaker than yourself.'

As those attending the trial, either as participants, media or spectators filed out of the court, it is fairly certain that not one of them believed a word of Bryant's outburst following sentencing. His cry of, 'I'm innocent – why will nobody believe me?' was greeted with almost audible derision in some quarters, whilst one of the prosecution team muttered to a colleague, 'Well, if he is innocent, he's going to the right place. They're all innocent in jail.'

One of those covering the trial for the media was Big Mac, who, despite severe pressure from the police, his editor and inducements from national newspapers, stuck loyally to his promise to his informant by protecting her identity. This caused a severe rift between the reporter and those managing the newspaper, and his position, which should have been secured by the exclusives he had obtained for them, was damaged to a point where he began looking for alternative employment soon after the end of the trial.

When the Woodland Strangler killings ceased following Paul Bryant's arrest and conviction, any remaining doubt there may have been over his guilt seemed to have vanished. Detectives in five other forces were able to mark their case files closed and amend their statistics by deducting one murder each from the total of unsolved crimes.

Not so the officers from three further forces, whose files relating to the rape and murder of three more women remained open. Although Bryant was a leading suspect in all three cases, the MO was slightly different, and with no corroborative evidence to back up their theory, they were unable to connect him to the crimes to an extent where they could present an acceptable case to the Crown Prosecution Service.

Detectives from the three forces attempted to interview Bryant on several occasions about these murders, but all he would do during the course of his interrogation was continue to protest his innocence of the prostitute murders. The similarity between the crimes they were attempting to solve and the Woodland Strangler cases lay with the fact that in all the cases, the jewellery worn by the women had been removed by the killer. There, the resemblance stopped. Whereas the Strangler victims had been garrotted with nylon cord, the other women had all been suffocated, probably, forensic officers speculated, using a pillow.

This argued that if Bryant was guilty of these murders as well, he had either taken the victims back to the cab of his truck or to the one-bedroom apartment he used when he wasn't on the road. Exhaustive forensic checks on both failed to yield any possible connection.

Some months following Bryant's conviction, a psychological profiler offered his services in examining all the cases with a view to being able to provide an informed opinion as to whether Bryant was involved or not. His long and detailed report was eventually used by one of the detectives in an attempt to secure a confession from Bryant, using the argument that as he was already serving a life sentence, he had little to lose by telling the truth. Despite a warning from his superior officer not to trust a convicted serial killer because they are known to be highly manipulative, the detective pressed ahead with the plan, and delivered a copy of the report to Felling Prison in North Yorkshire, where Bryant was now serving his sentence. Neither the detective who handed Bryant the report, nor the profiler who compiled it could have known the dramatic and violent course of events which would take place following Bryant's study of the contents.

The opening of the document, which was in the form of an overview, set out the classic personality and performance traits of the serial killer genre. Low achievement, both academically and in employment, a manual or menial job, violent, dysfunctional or non-existent family background, inadequate social skills, the inability to form stable and lasting relationships and a solitary lifestyle; all of these went into the makeup of the serial killer template.

From there, the profiler went on to analyze the crimes one by one and in great depth, citing the details of each of the victims, together with their background and suggesting how or where they might have come into contact with Bryant. In one or two of the cases the possible connections seemed tenuous or non-existent, but the profiler, whilst not ignoring the fact, appeared to minimize its significance.

He ended by giving a detailed assessment of Bryant, and pointed to the obvious and overwhelming evidence of how well he fitted the serial killer mould.

Bryant was an orphan, who had been abandoned by his mother shortly before she died of a drug overdose. His father was unknown, possibly a client of the mother, who had a record for prostitution. Bryant had been sent to a succession of foster homes and care facilities, and there was evidence to suggest that in one of these he had been sexually abused by an older boy. In another, Bryant himself had formed what was referred to rather vaguely as an unhealthy relationship with an older girl in the establishment.

At school his record was poor, both academically and athletically, although his intelligence was not below average. He was notably shy, especially around girls, and made few friends. On one occasion he had been in trouble for fighting, but apart from that there was little to indicate the violent conduct that was to follow.

On leaving school, Bryant had volunteered to join the army, and served without notable distinction for nine years. In commenting on this fact, the profiler failed to mention that Bryant didn't get into trouble of any kind during the period of his service, so presumably that fact was immaterial.

After leaving the army, Bryant took a job with a large haulage and distribution company, passing his HGV driving tests and becoming a reliable employee with a good attendance record. Once again the profiler paid scant attention to this part of Bryant's history.

His final paragraph, summing up all that had gone before, was a telling one, at least as far as the detectives studying the report were concerned. 'I have no doubt,' the profiler wrote, 'that although there is a slight variance in the methodology of some of these crimes, the perpetrator in each case was undoubtedly Paul Bryant, possibly the most dangerous and violent sexual predator I have ever encountered.'

In fact, the profiler hadn't encountered Bryant at all, merely studied the case files. However, the detectives read that summing-up and came to the logical conclusion that they need look no further for the man who had committed the murders. As for Bryant, he didn't read the full report. By the time he reached the foot of the first page he had learned all he needed to know about what the profiler had written.

Archie Lloyd was a thief. A highly professional thief moreover, one whose income from his nefarious activities yielded that of many within more conventional employment.

His success was such that his operations became a thorn in the side of police officers, especially those serving within forces in more affluent districts where Archie tended to concentrate his talents for entering and leaving other people's property unseen.

Archie's particular forte was jewellery and precious

stones, and shortly after Paul Bryant had been transferred to Felling Prison, Archie also arrived there, having finally made an entry in the criminal records by gaining his first conviction. The arrest followed a fairly devious sting mounted by North Yorkshire police following Archie's audacious theft of a diamond pendant from the home of a local landowner. For the first time, Archie had made a mistake. He entered the property in the belief that the owner and his family were abroad. Unfortunately for them, and for Archie as it transpired, the youngest child developed chickenpox and they had to remain at home. When Archie was about to open the safe he was confronted by the homeowner and resorted to his emergency plan. He took his gun from his pocket, tied up the man and his wife and locked them in the bedroom with their children.

When he was tempted by news of an even more expensive set of jewels that had been purchased by an internet entrepreneur for his wife, the temptation had been too great.

Archie's arrest, in the study of the businessman during the early hours of the morning, had left him unusually at a loss for words, even his agile brain failing to come up with a convincing explanation for his presence there. Identification by the householder who had suffered the undignified assault a few weeks earlier doubled the number of charges brought against Lloyd. His defence plea that he hadn't actually fired the gun and only used it to menace the couple, fell on deaf ears.

Although the prosecution could not bring evidence of the many other thefts carried out by Archie, their leading counsel managed, by skilful use of the English language to convey the impression that such a high-level of expertise could only be gained after assiduous practice over a long period of time; and that the sophisticated equipment Archie was carrying when detained were the tools of a highly proficient professional.

Lloyd's conviction, whilst upsetting for him, was equally distressing for his younger sister. Although she had been christened Mary, from an early age she was known to one and all as Marie, after the famous music hall star.

She and Archie were devoted to one another. Both their parents had died shortly after Marie's eighteenth birthday, and in the absence of other close relatives, Archie took it upon himself to look after his sibling. He did this so well, that when Marie graduated from university, her degree was to a large extent funded by Archie's burgeoning nocturnal career.

In the years that followed, Marie became increasingly successful in her chosen profession, which in contrast to that of her brother was strictly legal. Despite this wide difference in their lifestyles, she and Archie remained close, sharing an apartment in the affluent North Yorkshire market town of Netherdale.

Exactly how much Marie knew of Archie's burglary exploits is uncertain, but if his arrest and conviction distressed her, it by no means came as a complete shock. As soon as sentence had been passed, and Marie had learned that the place of his incarceration was within easy travelling distance, she wrote to Archie instructing him to set about providing visiting orders so that she could carry out the regular four-weekly, hour-long visits. At the same time she ensured her work schedule was such that she would be free for the time and date of those visits.

Marie had carried out three of these and had just received a visiting order for the next when events at Felling Prison took a dramatic and violent turn, one that affected the lives of Marie, her brother Archie, Paul Bryant, the so-called Woodland Strangler, and in the longer run a great many other people.

The prison population is ever-shifting, not only from new inmates and those being released, but via transfers that many in the outside world are unaware take place. One such order, signed on the day of Marie's third visit, brought a batch of new prisoners to Felling Prison. Amongst them was one whose crimes, although by no means as terrible as those Paul

Bryant had been convicted of, were sufficiently brutal to have him assigned to the high security wing of the jail. That brought him into close proximity with Bryant, and also with Lloyd.

Archie Lloyd's presence in such dubious company was not only a consequence of his carrying a firearm but his known ability to bypass such antiquated mechanisms as locks. Even the most sophisticated electronic protection was of little use against Lloyd's talent, and on reading his record, the warden had scrawled a note to the officers in charge of allocations to the effect that, 'if we hope to keep this prisoner inside the jail, he will have to go in the High Security Wing.'

The new inmate was an enforcer for a ruthless drugs cartel operating in the south of England. He had a long record of extreme violence. Ross Ashton's Christian name was rarely used, except on official forms – and by arresting officers when charging him, and later by judges passing sentence. Within his circle and a large section of the wider criminal community he was known as 'Ash the Bash', because of his ability to persuade reluctant people to an acceptable pattern of behaviour. Acceptable to his employers, that is. Using a sledgehammer to inflict pain, especially on vulnerable points on the human frame was Ash the Bash's speciality. In addition to a borderline psychopathic personality, Ashton was a rampant homosexual, with a penchant for tough and violent copulation, either with or without the consent of his chosen partner. On entering the High Security wing of Felling Prison, one of the first inmates he saw was Archie Lloyd. One look at the thief, with his fine-boned, handsome, almost effeminate features, and Ashton knew he wanted him.

Although much has been said and written about intimate behaviour amongst the prison population, in fact, the opportunity for such relationships to take place is far rarer than the popular myth. Such encounters, whether from willing participants or otherwise, are strictly forbidden, looked on with great distaste by the authorities, who set in place such tightly controlled routines as to make such an event virtually impossible to achieve. In a high security section of a prison especially, prisoners are of the type that have to be locked away alone for all but a brief period each day.

That is the theory, at least. In practice, although such occasions are extremely rare, the routine can be broken, given the devious and cunning nature of the prisoners, and the natural human response of their guardians to respond to a threatening situation that has arisen, rather than questioning whether its cause is a genuine one, or provoked by someone with an ulterior motive.

Ash the Bash had many contacts in the prison. This stemmed from the number of times he had been in similar establishments, and the desire of other inmates to court favour with both Ashton and his employers. A good turn done inside can be lavishly rewarded on the outside. The converse is also true, so, whether from the need for popularity or pure fear, he had little problem recruiting willing volunteers for his plan. Having first selected two close contacts to act as lookouts, Ashton approached a third inmate he knew wanted to get close to the cartel, and would act as his supplier when he returned to drug dealing after his sentence was complete. 'I need to get the screws out of the way. Ten minutes, at the most, will be more than enough.' He explained why he wanted this favour.

If the man had any scruples or reservations about becoming involved in such a horrific scheme, it didn't show. 'You need the screws out of the way so you can have a good screw?' he asked with a grin.

'You got it,' Ashton agreed. 'Any ideas?'

'A fight would be best, I reckon. Preferably one with steel involved. There are a few guys on the wing who owe me. I can call in some favours.'

Ashton put his hand on the man's shoulder, barely noticing the slight wince. 'I'll make sure you're looked after,' he promised.

Nothing more needed to be said. Two days later he got

the word. Everything had been arranged for the spell following exercise the next day. Even thinking about the possibility was already making him horny.

The fight was a three-way affair, and lasted little more than ten minutes. It would not have taken that long, or attracted the attention of all five prison officers on duty in the shower block had two of the combatants not produced makeshift knives.

The sound of raised voices gave Ashton, his supporters and other occupants of the shower area their cue. Two prisoners stood on guard; the others, warned in advance, slipped quietly past the sentinels and out into the corridor, ostensibly to watch the fracas going on there. As the warders pushed those inmates aside in their hurry to intervene and prevent bloodshed, Ashton approached Lloyd, dropping the bath towel that was his only garment on the floor.

'Now, honey, you're all mine.'

He slammed Lloyd face first against the rough concrete wall, one arm around his throat as his hand covered his target's mouth. Ashton, the two prisoners on watch and everyone else were too intent on the action, either within the shower area or in the corridor to notice the sound of a flushing toilet.

Ashton's attention was distracted by two piercing screams in quick succession. He turned his head to locate the source, but too late. As he moved, he felt a hand grasp one wrist. His arm was twisted, and, as he gave an agonized squeal, he felt a sharp blow on his elbow. Pain was immediate and like no other he had ever experienced. As he howled in agony, defenceless against further attack, his other arm was given the same treatment.

The returning officers were met by a scene of mayhem. They stared aghast in turn at the sight of two prisoners kneeling just inside the door, each clutching their face. One of the pair had blood trickling through his fingers. At the other side of the room, Ashton was slumped against the wall in a sitting position, his arms out to the side, elbows bent at an angle impossible to achieve for anyone not double-jointed.

In the middle of the room, in the eye of the storm he'd created, Paul Bryant, the so-called Woodland Strangler, was standing, one arm comfortingly round the shoulders of Archie Lloyd, who had a thin trickle of blood coming from his nose, which looked to have been broken.

'Ashton claims it was a totally unprovoked assault, as do the other two that Bryant assaulted. Both of Ashton's arms were broken at the elbow, forced out of joint and it will be months before he can get full use of them. For the time being he can't feed himself or go to the toilet unaided. The queue to assist in either of those operations isn't huge. As to the other two, one has lost the sight in his left eye; the other may suffer the same consequence.

All three reckon Bryant came out of the toilet and went berserk for no apparent reason. That totally contradicts what Lloyd told us. He says the two were standing guard whilst Ashton attempted to rape him. Lloyd admits he would probably have succeeded had Bryant not intervened. Lloyd says his nose was broken when Ashton forced him against the wall. I think that's called foreplay,' the officer concluded with a grin.

The governor winced. 'What a mess. Who do we believe?'

'I'm not sure. We know what a violent history Bryant has, but that's been against women. On the other hand, we know Ashton to be a raving queer. Everyone knows that, and there is a rumour he's had his eye on Lloyd ever since he arrived here, but you know what it is with prisoners, nobody is prepared to say anything openly.'

'What about Bryant?'

'He was the only one not to have a scratch on him. The officers who were on duty said when they came into the shower room he was standing there, cool as a cucumber, protecting Lloyd. That bit certainly tallies with Lloyd's statement.'

'What's Bryant's version of events?'

The senior officer shrugged. 'Your guess is as good as mine. All he's said so far is, "talk to Lloyd. There's no point asking me. Whatever I say; nobody believes me so why should I waste my breath". That was it; we couldn't get another word out of him, but the way he said it made him sound very angry and bitter.'

'I've been reading Bryant's file,' the governor said, 'and I noticed that he's always maintained he was innocent of all those crimes. Now that we have first-hand evidence of the level of violence of which he's capable, either with or without provocation, nobody is ever going to believe he didn't murder those unfortunate young women.' He gave a sigh of despair. 'I suppose I'd better ring the police and get the formal investigation under way. It's lucky that events like this are rare. All the extra work involved is a nightmare, and the upset it causes the inmates can be very unsettling.'

'Do you want me to contact North Yorkshire police, sir?'

'No, it had better come from me.' The governor frowned. 'We're under a different jurisdiction now, aren't we? Since they closed Bishopton police station, I mean?'

'Yes, sir, everything is channelled via their headquarters in Netherdale now.

Nash was seated in his office at Helmsdale with Detective Sergeant Mironova when the call came in from Superintendant Fleming. He listened for some time without speaking, but eventually responded. 'That's fine; but one thing I would like is a copy of the files for each of the inmates involved. If that's in order, I'll be there tomorrow to begin the investigation. I'll take Viv Pearce. What time should we go?'

After he put the phone down, Nash looked across at his colleague. 'Ask Viv to come in, will you, Clara. Tell him he's going to prison.'

When Pearce joined them, Nash explained. 'Apparently there was a serious assault at Felling Prison yesterday, but the circumstances were not as clear as usual in such cases.

Three prisoners were attacked by a fourth inmate and seriously injured, although none of the injuries is life-threatening. From what Jackie Fleming told me, one had both his arms broken, another has lost an eye, and it's touch and go whether the third will also be permanently blind in one eye.'

'Blimey!' Pearce exclaimed. 'What sort of weapon did the man use?'

'Only his bare hands, apparently.'

'Who is he, Superman or a devotee of Bruce Li?' Mironova asked.

'Neither.' Nash's expression was sombre. 'I'd normally have no qualms about taking you along with me, Clara, but given the identity of the attacker I wouldn't even consider it. The prisoner accused of committing the assaults is Paul Bryant.'

'Bryant? Isn't he the—?'

'The Woodland Strangler,' Nash confirmed. 'Now you understand why I refuse to let you go along. I wouldn't let any woman near that sadistic pervert.'

Chapter Three

Having met with the governor and examined the files of all the prisoners involved in what Pearce referred to as the shower room incident, they began questioning Archie Lloyd. His story differed widely from the version of events they would receive from the inmates and prison officers. Their next interviewee, Ashton, was surly and for the most part uncommunicative. He was obviously in some pain, which might have explained his taciturn lack of response to their questions. The presence of other inmates in the prison hospital ward where he was being kept obviously didn't help.

Nash and Pearce had already been told that their questioning of the two men who had suffered eye injuries would have to wait, as they had been transferred to Leeds for specialist treatment.

When they had finished with the officers involved, they braced themselves for the final encounter of the day. After Paul Bryant was ushered into the small room they had been assigned, whatever preconceived notions they might have entertained about the serial killer were soon to fade in the face of reality. Bryant appeared calm; quiet and polite, and surprisingly normal. Moreover, he was extremely bitter and antagonistic in his attitude to authority, which surprised the detectives.

'Tell us your version of what happened,' Nash invited him.

Bryant's response was similar to that reported by the prison officer who had questioned him immediately after the incident. He leaned back in his chair and sighed wearily. 'What does it matter? You won't believe me. You'll already have made up your minds that I'm guilty. Nobody listens to me or believes a word I say, so why should I waste my breath? I'm a notorious killer, remember? That means I'm obviously incapable of telling the truth.'

The prison officer who had accompanied Bryant was about to intervene, but Nash put his hand up in a warning gesture. 'Why don't you try me?' he suggested quietly. 'I've never met you; I've no reason to doubt your version of events. Remember, this isn't just about you. Lloyd could also suffer as a result of this investigation should you fail to say anything. He could be charged as an accessory, or an equal participant.'

'That sounds to me like blackmail.'

'Call it what you like. All I'm after is the truth. It was so much easier in medieval times, when I could have put you on the rack and got the truth out of you. Now, we have conventions regarding the questioning of prisoners that forbid such practices.'

Oddly, it seemed that Nash's absurd suggestion actually swayed Bryant, although his first reaction was a disbelieving laugh. 'Truth – that's an interesting word to use.'

Pearce was beginning to think they were not going to get anywhere with Bryant, and that they were wasting their time, but Nash waited in patient silence. As the seconds grew into minutes the silence got more and more oppressive, until Bryant suddenly leaned forward in his chair. 'OK, but remember this; when I was in court at my trial, I gave my version of events and nobody took any notice. Their minds were already made up before I entered the courtroom.'

'Yes, you've already said that, and my answer is still the same. Let me judge for myself, and remember, I said judge, not pre-judge.'

'What happened is simple. Sordid, but simple,' Bryant began. 'There was a fight; a put-up job to distract the officers on duty so that Ashton could get at Lloyd. From what I've heard since, Ashton had already marked Lloyd down for his special attention.'

The prison officer standing in the corner gave a surprised gasp, which in turn made Bryant smile. 'A lot of prisoner gossip doesn't reach the ears of the officers,' he explained. The two whose eyes I poked were acting as lookouts. Ashton had Lloyd up against the wall, and was trying to force himself on him when I came out of the toilet. In all the excitement, the officers had forgotten the serial killer was taking a shit at the time. As soon as I came out I could tell what was happening. I got shut of the lookouts and then dealt with Ashton. I probably used too much force, but I have no regrets. Ashton is an evil bastard, and I was taught not to take any chances in such situations.'

'Taught?' Pearce asked. 'Taught by whom?'

Bryant gave a faint smile. 'The British army. They're rather good at that sort of thing.'

'Why did you think we wouldn't believe you?' Nash asked. 'Your version of what happened tallies exactly with Lloyd's statement.'

'Force of habit, I guess.'

'You still maintain you didn't kill those women, even though you've been tried and found guilty?'

Bryant's expression darkened. 'He looked at Nash, to be met with a stare that held his own; challenging him. 'Yes,' he said eventually, 'I do. Whatever you heard, saw or read about me isn't the truth. I was convicted purely and simply because I was lonely and paid that poor woman for sex. I didn't garrotte her; or any of the others. Anyway, it's immaterial now, isn't it?' For a moment it seemed as if Bryant was going to add more, but he fell silent, and despite further questions from Nash would say nothing further.

Nash was very quiet as they drove back to Helmsdale. 'What do you make of Bryant?' Pearce asked eventually.

'To be honest, I'm not sure what to make of him. He's either a very good actor, who has learned how to channel his body language, or he's telling the truth. He showed none of the signs we're trained to look out for when someone is lying. Alternatively, it could be that he's sick enough to believe that what he's saying is the truth.'

'You mean he could be too mad to differentiate between truth and fantasy?'

'It's happened before.'

'Lloyd's statement bears his story out,' Pearce

commented.

'Oh yes, I'm in no doubt about that part of what Bryant told us. I was referring to his denial of responsibility for the Woodland Strangler murders.'

Pearce stared at him in surprise. 'You think there might be a possibility that he didn't commit the murders he was convicted of?'

'I wouldn't put it as strongly as that; certainly not without a much closer knowledge of the case, but Bryant didn't come across as guilty. Most serial killers are sick enough to take pride in describing their exploits, sometimes revelling in the revolting details. There are very few that I've read or heard about that continue to protest their innocence even after they've been convicted and sentenced.'

'I have to admit, Bryant wasn't at all what I expected. He seemed ... well... normal,' Pearce added.

'One thing that does intrigue me. If Bryant did commit those murders, why did he use a garrotte?'

'I don't get you.'

'Look at it this way, Viv. You've just heard first-hand evidence of how he dealt with three men in a fight. He told you himself, or as good as, that he'd been trained to kill with his bare hands. That means he had both the strength and technique to kill those women without need for a rope, or wire, or whatever was used. Of course, the court would have had no knowledge of any of that. They wouldn't have the evidence of his strength that we have, nor, unless his counsel was crazy, would his unarmed combat training have been brought out. However, that's not our priority, at the moment all we're concerned with is the prison incident.'

'At the moment? The killings are nothing to do with us, surely? We can't get involved with them now that the case has been tried, can we? The murders didn't even take place in our territory.'

'I appreciate that, Viv, but if you want to split hairs, Bryant is in Felling Prison, and that does fall within our jurisdiction. More important though, if we suspect that there has been a serious miscarriage of justice, we are duty bound to investigate it. That, in my opinion, is exactly what we're employed to do.'

'I still don't think we ought to go poking around the murders, Mike.'

Nash glanced sideways, a look that made Pearce shiver. 'No? What if Bryant is innocent?'

Pearce shrugged. 'He wouldn't be the first man to be wrongly convicted. I don't see it as our job to attempt to put things right, even if he isn't guilty. Surely that's a matter for his legal team and the court of appeal.'

'Is that what you think? Have you taken time to consider the implications?'

'Sorry, Mike, I'm not with you. What implications?'

'Well, first we may have a miscarriage of justice. That's bad enough to begin with. However, far more serious is the possibility raised if Bryant is innocent.'

'And that is?'

'That the real killer is still at large, free to kill; whenever and wherever he wants.'

'Good Lord! I hadn't thought of that.'

'I didn't think you could have. But whatever the true version of the murders might be, we have to decide whether Bryant's actions in Felling were justified, or whether he overreacted. Thankfully, the final decision for that won't be ours, it'll be down to the CPS. That might not be good news for Bryant.'

It wasn't long before news of the disturbance at Felling Prison got into the public domain; fuelled as it was by the notoriety of at least one of those involved. The level of violence used by Bryant convinced any who might have doubted his original conviction, even without the hyperbole employed by the media, whose reaction was for the authorities to clamp down hard on Bryant. This was followed by a campaign for tougher sentences, complete segregation of category 43 prisoners and a demand that the Woodland Strangler should never be released despite the limitations of the British sentencing policy.

One of the leaders of the protests directed at Bryant came uncomfortably close to home for Nash. The local paper, the *Netherdale Gazette* was at the forefront of calls for the full weight of justice to be brought down on Bryant. Their headlines and the articles below them caused a slight rift between Nash and the paper's temporary editor. Becky Pollard had returned from her post in London with one of the Nationals to take control of the family-owned paper. Her uncle, the editor, had fallen down the office stairs. The resultant stay in hospital for a necessary hip replacement meant she would be in Netherdale until he was fit to return to work. More than one resident took pleasure in her, albeit short-term, return. She was the goddaughter of the chief constable and she also had a long-term relationship with Nash. Now it seemed as if the paper's stance would endanger this.

'Look, Mike,' Becky told him when he protested, 'I didn't write these articles. That's all down to the paper's crime reporter.'

'But you could have used your authority to suppress them,' Nash countered.

'I could have done, but that wouldn't have been in the public interest. People are scared by monsters like Bryant. Besides which, I'm only here in a caretaker role. If I was full-time editor, I might have had it toned down a bit. The public want to know that they can feel safe whilst he's locked away. They don't want to hear about him being able to go on the rampage in Felling, simply because they're afraid of what he might do if he escaped.'

Although Nash argued the unlikelihood of such an event, it seemed he was fighting a losing battle, and there followed a coolness in the couple's relationship. He concentrated his mind on the report he had to write following his interview with all the inmates and officers involved in the incident in the High Security Wing. His written statement for the CPS contained a guarded summary of what had taken place, which he followed with his opinion regarding the course of events.

'There seems little doubt,' Nash wrote, 'that the fight that took place in the corridor was staged simply to distract the officers on duty within the shower block and draw them out, leaving the room unguarded. This would support the statements of Lloyd and Bryant that the diversion was created in order that Ashton was given the opportunity to stage a sexual assault on Lloyd. Given the respective physiques of the two men, there seems little doubt that this would have succeeded, had it not been for Bryant's timely intervention.

'However,' Nash's report continued, 'the level of violence used by Bryant in defence of Lloyd must appear to outsiders as excessive. Bryant himself tacitly acknowledged this, but in his own defence explained that it was the way he had been trained to deal with such a situation during his time in the army. Having checked his army records and spoken to his former commanding officer, I am able to confirm that this is the case, and that Bryant was trained in unarmed combat, in which he became highly proficient. The methods he used, which I described in detail, are apparently standard procedure. Whether Bryant's actions warrant a further prosecution, I leave for CPS to decide.

'One further point I should make is that a prosecution of Ashton for the attempted sexual assault on Lloyd should be considered. Although the assault was unsuccessful, it would have been a completely different story had Bryant not intervened.'

Despite Nash's comments, he received a note from CPS a week after submitting his report informing him that paperwork was being prepared for Bryant to answer three charges of occasioning actual bodily harm, and that Nash should make himself available should it be deemed necessary for him to give evidence once a date had been set for the court appearance.

The day after Bryant was told that he would have to go to court to answer charges of assault, he received a letter. He stared at the envelope for some time. The handwriting was unfamiliar, which was hardly surprising as Bryant had no friends or relatives. During his time in prison he had received only one communication from the outside world, a piece of hate mail from the sister of one of his victims. Was this another such, he wondered? Such mail would normally not get past the censor, but human nature being what it is, Bryant was sure the officers charged with inspecting the mail would be quite happy to allow anything past that might cause him distress.

He slipped the letter from within the already opened envelope and began to read. He was surprised to find that it contained, not the hate he had expected, but an outpouring of gratitude for what he had done to defend Lloyd. He turned the sheet of paper over, and deciphered the signature on the reverse. The letter was from Lloyd's sister, Marie. He continued to read and was surprised to see that she wished to visit him to express her appreciation properly.

Bryant thought about the letter for several days before replying. During that time he kept her letter safe, taking it out now and again to read it over, and occasionally sniffing the paper. Her scent was on it; the clean scent of a woman. Despite his grim surroundings he felt his excitement growing. He hadn't been near a woman for a long time. Lloyd was a good-looking man; would his sister be even more attractive? Would she be the sort of woman he liked; wanted?

Eventually, he replied, and as he wrote he kept the tone of his note casual. The last thing he wanted was to scare her off. If she did come to visit, he would get that lovely scent again. Perhaps she would allow him to touch her, if only to shake hands. He stated that he didn't think a visit was necessary if only to say thank you, but if she was prepared to make the effort, he would be pleased to see her. He ended by saying that the time and date didn't matter, as he was always at home. He enclosed a visiting order which he had signed.

The last sentence made Marie smile when she read it, and as she started to fill in the visitng order she felt slightly more relaxed, although the prospect of coming face to face with a serial killer was still daunting.

When she arrived at Felling Prison, Marie spent the first few minutes of the hour-long visit reiterating her gratitude; explaining how close she and Archie were, and the reasons for that. Bryant sympathized, and told her that he understood because he had never known either of his parents, having been abandoned to an orphanage within weeks of his birth. 'Even my name isn't my own,' he told her. 'It was one that was given to me.'

Although Bryant had initially accepted the visit as a chore and out of curiosity mixed with the desire to be in the company of a woman again, after only a few minutes in Marie's company he felt urges that he had long repressed growing within him.

Marie was upset when Bryant told her that he was going to face further trouble on account of his defence of her brother, but he merely shrugged and said, 'They've got me locked up for life. What more can they do to me?'

The comment gave Marie the opening she had been looking for. With a great deal of trepidation she broached the subject of his conviction, and the crimes that had led up to it. He began to tell her his side of the story, his explanation a halting one, sometimes rambling, sometimes almost drying up. If Marie found the revelations shocking she managed to control her emotions sufficiently to hide any revulsion from Bryant.

Ten days after Marie's visit to Bryant, her brother Archie was on the receiving end of a snide remark from a fellow inmate. The man was thin, weedy and undersized, presenting nothing of the threat that Ashton had posed. Archie cornered the man and demanded an explanation for his comment.

At the first opportunity, Lloyd sought out Bryant. Getting to speak to him had been hard prior to the incident; now it was doubly difficult. However, Lloyd managed it, passing the news quickly, his voice little more than an urgent whisper.

'Word is there's a contract out on you because of what

you did to Ashton. His boss has ordered the hit because you dissed one of his men. Better be on your guard at all times.'

Until recently, the news might not have troubled Bryant unduly. But since Marie's visit his attitude had changed somewhat. He had thought of little else since she had left. He wanted her, as he hadn't wanted a woman for a long time. However impossible to achieve, that didn't prevent his thoughts from returning to her face, her body, concealed though it was by her clothing; thinking of what was beneath those garments, his desire to be with her growing with each memory. He clung desperately to the promise contained in her parting words, and the prospect of her coming to visit him again as soon as she was able.

*

Three days after the snatched conversation between Lloyd and Bryant, Marie was back at the prison visiting her brother. She began by telling Archie about her time with Bryant. 'He wasn't anything like the monster I imagined,' she said, 'and I still can't believe he did those dreadful things. Although he did tell me something that made me wonder if I was prejudiced because of what he did for you. He told me he didn't kill any of those women. And I was halfway to believing him, but then he said something that brought all the doubts back and made me wonder if all those protestations of innocence were nothing more than a pack of lies, designed to impress me. Perhaps after all, he was only playing on my gratitude and saying what he thought I would want to hear.'

'What exactly did he tell you that upset you so much?'

'As you know, all along he's maintained that the only evidence connecting him to those murders was the fact that he'd had sex with the last victim at some point before she died. He also said that as far as the police and everyone else is concerned that was his only connection with any of the dead women. But then he told me that one of the Woodland Strangler's other victims was his first girlfriend. He knew the girl when they were at school together. Bryant said he hadn't seen her for years. Now I don't know what to believe.'

'On the face of it, I think you're right to suspect the worst. Better to be safe than sorry. Don't have any more to do with him, Sis. By the sound of it, he's got more on his plate than he can handle. Far worse than the court case. He'll be lucky to see the year out, I reckon.'

'What do you mean?'

Archie explained about the contract. If he thought that would deter Marie, on top of the warning about Bryant, his reading of female logic was totally wrong. The news that Bryant was in danger, far from discouraging Marie, made her determined to continue their contact. As she was about to leave, Archie said something that gave her food for thought. 'One thing I don't understand, Sis. Bryant isn't the bragging type, right? That being the case, and if he denies he committed the murders, why did he tell you about his old girlfriend? He must have known that would make you suspect the worst. If he wasn't telling the truth you'd have thought he'd keep information as damaging as that to himself, wouldn't you?'

Despite her brother's warning, Marie visited Bryant twice more in the period prior to his court appearance. He acknowledged her concern for his welfare following the threat to his life from the contract rumoured to be out on him. Her interest in his wellbeing heightened his excitement. Marie was unaware of this, or the mounting frustration her proximity was causing him.

He had been without a woman for such a long time, it had ceased to worry him, or, more accurately, he had schooled himself not to think of women. Now that had all changed. With each visit the old desires were re-awakened and intensified. Soon, Bryant knew, he would have to deal with this. But in order to do that, he would have to escape from the confines of Felling Prison. Escape – the thought hadn't occurred to him before. Now, suddenly, the idea filled his mind; that, and the need for a woman.

Chapter Four

On the Saturday prior to Bryant's trial, Nash took his son Daniel to Headingley to watch the Test match, a treat he had promised Daniel months earlier.

As Nash emerged from the toilets adjacent to one of the bars during the lunch interval, he encountered someone he recognized. Apart from a nod of acknowledgment, the two men didn't speak. At any other time they would have stopped for a chat, but Nash was aware that, as the judge hearing the Bryant case and the police officer who would be giving evidence, any contact between them, however innocuous their conversation might be, could be construed as improper.

Nash settled back into his seat as play was about to recommence. He helped himself to a sandwich from the selection he had purchased and they sat back to watch the entertainment. Daniel's excitement grew as the afternoon session of play provided a rare treat. England's middle-order batsmen were taking the opposition bowling attack apart, and in an attempt to achieve a breakthrough, the visiting captain turned to his off-spinner. The man's first delivery was over-pitched, and the hard-hitting number six seized on the half-volley with glee, sending the ball rocketing back over the bowler's head into the stand, causing several spectators to duck for cover.

Nash watched the judge take avoiding action and chuckled to himself. Back in the office on Monday morning, he remarked to Clara, 'We almost had to postpone Bryant's trial.'

'Why?' Clara was mystified by the remark until Nash explained what had happened at the ground.

'Perhaps Bryant's defence is paying the batsman,' she suggested.

The prosecution presented their case factually. If their star

161

witness, 'Ash the Bash' Ashton, made a less than favourable impression on the jury, his vehement denial of any wrongdoing was unshaken, despite the severe cross-examination of defence counsel.

The first witness for the defence was Archie Lloyd. By contrast with Ashton, who had appeared calm and unruffled in the witness box, Lloyd was far more hesitant. This might have been due in part to having to describe the attempted sexual assault he alleged he had suffered.

When prosecuting counsel rose to cross examine Lloyd, his first question seemed somewhat irrelevant. 'How long have you known the defendant?'

'I don't know him,' Lloyd replied, 'I've only spoken to him a couple of times.'

'Really,' the prosecutor's voice was a drawl of disbelief. 'Then how do you account for the fact that your sister has visited him three times in the past four months? That's once more than she's visited you.'

'I ... er ... I don't know. I think she was grateful for what he did for me.'

'So grateful, that between the three of you, you concocted a story that would allow Bryant to escape punishment for his violent actions? Isn't that the reason she visited Bryant so frequently?'

Although Lloyd denied the allegation, it was clear that the jury had taken the point, prompted by counsel's implication that Marie was never off the doorstep of Felling Prison. Defence counsel glanced at Bryant to see how he was taking this unexpected development. His casual glance turned into a stare, as he noticed with slight puzzlement that Bryant seemed oblivious of proceedings.

Instead of listening, Bryant was gazing fixedly towards the press gallery on the opposite side of the court, a curious expression on his face. As counsel followed the direction of Bryant's eyes, he recognized the woman seated in the front row. The barrister was a local man, and most of the members of the press were well known to him; certainly someone as important as Becky Pollard. But why was Bryant staring at the editor of the *Netherdale Gazette*? And what was that expression? Lust or loathing? Even the counsel, who was used to interpreting people's facial movement, was unable to fathom that out.

The only other witness called by the defence was Nash, who had been passed over by the prosecution, whose counsel deemed his evidence unnecessary, or possibly damaging. His evidence began by concentrating on the fight in the corridor, which Nash suggested had been staged to distract the officers on duty in the shower area. When prosecuting counsel rose to challenge this, Nash informed him that two of the inmates who had been in the shower area at the time had made statements to the effect that they had been instructed to leave once the altercation began. Counsel sat down abruptly.

The exchange and Nash's victory obviously made a deep impression on the jury. When cross-examination began, prosecution counsel asked Nash to explain the excessive level of violence used by Bryant. If he had hoped that Nash would be flustered by the question, the barrister was disappointed.

'Excessive is your word; and I venture to suggest is a matter of opinion. However, in answer to your question, I believe it to have been no more than a reflex action on Bryant's part. By that, I mean something he was trained to do. To such an extent that when called upon to act, his training took over and he responded in the only way he knew.'

Nash paused and turned slightly, so that he was facing the judge. 'It's a bit like a bowler sending down a half-volley to a top class batsman and expecting him not to hit it for six.'

The judge put his hand over his mouth to conceal a smile, but when it came to his summing up it was clear that Nash's evidence had convinced him. The jury took longer to make their minds up but when they filed back into the courtroom three hours later, the foreman announced that they found the defendant not guilty. The judge commended them on their decision and told Bryant he was free – to return to his prison cell.

That evening, as Nash and Becky were enjoying a barbecue at Nash's home, Smelt Mill Cottage, on the outskirts of Wintersett village, Becky told him that despite the verdict, and in spite of Bryant's continued protestations of innocence, she was more than ever convinced that he had committed the Woodland Strangler murders.

'Why do you say that?'

'I know you have reservations, Mike, but you're a man. Bryant doesn't look at you the way he looks at women. All the time you and Lloyd were giving evidence, Bryant was paying no attention to what was being said. He was staring at me. I tell you, Mike, creepy is the only way to describe the way he looked at me. Almost as if he was trying to tell me what he would do to me if he was free.'

'Are you sure? Could it be that because you know the crimes he's been convicted of, your mind is suggesting the rest?'

'No, Mike,' Becky insisted. 'He was staring at me all that time. If I could have read his mind I feel sure he was thinking "you'd be my next victim, if only I could get at you". That's how bad it felt.'

Nash refilled her wine glass. 'It doesn't matter one way or another, does it?' he comforted her. 'He's never going to be free – at least not until he's far too old to pose a threat to women, so you can relax. Relax and forget about him. He's safely tucked up in Felling for at least another twenty-four years.'

Even as he was speaking, Nash remembered Bryant's changed attitude when he spoke to him after the verdict had been returned. There had been a marked change in Bryant's demeanour; an almost gloating triumph in his expression. Was that connected to the way he'd been staring at Becky? Nash decided not to spook her further by mentioning it.

Shortly after returning Bryant to his cell, one of the prison officers who had escorted him from the court, glanced in to see the prisoner scribbling furiously on a writing pad. He wondered briefly who Bryant could be writing to. His legal adviser, perhaps? The officer was aware that Bryant had no relatives and few, if any, friends.

When Marie Lloyd received his letter a few days later, it took some time for the sense of what he had written to sink in. This wasn't helped by his handwriting, which only the most generous would have described as a scrawl. When she finally did understand what Bryant was trying to convey, she went straight to her computer and began entering search terms to retrieve the information he had asked her for. Only when she had got it and printed it off did she start to fill in the visiting order he had enclosed.

If her wait for the day of her next visit was agonizing for her, she wondered from time to time how much worse it must be for Bryant, cooped up in his cell. If what he had told her was correct, it must have been bad for him before, but now, with the knowledge he had gained fresh in his mind, the torment must be close to unbearable. At no time in the period leading up to that visit did any doubt creep into Marie's mind. That would come later.

When she reached the prison, her first task, having greeted Bryant, was to hand him the paperwork she had brought along. This was given a cursory glance by the supervising officer before he granted permission for the hand-over.

Bryant scanned the content eagerly. 'I thought so,' he told her once he'd finished reading. He seemed subdued, rather than excited by the news, which both surprised and puzzled her.

'What are you going to do about it?'

Bryant looked round at the drab room and shrugged. 'There's nothing I can do in here. I'm not at all sure there's anything I could do even if I was on the outside.'

'You could try talking to the police, couldn't you?'

He laughed, but there was little humour in it. 'What good do you think that would do? They didn't believe me before; so if I took a story as fantastic as this to them, they'd dismiss it out of hand. Once they'd stopped laughing, that is.'

'That detective who gave evidence at your trial last month, he believed your story about the attack on Archie. What's more he convinced the jury that you were telling the truth.'

'Yes, he did, but that was only because the evidence was on my side. Not only my own word, but your brother's statement and the put-up job of that fight in the corridor.' Bryant tapped the papers. 'What we have here isn't evidence. It's a theory based on coincidence, little more than that. I'm probably the only one who doesn't believe there's any coincidence involved.'

'OK, I accept that there isn't any evidence at the moment, so how do we go about collecting some?'

Bryant paused for a few seconds before replying, savouring with some excitement Marie's use of the word 'we'. He chose his words carefully, not wanting to show how much her presence disturbed him. 'There's no way I can, as long as I'm in here. And even if I was free, and there is evidence to collect, getting hold of it wouldn't be easy. That's always assuming it exists. I've been thinking about all that was said at my murder trial; all that they accused me of. And there are one or two possibilities. Even if that evidence hasn't been destroyed, getting hold of it might prove close to impossible. For one thing, we wouldn't know where to look. A needle in a haystack might be simpler to find.'

Bryant watched Marie carefully as he spoke. He had thought over the possible outcome of this meeting for days, and wanted to be sure she had taken the carefully planted bait. The last thing he wanted to do at this stage was to frighten her off. He needed her to achieve what he had in mind. After that, well, that was another matter altogether.

The rest of the visit was spent discussing and discarding various ideas, but during that time Bryant managed to insidiously suggest that getting him out of Felling Prison represented the only chance of achieving their aim. It was only when visiting time was nearly over that Marie came up with a possible way ahead; and with it Bryant knew that his plan had worked. 'I think I should talk to Archie,' she suggested.

'What good would that do?'

Marie explained, and her explanation not only interested Bryant for the practical possibility it contained, but for an indication of the lengths she might be prepared to go to in order to help him. Back in his cell, he thought about Marie. His excitement at her idea, the possibility of freedom and his desire for her, thoughts of what he would do with her if they were alone together all mingled in his head, setting his pulses racing.

Over the course of the next two months, Marie visited Felling Prison as often as regulations permitted, alternating between Bryant and her brother. If Archie had been sceptical at first, he was eventually won over by his sister's obvious belief in Bryant. Once he had accepted the ideas she put forward, their thoughts turned to the ways and means by which they could achieve their objective. Even now, with the fresh information put forward by Bryant, they were both beset by doubt from time to time. Were they being hoodwinked? Led down a false trail by a cunning and manipulative serial killer? And if that was the case, and they managed to achieve what they had set out to do, what might the consequences be once Bryant was at large once more? Would their actions lead to the release upon society of the most dangerous menace for years, a man who had killed and killed again, without remorse or acknowledgement of guilt?

Even worse, might their complicity in his scheme lead to the death of yet more innocent victims? If that was to happen, how could they live with the knowledge that those women would not have died had they not been gullible enough to fall for his machinations?

Several times, as Marie set off for the prison, she was determined to tell Bryant that she could not go through with the plan, which by now was rapidly taking shape. Each time her nerve failed; each time she left the jail the plan was still in place.

Several times, as Lloyd prepared for his sister's visit, he

was determined to convince her that she must drop the scheme, for her own safety and that of others. But somehow, the opportunity didn't arise, and the visit ended with the plan securely in place.

'Bryant's ill. I've sent for the duty doctor,' one of the officers told his replacement at shift changeover.

'That fucker's sick at the best of times. He's getting to be a bloody nuisance. What's up with him?'

'Not sure. Vomiting, diarrhoea, fever, he's got the lot.'

'I hope he snuffs it. Not on my shift though – and not on yours,' he added charitably.

'In that case you'd better look after him as if he was your own son. He's not in good shape at all. To be frank, I'm quite worried that someone might have slipped him some poison in his food.'

The doctor examined Bryant. 'Any abdominal pain?'

Bryant nodded; the slight movement causing sweat to trickle unchecked down his face. His reactions seemed slow and he didn't appear to notice this. The doctor kneaded his stomach and saw Bryant wince. He took the prisoner's pulse, a frown of either disapproval or concern on his face. After a minute or so he let go of Bryant's wrist, and watched his arm flop limply to his side. He stared at the prisoner for a few moments before turning to the officer, who by now had taken in the gravity of the situation and was looking suitably worried. 'We need to get him to hospital.'

'I'll get a couple of men to help carry a stretcher.'

'No, you miss my point. We can't treat him here. He'll have to go to Netherdale General.'

'Why? What's wrong with him?'

'I can't be certain, and I don't have the facilities to make a test, but I think he may have septicaemia.'

'Septi...?'

'Blood poisoning to you; if I'm right there's no way we can treat him here.'

'I'll have to speak to the governor, and then we can make arrangements for him to be moved tomorrow.'

'You could do,' the doctor agreed, 'but if his condition continues to worsen overnight, you could be moving him in a hearse; not an ambulance.'

The officer didn't appear unduly worried by this idea. He shrugged. 'I don't think he'll be missed.'

'Maybe not,' the doctor smiled thinly. 'But I take it from your remarks that you've never had to face an HMP Inspectorate conducting an internal inquiry into a death in custody?'

The officer shook his head.

'I thought not,' the doctor continued. 'Believe me, Torquemada and the Spanish Inquisition could learn a lot from them.'

'Oh, right, I'd better get on with it then.' As the officer swung the door open, the doctor cast a final glance at Bryant. His patient appeared to have taken in little of what they had discussed about his welfare. If that was so, it wasn't a good sign at all.

Bryant listened carefully to the two sets of footsteps receding down the metal staircase. He gave a quiet smile if satisfaction, before reaching across to take a tiny capsule from its hiding place. He had to ensure he didn't appear to be recovering, and the capsule would continue to provide the symptoms of his 'illness'. As he swallowed it, he was thankful that the doctor had been insistent. One more tablet he could manage, but having to maintain the pretence for another day would not have been pleasant. He settled back to await events. The officers, who looked in regularly on the instructions of their senior, were mildly alarmed by his semi-catatonic state, his grey complexion, the sweat that continued to pour from him. One of them even remarked to a colleague that Bryant might not survive the ambulance ride.

Netherdale General Hospital was quiet at that time of night; if a hospital is ever truly quiet. Apart from a couple of patients awaiting treatment for minor injuries, even the A & E unit appeared deserted. The lack of activity contrasted strongly with weekends, when it was standing room only in the waiting area and every cubicle was curtained off to protect the privacy of the patient within.

The ambulance pulled up outside and Bryant was removed from the back by two paramedics, watched by a pair of prison officers who walked alongside the trolley as it was wheeled indoors, like police outriders for a Presidential motorcade. The paramedics, after consultation with the prison doctor, had decided he was far too weak to walk, hence the trolley, and evidence of his illness was plain by the small container into which he had vomited several times on the journey from the prison and the drip hanging above the him. Despite his condition, it was obvious the prison authorities were taking no chances, given his violent nature and had secured him to the stretcher bed with handcuffs fastening both his wrists. As they entered the A & E unit, the paramedic informed the reception that this was a medical transfer and one of the officers was immediately seized on by the admissions nurse, who demanded details of the patient for the hospital record.

As he was beginning to give her the facts from Bryant's prison record, a doctor came hurrying through the double doors alongside the admissions area. As she approached, the officer standing alongside the trolley noted her white coat, which was open to reveal a blue top and slacks. The ensemble was completed by the stethoscope the woman was wearing draped scarf-like around her neck. 'Patient Bryant from Felling Prison?' she enquired in a sharp tone of voice. 'Suspected septicaemia?'

The officer nodded, at which the doctor seized one side of the trolley and gestured to the officer to help. 'This way,' she demanded, setting off in the direction of the doors. The officer looked round, but the paramedics had vanished, and he remembered their conversation on the journey about the break they were about to take, and speculation as to whether there would be anything worth eating in the canteen. He had no choice but to help the doctor push the trolley through the doors and down the corridor; then turn left until they were faced by another set of double doors. 'This is as far as you go,' she told him. 'Beyond here is a sterile area, so I can't let you in.' As she spoke, the doctor drew a surgical mask up around her mouth and nose.

'I can't leave the prisoner,' the officer protested.

'You'll have to, or stay inside there as long as he does, and risk catching whatever it is he's got. It may be septicaemia; or it could be something far more contagious. We won't know until we take some tests and get the results back; and that could be several days from now. It's up to you if you're prepared to take the risk.'

The officer hesitated, his indecision apparent. He looked at Bryant, who appeared to be unconscious. He noted the prisoner's grey complexion and saw the beads of sweat on his forehead and upper lip. He checked that the handcuffs were secure and then nodded reluctantly to the doctor. 'OK, but I'm not prepared to release these.'

'Very well.' The doctor took control of the trolley and use it to push the doors open. The officer had only chance to catch a glimpse of the corridor stretching beyond the doors before they swung to. He returned to the A & E unit to report to his colleague, who had by now completed the questionnaire for the admissions nurse. They waited for fifteen minutes or so until a young man in doctor's uniform approached them. 'Sorry to have kept you waiting,' the man apologized, 'are you from Felling Prison?'

They nodded, both thinking that their uniforms should have made the question superfluous. 'OK,' the doctor continued, 'where's the patient? Have they put him in a cubicle?'

The officers looked at one another in alarm. 'But you've already got him,' the senior of them objected. 'One of your colleagues came for him a while back and took him off to a special sterile area. We weren't allowed to go with him.'

The doctor looked at them for a moment. 'Are you sure? Because for one thing, I'm the only non-surgical doctor on duty, and for another, this isn't an isolation hospital – we don't have a sterile area.'

The prison officers retraced the route along the corridor

to the double doors where Bryant had last been seen. The doctor accompanying them went through without hesitation. Halfway along the corridor they came across the stretcher bed, which was empty now apart from the handcuffs; still secured, but only to the trolley frame. The only other items on the stretcher apart from the blanket and drip were the prison uniform Bryant had been wearing when he had been admitted.

The doctor pointed to a sign on the door opposite the trolley. It read, 'Kitchen'. 'I suppose you could call that a sterile area,' he said.

The humour was completely lost on them.

Although the headquarters in Netherdale was open twenty-four hours, Helmsdale police station closed at night. Detective Sergeant Mironova was on overnight call. The control room in Netherdale had tried Detective Superintendent Fleming's number, but on failing to get a reply from either her landline or mobile, they reverted to the duty officer.

Clara was at home, the evening having been spent decorating the lounge of her flat, ably assisted by her fiancé David on leave from his specialist duties with HM armed services. When her mobile rang, it took a moment to locate it, eventually unearthing it from the protection of the dustsheet covering the dining table. 'Work,' she told David with a grimace as she answered the call.

From habit, Clara glanced at her watch and noted with some surprise that it was well after midnight. Whatever the reason for the call; it wasn't going to be good news. She listened as the operator gave details of what had happened, and David saw her expression change, from surprise to incredulity and a touch of something else that he thought looked almost like fear. 'OK,' she told the operator, 'phone Sergeant Binns and get him to mobilize uniform branch. I'll get hold of DI Nash and the chief constable.'

She listened for a moment before continuing, 'No, you wouldn't have been able to raise Superintendent Fleming.

She's in Tuscany. And right at this minute, I wish I was there with her.' She ended the call and immediately pressed the short code for Nash's home number. As she waited for him to answer she looked across at David. 'Sorry, looks like you'll have to warm the bed yourself tonight. You'll understand why in a minute.'

After several rings, she heard the sleepy voice of her boss mumble, 'Nash.'

'Mike, sorry to disturb your beauty sleep.' She took a deep breath. 'Bad news, I'm afraid.'

Nash had only been asleep a few minutes when Clara's call woke him. He listened to her in silence, reaching across to switch the bedside lamp on, despite the sleepy protest of his companion. She sat up, rubbing her eyes. 'What is it? What's happened?'

Nash ignored her, and continued to listen to his sergeant. By the time Mironova finished, he was seated on the edge of the bed reaching for his clothes. 'OK, Clara, I'll meet you at Netherdale General. Have you got Jack organized? And the chief? Good, I'll be there ASAP.' He replaced the handset on its cradle, stood up and began struggling into his shirt.

'What's matter, Mike?'

Nash looked across at Becky Pollard. 'I shouldn't tell you this really, but no doubt you'll find out what's happened soon enough, and by morning the whole country will know. God, this is going to be some media circus.' He hesitated. 'Tonight, a prisoner from Felling Prison was taken to Netherdale General. He was suffering from some sort of suspected poisoning. All I know is that he somehow managed to escape, even though he was handcuffed to a bed.'

'That sounds serious, but why do you say it will be a media circus. And why were you reluctant to tell me?'

'Because that's not the worst of it, I was saving that 'til last. The prisoner who escaped is Paul Bryant. Which means, we have a convicted serial killer at large.'

Chapter Five

The flash message came via the Press Association. In the newsroom of the *Netherdale Gazette*, only a sub-editor and his junior were still working. It was that dead hour in a local newspaper, the middle of the night, after the night's final edition had been published and before work started on next day's copy. Or, as one cynic put it, 'Between printing today's lies and thinking up more for tomorrow.'

One of the men glanced at his computer screen, more from habit than in expectation of seeing anything of interest. The first few words of the message on screen changed that. He read on, his breathing accelerating with each sentence. 'Holy shit!'

His colleague looked up. 'Won the lottery?' Failing to get a response, he changed tack. 'What's happened? It was obviously something momentous, nothing less would provoke such excitement.

'The Woodland Strangler's escaped.'

'What?'

The sub-editor read aloud, 'Unconfirmed reports say that Paul Bryant, the serial killer nicknamed The Woodland Strangler, has escaped from Felling Prison, where he was nine months into a life sentence for the murders....'

He didn't need to repeat the rest of the piece. They knew it only too well. It had been the investigation conducted by the man who had become their crime reporter six months ago that had brought the Woodland Strangler to justice. 'Where's Big Mac?' The reader glanced round, as if expecting to see their reporter in the room. The nickname was doubly appropriate. Added to his surname of MacDowell, he was over six feet tall and weighed in excess of seventeen stone.

'He's on holiday of course. It's nearing the end of the trout fishing season. World War III wouldn't keep him away from his favourite stretch of river whilst he's still got

174

chance.'

'A story about the Woodland Strangler's escape might.'

'Well we'd better get hold of him. Before that though, we should call Ms Pollard. She's bound to—'

His colleague looked across, wondering why he'd stopped in mid-sentence, only to stare in amazement at their boss, who was standing in the doorway.

'You've heard, then?' Becky asked.

'Yes, the message came in a couple of minutes ago and we were about to call you. How did you find out?'

The moment he'd said it, the sub-editor realized and was in the process of kicking himself for his lack of tact when Becky replied. 'I was with Mike Nash when he got the news. Raise Big Mac and get him outside Netherdale General. I want him to pick up on any gossip. Tell him to interview members of staff and to get all the background before the Nationals and radio and TV arrive.'

'He's on holiday.'

'Not any more, he isn't.'

However, despite several attempts to call his mobile and home number, they were unable to contact the reporter.

By 8 a.m. the following morning, the media contingent camped outside Netherdale General was matched by another of similar size at Netherdale police headquarters. Inside the building, Nash and Mironova were briefing the chief constable on what had happened.

'Bryant had an accomplice; that much was obvious from the start. Someone, who was able to pass themselves off as a doctor. It has to be someone with a detailed knowledge of the hospital. Not only did they take Bryant to a part of the building which would have been deserted at that time of night where he could remove the handcuffs without being disturbed. But they would have to be someone who knew that the kitchen entrance is the only way in and out of the building that isn't monitored by CCTV.'

'Any idea who this accomplice might be? Or how Bryant managed his Houdini act?' O'Donnell asked.

'The answer is yes on both counts. Bryant's only visitor

over the time he's been in Felling has been Mary Lloyd, the sister of the prisoner he protected from the sexual assault. That's Dr Mary Lloyd, to give her full title. She's a junior doctor at Netherdale General. As to the escapology, Dr Lloyd has also been visiting her brother regularly, and by all accounts what Archie Lloyd doesn't know about picking locks isn't worth knowing.'

'That sounds logical. What action have you taken; and what more can we do?'

'As soon as we got the information from Felling that established the connection, we raided Dr Lloyd's apartment a couple of hours ago, but there was nobody at home. Her car was parked outside, and the car keys were inside the flat, so she's obviously not intending to use her own vehicle. So she either has access to another vehicle or the pair are on foot. If it's the latter, we should have no problem picking them up. However, until we do, we must face the fact that Mary Lloyd is on the run with a depraved pervert who has already murdered at least six women. She's in the most terrible danger.'

When Nash and Mironova returned to Helmsdale, after facing an impromptu and fairly hostile media conference on the steps of Netherdale station, they had to run the gauntlet of one or two more media inquisitors on their way into the station. Nash saw the look of distaste on Mironova's face and laughed. 'This is only the tip of the iceberg,' he warned her. 'It will get worse and worse until Bryant is recaptured. My guess would be that by tonight there will be three or four times as many reporters and TV crews loitering outside both stations and the hospital. Forget them. Our main concern is trying to discover where Bryant is – and what he's done with Dr Lloyd.'

Once inside, Nash told her, 'I want the files from Bryant's murder trial. I need to learn as much as I can about how his mind works. I'm also keen to find out what made him suddenly so desperate to escape. I don't believe this was a sudden decision. It was far too well planned to be a spur of the moment thing. It might be worth asking the officers at

Felling to search his cell again. No, on second thoughts, get Pearce to do it, and whilst he's there, ask him to question the officers who were present when Bryant met up with Dr Lloyd.'

'Anything else?'

'No, but when you contact West Midlands police, ask them to e-mail their files in the first instance and send the hard copy through afterwards.'

Clara knew how intuitive Nash was, and how he could often deduce the truth from a mere handful of facts. However, when the truth came out, she realized that even Nash, with all his ability, would never have been able to guess Bryant's location, or what he and Marie were doing.

The media feeding frenzy predicted by Nash was far in excess of even his expectations. Twenty-four hours after they had faced reporters for the first time, he and Chief Constable O'Donnell, prepared for another grilling from the representatives of the press, radio and television.

The contingent of news-gatherers had been growing dramatically throughout the time that Bryant had been at large, and was now so great that there were no rooms within the Netherdale police headquarters capable of housing the conference. Instead, the chief constable had managed to come to an agreement with the headmaster of Netherdale High School, who had generously consented to loan them the use of the school sports hall on the proviso that all attendees were clear of the grounds before pupils began arriving for the day's lessons. With that in mind, the media conference had been set for 7 a.m., which as Nash remarked would come as a shock to several of the reporters, who were unaware there were two seven o'clocks in a day.

Although the chief constable had erred on the side of caution when setting the time, Mironova commented that they could probably have opted for a far later start; given that they had little of anything new to report. At 7 a.m. promptly, Nash took his place alongside the chief constable and waited for the chatter of conversation to die down before the chief began her opening remarks.

O'Donnell started by introducing Nash to those reporters who didn't already know him and explaining that, in the absence of Superintendent Fleming, who had been recalled from holiday, Nash was the lead detective involved in coordinating the hunt for the missing prisoner. He would bring the media up to date with what few developments there were to report. Attention swung to Nash, who waited for a few seconds before speaking.

'Obviously, the question you all want answering most urgently is, has Paul Bryant been recaptured? Regrettably, I have to report that the answer to that question is no. Although there have been several calls by people who have claimed to have seen him; all of these supposed sightings have been inaccurate. Most of them were well-meaning cases of mistaken identity. However, I have to tell you that there have been some that I can only describe as hoaxes. The people who made those calls have been identified, and I hope they will suffer the consequences of their irresponsible behaviour. When one of these calls comes in, the report has to be investigated and that costs a good deal of time and diverts much needed manpower resources from the search for Bryant.'

Nash paused briefly to allow time for this to sink in; no doubt hoping that as many of the reporters present as possible would repeat his message. He then gave brief details of how Bryant had achieved his escape. 'There is absolutely no doubt that he was assisted, and we believe that the young woman who helped him escape is a doctor working at Netherdale General Hospital.'

There was a restless shuffle of movement and some low whispers of excitement amongst the reporters, most of whom were getting their first titbit of new information with Nash's announcement. Nash allowed the noise to subside, before glancing to his right, where a uniformed officer was standing behind a projector linked to a laptop computer. Nash nodded, and a couple of seconds later a photograph of Marie Lloyd was displayed on the screen behind Nash.

'This is the woman we believed acted as Bryant's accomplice in his escape. Her name is Dr Mary Lloyd, more usually known as Marie. We know that Dr Lloyd has visited Bryant over the past few months. We also believe that she was able to assist Bryant in convincing the prison authorities that he was in need of medical attention.

'In the light of that, the decision to transfer Bryant to Netherdale General was quite justifiable. However, we now believe this was the first part of a very cunningly thought out plan and in fact was designed purely to give him the opportunity to escape. The only person to see her at the time was one of the prison officers, and he has confirmed her identity from that photograph.'

Nash indicated the image behind him and maintained that pose as he delivered the final part of the statement he had agreed with the chief constable beforehand. 'Since leaving the hospital, there has been no trace of either Bryant or Dr Lloyd. Her flat is empty; her car is parked outside and we have had no reports of any vehicles having been stolen. We are not aware of anyone else in the area who might have assisted them. But in the meantime our major concern is for the safety and welfare of members of the public; and in particular for that of Dr Lloyd. She has been alone with him for over twenty-four hours; alone with a man who has been convicted of a string of sex-motivated murders.'

Nash sat back and waited for his final sentences to sink in before giving details of the searches that had been carried out. 'We have visited every caravan park within a twenty-five mile radius of here; and as I speak, officers are continuing to check barns, empty farm buildings, allotment sheds and any other possible place where the couple could be hiding. We ask members of the public to be on their guard and report any suspicions to us.'

The camera lenses continued flashing as the press began shouting questions in a tumult of noise. 'Inspector Nash, how long as this woman known him?' 'What was supposed to be wrong with him? Why did he need to go to hospital?' 'When you said you fear for the doctor's safety – do you

179

think she's dead?' 'How did he fake it, Inspector?' 'Do you think he's killed the woman you believe helped him to escape?'

Nash glanced at O'Donnell who nodded her head as if in agreement with him. He raised his hands to request silence. 'I am not prepared to answer any more questions at this stage. As soon as there is any further news you will be informed through the normal channels.' With that, he and the chief stood and left the hall, ignoring the barrage of further questions hurled at them by reporters as they headed back to their respective cars.

As they came away from the meeting, Clara, who had been standing at the edge of the hall watching proceedings, thought that, given the spread of reporters there, it might just be possible that by the end of the day, the only people who had not heard the dramatic news might be those living in an Amazon rainforest or a Bedouin tribesman wandering the Sahara. Apart from such as them, the whole world would know that the Woodland Strangler was at large.

Once they returned to Helmsdale, Nash informed Clara that he intended to use the time before the station got busy to study Bryant's file again. 'I only had chance to flick through it yesterday; now I want to go through it in depth.'

'I suppose that means you want me to make coffee?'

'That sounds like a great idea. You know, when I remember some of the poisonous brews you used to concoct, buying that coffee machine must rank as one of my shrewdest investments.'

'You mean you actually trust me not to ruin it?'

'You haven't managed it yet.'

When Clara entered Nash's office, he was sitting behind his desk staring at the open file in front of him. He didn't respond, even when she placed his mug on a coaster near his elbow. After a few seconds, Clara asked, 'Have you found something important?'

'I'm not sure. It might be something, or then again I could be reading too much into what probably has a simple explanation, but you know how I dislike loose ends. There is one thing in all this lot,' he indicated the thick folder, 'that somehow doesn't ring true.'

'Care to tell me?' She sat down, ready to listen. Sessions like this with Nash were always constructive and often led to healthy debates with positive conclusions.

'OK, from what you know of the case, I think you'd agree that the Woodland Strangler is obsessive, wouldn't you?'

Clara shuddered. 'I think obsessive is the understatement of the year, but yes, I'd say obsession was obviously a prime motive for the murders.'

'And how would you suggest that obsession manifested itself; apart from the actual killings, that is?'

Mironova thought it over, trying to recall the facts of the case. 'Didn't he collect things? Is that what you're referring to? The victims' clothing and jewellery, wasn't it?'

'That's correct. Every item of clothing, including their shoes, every piece of jewellery, their earrings, watches, bracelets or bangles, chains, necklaces, the lot. Some, quite valuable; others virtually worthless, a vast proportion without any resale value at all. He removed them from the dead bodies and took them away with him.'

'OK, but all that came out at the trial. I don't see what you find so interesting in it, Mike.'

'My point is; where are they?'

'Sorry, I don't get you.'

'Where are they? Where is this extensive collection of clothing and jewellery? Bryant's flat, his wagon, his car, his locker at work were all searched, not once but several times. Everywhere he might have concealed that macabre set of trophies; but no trace of them was found.'

'Oh, come off it, Mike. You're putting two and two together and making five. He could have thrown them in a skip, or hidden them somewhere so obscure that no one would ever find them.'

'I'd go along with that idea; but for what we agreed at the beginning of this conversation. You have to understand the true nature of obsession. If Bryant took those items, which were the most private and personal belongings of his victims, he would want them somewhere close at hand. Somewhere he could take them out whenever he felt the urge. Somewhere so close he could touch them, stroke them, fondle them, smell them; feeling the lust and excitement growing again; recreating what he'd done to those women. That being the case; where are they?' Although the police at the time searched every place remotely associated with Bryant, they came up with nothing.'

'What are you trying to suggest, Mike? That Paul Bryant didn't commit those ghastly murders? That he isn't the Woodland Strangler after all?'

'I certainly wouldn't go so far, Clara. I'm just saying it's curious. It's a loose end, and I—'

'Don't like loose ends. I know, Mike. But that's not our priority, is it? We've got to find Bryant – and Dr Lloyd. If she's still alive.'

Now, following the escape, the killings could begin again. He hadn't realized how much he'd missed the thrill, and how he was looking forward to his next victims.

He would start with the woman who was close to him; the woman who'd come into his life so unexpectedly. After that, as long as he remained at large, the list of victims would continue to grow. After all, if he was going to remain locked away for the rest of his life, the Woodland Strangler would have to make use of the window of opportunity; the window of freedom.

When four days had passed with Bryant still free, and no rumoured or confirmed sightings, even the media had reduced both the level of their hysteria and their physical presence. Mentions in the press and on radio and TV bulletins were reduced from screaming headlines and opening news items to inside page paragraphs and tail-end one-line announcements.

A rumour that was started as the search entered day five, helped revive interest, if only slightly. Where the story began isn't clear; it seldom is in such cases, but word soon got around that the couple might have fled the country. Quite how they achieved this feat without passports isn't clear, but the tale gained credence from the number of newspapers, radio and TV stations that repeated it.

Concern for Dr Lloyd's safety remained high within those most actively involved in the hunt for the pair. Detective Sergeant Mironova had suffered a recurring nightmare that she would be called out to a crime scene only to discover that the body of a murder victim was that of the young woman who had been misguided enough to trust the man, Clara now thought of as a maniac.

Although Nash's anxiety about Dr Lloyd didn't reach such dramatic levels, he was worried, not least by the apparent ease with which Bryant and his accomplice had managed to disappear so completely. Was someone hiding them, he wondered, time and again? If so, who could that be? Bryant had no friends or relatives, and Dr Lloyd, apart from a few workplace acquaintances, appeared to have lived a solitary existence. A darker thought entered his mind. Could the couple, far from seeking shelter from someone they knew, have entered the home of complete strangers and be holding them captive, or worse? Try as he might, Nash could not rid himself of a stray and peculiar notion. Could it be that Dr Lloyd, far from being in danger, was actually enjoying what to her might have seemed like a great adventure; and would that adventure end tragically? During the period of Bryant's freedom, armed police units were on constant standby. Caught in the middle of a showdown between Bryant and those seeking to capture him, there was an extra element to the perils Dr Lloyd faced.

Superintendent Jackie Fleming had come to Helmsdale to get an update from the team. Nash, along with DC Pearce, had the advantage of having met Bryant and interviewed him at great length. During the meeting Nash sought Pearce's opinion.

'You've met Bryant,' he said to the DC, 'what was your impression of him?'

'To be honest, Mike, I'm not sure. I've been mulling it over during the last few days. Somehow, I'm struggling to equate the man we interviewed with the monster portrayed by the media, and the man we know to have committed those dreadful murders.'

'But surely that's the case with a lot of serial killers,' Fleming objected. 'After they're caught and the truth comes out, friends, neighbours and people who work alongside them all say what normal, quiet, well-behaved men they are, and that they can't believe them guilty of such horrible acts.'

'It isn't only that,' Pearce responded. 'When Mike asked Bryant about the murders, he maintained that he was totally innocent. Now you could say he was merely keeping up the pretence, but I was in the position of being to one side of him as he talked, and I was convinced he was telling the truth, or what he believed to be the truth. Whether that's some form of schizophrenia, I don't know, but Mike couldn't see from where he was sitting, that Bryant's hands were clasped together under the table, and his grip was so tight the knuckles were showing white. Add to that, the bitterness in his voice, which came across strongly, especially when he talked about his conviction, and I don't think you can put that down to good acting.'

'Viv's right, Jackie, he did sound really bitter,' Nash agreed. 'However, there's something else as well. Viv and I spoke to him a second time, immediately after his court appearance, just before he was transferred back to Felling. I've been replaying that second interview over in my mind.' He turned to Pearce. 'Do you remember, Viv? It was when we were talking about what had just gone on in court. There was a moment when I think Bryant was about tell us something, but then he suddenly clammed up, as if he'd had a last-minute change of heart.'

Pearce thought it over for a moment. 'I think you're right, Mike. I knew there was something troubling me about that conversation, but I couldn't put my finger on it. However, I've absolutely no idea what it was that Bryant was about to tell us. Do you?'

'I'm not sure, but there was something odd about the way he said it. He didn't say, "There's something else I can tell you", he said, "There's something else. I can tell you—". Two distinct statements. Also, his attitude when we met him was different. At the time I put it down to relief that he'd been acquitted, but that can't be right. He's already serving a life sentence; being found guilty of an assault wouldn't have made any difference. However, when we saw him after the court appearance, he looked for all the world like someone who has had an immense weight taken off their mind. That can only have happened within the confines of the courtroom, but if it wasn't the acquittal that had excited him, what was it?'

'Well whatever it was, speculating won't help us find him,' Jackie added.

Chapter Six

'Ms Pollard, I need a word.'

Becky Pollard looked up from her study of the computer screen on the desk in front of her. The office she used had changed little since the days when her grandfather had owned and edited the *Netherdale Gazette*. Only the computer and a modern telephone would have puzzled the previous incumbent. Becky noticed the worried expression on her deputy's face and gestured to a chair. 'What's the problem?'

'I still can't raise Big Mac,' the assistant editor explained. 'Since Bryant escaped I've left messages on his home phone and on his mobile, sent him texts and emails, but without a response. So I thought I'd better go to his house to check. It didn't help that he lives out in the wilds, but I went there on my way into work this morning. It was all locked up, and his car was missing. In view of the past history and the connection with Bryant, I'm concerned that he hasn't got in touch. You'd think that he, of all people, would be keen to know all the latest, given that he was instrumental in having him put away.'

Becky frowned. 'You're right, it does seem strange. However, he said he was going on a fishing trip, so maybe he doesn't even know about Bryant yet. If he hasn't been home, or switched his mobile on, he won't have picked up your messages. Fishing's a solitary occupation and he might not have even taken his mobile with him. And if the place he's gone is off the beaten track, he may not have access to TV and radio.'

'There will have been newspapers though, and Bryant has been on all the placards for days.'

'Do you read newspapers when you're on holiday? I certainly don't; in fact I make strenuous efforts to avoid them. However, I agree that it is a long shot that Big Mac won't have seen or heard or read something about Bryant. I'm having dinner with Mike this evening and I'll mention it to him, although he's got more than enough on his plate at the moment. Thanks for telling me, and try not to worry too much

Although it wasn't late when Becky left the office, it was already dark outside. As she crossed the street from the *Gazette* building to the car park opposite, one or two dead leaves, blown on the freshening breeze, fluttered around her feet. The shorter days and the falling leaves were two reminders that summer was over, Becky thought, and the autumnal nip in the air was another. Before long the clocks would change. Once they were set back an hour, the dark winter nights would be upon them. For some reason, she always found this time of the year depressing.

Her thoughts switched to Nash, perhaps in a subconscious effort to cheer herself up. Becky knew he was worried by the failure to catch Bryant. More concerned still, for the fate of Marie Lloyd. Perhaps this evening Becky would be able to take his mind off the case for a few hours. She knew exactly how to do that, and smiled in anticipation at the idea. Even if it didn't totally succeed, at least it would be fun trying.

The car park was all but deserted as she headed for her yellow Mini, parked in the far corner in the section reserved for members of the *Gazette* staff. She had just pressed the button on her remote to deactivate the central locking when she heard a footstep behind her. Becky turned, but as she did, something heavy hit her on the side of the head. She slumped, unconscious, and would have fallen to the ground had her attacker not caught hold of her about the waist.

He hoisted her effortlessly over his shoulder and carried her the short distance to where a van was parked. Two minutes later, the van drove away, leaving the car park near silent, the only sound being the rustling of leaves.

Nash waited at Smelt Mill Cottage. The casserole he had prepared the night before had been in the slow cooker all day. He loved that device; it was perfect for someone like him. He could switch it on before leaving for work and know that no matter how late he finished his evening meal would not be ruined.

On this occasion however, it was Becky who was late. That was by no means unusual; the time constraints on her job as a newspaper editor were almost as bad as that of a detective. It was only when he heard the clock in the lounge strike eight times that Nash considered ringing the *Gazette*. Before making the call however, he wondered if some late story might have delayed her, and even checked the TV channels for a breaking news item. He failed to find anything, and realized that if she had been kept back at work, she would have phoned to let him know. This only served to heighten his concern, and he hurried through to his study to make the call.

The paper's switchboard had long since closed, and the only person in the newsroom was the night editor on the news desk. He answered the phone, but was unable to help Nash. 'No, she's been gone a couple of hours at least. She didn't mention anything before she left.'

'That's strange, she was supposed to be coming to my place for a meal. She should have arrived before now. I'd better phone my people. There may have been an RTA that's held her up.'

Ten minutes later, Nash was back on the phone to the newspaper office. 'There are no reports of any incidents between here and Netherdale. I tried her mobile, but I think it must be switched off, because it went straight to voicemail. Let me know if she rings in, will you?' He gave the man his home number before ending the call.

Time crawled by; Nash's anxiety heightening with every passing minute. He considered ringing her godmother, the chief constable, and even picked up the phone twice to do so, but changed his mind. He thought it would be unfair to worry her for no reason. Better not to alarm her when Becky would probably walk through the door at any moment.

She didn't, and by ten o'clock his anxiety had become alarm and had risen to fever pitch. He checked with Netherdale General Hospital, but they had no reported admissions or female outpatients in A & E matching Becky's description. He also ordered Netherdale control room to send a patrol car to check the route she would have taken to reach his house, but their report came back correspondingly negative. In desperation, he tried the *Gazette* again.

The night editor confirmed that they had heard nothing either. He was about to ring off when he had an idea. 'I'll go check the car park if you like. Give me five minutes and I'll call you back.'

The five minutes seemed more like an hour, but eventually Nash's phone rang. 'Her car's still here,' the newsman reported. 'The doors are locked.' He paused, agonizingly, before adding the worst part. 'But as I tried the car doors, I kicked something with my foot. I picked it up. It was a bunch of keys. I tried the key fob on her central locking system. It opened it, so those must be her car keys. I'm sorry, Inspector Nash, but it looks like something has happened to Becky. Something bad.'

By the time he spoke the final words, the night editor was speaking to himself. Nash had already ended the call and was dialling the Netherdale control room.

At two o'clock in the morning, there are few pedestrians about in Helmsdale town centre. Most of the residents are safely tucked up in bed. Any who may have been roaming the streets at that hour would have been surprised to see the police station with all its lights on. Given that Helmsdale station usually closes overnight, they might have wondered briefly why this unusual activity was taking place, before concluding that it must be connected to the hunt for the Woodland Strangler.

Inside the building, a hastily-convened meeting was in progress. Nash had returned from Netherdale, having examined the car park from where Becky had disappeared, and been joined by the other members of the Helmsdale team. Also present were the chief constable and Detective Superintendent Fleming. Helmsdale had been chosen for the venue because it was more convenient for most of the senior officers, and because they could be assured of being undisturbed by the activity of other branches of the service, notably uniform and traffic divisions.

It was Jackie Fleming who voiced the fear shared by everyone in the CID suite. 'We have got to assume that Becky was abducted,' she stated, her voice devoid of emotion. 'Any other explanation simply doesn't fit the facts as we know them. The only questions that remain are, by whom, and for what motive?'

'She could have seen something suspicious, or interrupted some illegal activity, such as a drugs deal,' Pearce suggested. 'A deserted car park in the town centre during the hours of darkness would be a natural place to choose for something like that.'

'That's certainly a possibility,' Fleming agreed. 'There is one other explanation that springs to mind. One that I certainly don't like having to consider, but one we cannot afford to ignore.'

'You think Bryant might have been responsible?' Mironova asked.

'I certainly don't think we should discount the idea.'

Everyone glanced towards Nash, aware of his intimate relationship with Becky, conscious of the pain he must be suffering at this moment. He had remained silent thus far, and when he spoke, his voice was muted, his thoughts obviously elsewhere. 'Becky told me that when she attended Bryant's trial on the assault charge she had been very uncomfortable because she was in the press gallery, directly opposite where Bryant was seated, and that all through the proceedings, he was staring at her in a very unpleasant way.'

There was a moment's silence as they all digested this unpalatable fact, before Pearce suggested, 'Might that have had something to do with his attitude when we spoke to him immediately after he came out of the court?'

'I'm not sure, who knows what goes on in the mind of someone like that,' Nash said soberly. He paused before adding, 'No, I don't think it did, Viv. By what he said to us, and the way he looked as he was speaking, I'd say it was more as if he'd found out something really important. However, that can't have been the reason he was staring at Becky because she has never had any connection with Bryant, and he wouldn't have recognized her....' Nash's voice tailed off into silence.

The others waited, aware that he was thinking, unwilling to disturb his thought processes. After a moment, her anxiety caused O'Donnell to break the silence. 'What is it, Mike? What have you just thought of?'

Nash resumed as if there had been no interruption. 'Unless Bryant wasn't looking at Becky at all. Unless he was staring at someone else. Someone seated close to her. That might explain why Becky thought his expression was strange. Because although she thought he was looking at her, in fact Bryant was staring at someone else, someone he did recognize.'

'If you're right, Mike, that would tend to discount Bryant as a possible suspect if Becky has been kidnapped,' Pearce pointed out.

'It might do; but then again, perhaps not,' Nash said confusingly. 'I want to look through Bryant's file again. There's something niggling me. I have a feeling I've missed something in there, but at the moment although it's at the back of my mind, I can't work out what it might be.'

The phone rang, startling everyone. Mironova, who was closest, answered it, and after a moment covered the mouthpiece. 'It's the night editor of the *Gazette* for you, Mike. He's very insistent. So much so that the operations room in Netherdale gave him your location. He says he has some information that could be both important and urgent.'

Nash took the receiver from her and listened to what the newsman had to tell him. After a few minutes, they heard him say, 'Yes, OK, we'll look into that as well. Thank you for telling us. No, there's no news yet. I'll let you know if there are any developments.'

He put the phone down and looked around. 'Apparently, when Becky set off for my house tonight she had something to tell me. It seems that the *Gazette's* crime reporter has also gone missing. He's supposed to be on a fishing holiday plucking trout from a stretch of the Helm further up the dale where he has fishing rights, but although the Bryant news broke whilst he was away from the office, he hasn't been in touch with the paper, even though they've tried to contact him. They've left messages, and now they're concerned for his safety because he was instrumental in helping the West Midlands police catching Bryant in the first place.'

'Why was that? I haven't had chance to read Bryant's file,' Fleming asked.

'The reporter, whose nickname is Big Mac, got a tip-off from a prostitute who alleged that she had been assaulted, and only narrowly escaped being strangled. She told him where the assault took place, and he went to the police with the story. They were already looking for another prostitute who had been reported missing, so they decided to search the area of woodland close to where the reporter's informant said the assault took place. They found the missing woman's body, and it hadn't been there long enough for the evidence to be degraded. They got a DNA match from semen found in and on the body, and arrested Bryant as a consequence. Bryant admitted that he had paid the woman for sex, but always denied having killed her, maintaining that he had been set-up.'

'Are you suggesting this Big Mac person has fallen victim to Bryant? Some sort of revenge? Or are you implying Bryant was set-up? If so, that sounds ludicrously far-fetched. Why would anyone pick Bryant out to frame him? And why would a reporter go to the trouble of paying a prostitute to make a false statement about being assaulted?'

Nash looked at Fleming. 'That's a very interesting question, Jackie, and one I've no—' He stopped dead, and his expression changed. 'Of course; that's it, that's what I couldn't recall,' he said, as much to himself as the others.

He stood up abruptly. 'If you wouldn't mind waiting here,' he told them, 'I need to confirm some facts. Clara, will you help me. I'm going into my office to make one or two phone calls. It shouldn't take long, but some people are going to have their beauty sleep disturbed.'

As he and Clara reached the door, he paused. 'Someone might think of switching the coffee machine on,' he suggested.

Pearce stood up and headed towards the kitchen, aware of his lowly position in the pecking order, which made him the highest ranking coffee maker on duty. As he left the room, Fleming nodded towards Nash's office. 'That's a good sign,' she told the chief constable. 'If Mike is asking for coffee, it's obvious he's making progress.'

If the thought consoled O'Donnell, her expression didn't show it.

Chapter Seven

Becky's first sensation was of feeling cold. She opened her eyes, struggling to remember what had happened. It was dark; thick, impenetrable blackness. She sensed, rather than knew, that she was inside a building. Her arms were aching from being stretched above her head. She attempted to lower them, but found that they would not move. Her wrists were fixed, tied fast to something. Panic set in, and as if spurred by the surge of adrenalin, her memory returned. She had been on her way to have dinner with Mike; had something important to tell him. Then, as she was walking towards her car, someone had come up behind her. And that was the last she remembered. As if provoked by her recollection, Becky felt a throbbing pain in her head. Had she been struck from behind, or hit her head as she fell to the ground?

It scarcely mattered; the result was the same. Imprisoned in some dark, cold place that smelt vaguely of damp. Damp and something else, something familiar; although Becky was unable to put a name to the aroma.

Questions flooded her brain, a sign that full consciousness was returning; the unanswered posers heightening rather than lessening her fear. Who? Why? Where? Who had abducted her? Why had she been taken? Where were they keeping her? Other questions followed in natural succession. What was the reason for the kidnap, and why choose her? Or was it just a random abduction? It could have something to do with her work; or it might have been done to extort a ransom from her family. Worst of all; was the abduction merely the prelude to other, more dreadful crimes?

At this final thought, a face appeared in her mind. Her mental image was of that day in Netherdale court, when the man acquitted of assault had stared so fixedly at her. Paul Bryant, the Woodland Strangler. If he had taken her, then she knew her chances of survival were less than slim. She was only too well aware of the ordeal his other victims had undergone before he killed them; their suffering had been graphically described at the time, and repeated with relish following his escape, by radio, television and in the nation's press; even in her own newspaper.

Becky wondered how long she'd been unconscious, how long she'd been tied up here; wherever here was. She wondered if Mike had realized that she was late for their dinner. Perhaps even now he was raising the alarm; searching for her. The thought should have comforted her, but somehow it didn't for it only led to another unpalatable fact. How could Mike hope to find her? He didn't know where she had been taken. Even she didn't know where.

She knew it had to be somewhere remote because of the silence. In cities, even in small towns and villages there is always sound of some sort. But here there was nothing. Or so she thought, but even as she was trying to reason it out; into that silence came a sound. Faint and intermittent, but as Becky strained to hear, it was repeated. As with the smell; she felt she should know this sound, but before she could place it, another noise, closer and more identifiable took precedence. Although she knew instinctively that the sound came from outside the building, her sense of direction had gone, until another, louder noise supplemented it.

It was a sort of metallic scraping or scratching sound. At the same time, Becky saw a light, the first since she had woken up. She couldn't work out what it was though, merely a slender rectangle that stretched from the ground to a point above her head. She stared over to her left, towards the light; towards where she was now certain the sound was coming from. Suddenly, the metallic sound ceased and a voice said quite clearly, 'Got it.'

A second later, the rectangle of light disappeared and was replaced almost instantly by the powerful beam of a torch that shone across the interior of the building, moving from side to side until it located and held Becky; temporarily blinding her.

As her vision adjusted, Becky saw the figure of a man

195

standing in front of her. Then she saw his face. Even in the dim reflection of the torch he was holding, it took only a split second for recognition to come. Recognition of the face that had stared from the front page of every newspaper in the land. The face that her own newspaper had featured so heavily. The face that had introduced every TV news bulletin for the past week. The face of the man who had stared so fixedly across the courtroom at her. The face that had haunted her dreams ever since. The face of Paul Bryant. Becky's fear reached terror level as she realized she was face to face with the Woodland Strangler.

The coffee Pearce had made was only a memory, the mugs cold by the time Nash and Mironova came out of his office. 'We haven't quite got the whole story,' Nash told them, 'but we do have enough to act, I think.'

O'Donnell saw his face was animated with the need to impart the news, and the urgency of the situation. 'I think I know where Becky is,' Nash them. 'We need to move fast. Every minute could be crucial.'

He explained what he had discovered from the phone calls he had made, which had been supplemented and cross-checked by Mironova from the case file on Nash's desk. Even before Nash had finished, O'Donnell was on the phone to Netherdale to order up an armed response unit, her instructions clear and concise. She paused only once, to spell out the address from a slip of paper provided by Mironova.

By the time she ended the call, the team was ready to leave. 'Two ARU units will meet us there,' she told them.

Pearce turned to Clara. 'What about a warrant?' he asked.

'We believe the suspect and the kidnap victim to be on the premises. As long as there's a senior officer present, we don't need a warrant.' Clara gestured to the others. 'And I think we've enough senior officers to satisfy regulations. That might be a liberal interpretation of PACE,' she admitted, 'but I for one wouldn't care to argue with either Nash or God at the moment, the mood they're in.' Clara lowered her voice as she mentioned Gloria O'Donnell's nickname.

The journey to their meeting point with the ARU teams seemed to take an age, especially for Nash, whose stomach was churning with anxiety over what they would find at their destination. He had managed to control his emotions as he'd developed the theory that had set them on this course, but that was all it was, a theory. They had no proof to substantiate it, and they could be wasting valuable time on a wild goose chase. Time that Becky didn't have. Time that might make the difference between finding her safe, well and unharmed or.... Nash didn't want to dwell on the 'or' but knew it was a strong possibility, and even worse; the chance of not finding her at all until they got a phone call. A phone call such as officers in other forces had received, directing them to the site of a victim's remains. The difference was, that for Nash it was personal.

Eventually, they arrived at the meeting point which was little more than a gap in the hedge alongside a deserted country road at the top end of the dale. To their right, Stark Ghyll towered broodingly over the gentler countryside near at hand. The gap in the hedge was in fact the beginning of a track that ran alongside a belt of trees marking the edge of a large plantation. At the end of the track, within yards of their vehicles was a tiny cottage that Mironova speculated could once have belonged to a gamekeeper or some other estate worker. The building was in darkness; the occupants no doubt fast asleep, oblivious of what was about to happen nearby. That didn't matter; it wasn't this house they were aiming for. They pulled up to find that one ARU was already in position, and as the detectives got out of their cars, the leader of the team emerged from the van.

'We're two teams of six,' he told them. 'The house we're after is halfway along this track which eventually leads to the River Helm. I sent a couple of the lads ahead with night glasses to take a look, the rest have taken up a watching position. All appears to be in darkness, although we can't be sure about the back of the building.'

'OK,' Jackie Fleming took charge as the senior

operational officer, 'no time to waste. Straight in with the big red key, front and back. Three armed men at each entrance. I'll go in the front with Clara once the ARU has cleared the way. Pearce, you take the back with the others. I want some of the ARU team to stand guard by the vehicles, and I want you to remain with them ma'am; and you Mike. She saw Nash was about to object and raised a staying hand in his direction. 'No Mike, you're personally involved.' She continued, 'I want the rest beyond the building to block any chance of escape. Everyone clear on that?'

She waited, but her tone had effectively discouraged any argument, even from the chief constable. 'OK, let's go.'

Close to, the house looked secure, quiet, with no sign of life or movement. That all changed when the leading ARU man got within twenty yards of the front of the building. A PIR security light, activated by the motion sensor, bathed the front of the building in bright white light, dazzling those in front of it. They waited until their vision adjusted, then the leader urged them forward. 'Go, go, go,' he yelled into his radio.

Two of the armed officers swung the door enforcer, a heavy steel bolt with handles as their colleagues stood guard. At the second blow, the heavy oak door gave way amid the crashing sound of splintering wood, which was echoed by a similar sound from the rear of the building. A second later the hall light was switched on, and the waiting detectives head one of the ARU shout over his radio, 'We're in. Armed police, do not move. Armed police.'

After a minute or two it seemed as if he had been talking to himself because there was no response, apart from the sound of their colleagues entering the rear of the property. As Fleming and Mironova entered the hallway behind their armed guard, they were met by one of the officers from the back. 'Ground floor clear,' he announced into his radio on seeing them.

Seconds later they heard the voice of another of the armed team shout, 'Upper floor clear. There's no one at home.'

Their inspection of the property had revealed that there was no garage, shed or other outbuildings. It appeared as if the gamble had failed. The property was deserted. No sign of their suspect, or of the victim. The sense of deflation was apparent. Chief Constable O'Donnell and Nash entered the building once the all clear had been given, could see it clearly on the faces of Fleming, Mironova and Pearce. Nash's face was compounded by a look of abject misery. O'Donnell voiced the question that was in all their minds. What now?'

They had congregated in the lounge of what was a conventional small rural cottage, very similar to the one they had passed at the end of the track. Even the solid, traditional furniture seemed totally in keeping with their location. Nash glanced round, partly to seek inspiration, partly to avoid embarrassing eye contact with his colleagues, whose sympathy he could not have tolerated at this moment of total defeat.

Inspiration wasn't long in coming. As he took in his surroundings, his attention was drawn to an object fixed to the wall alongside the large stone fireplace. Something stirred in Nash's memory. Something he'd been told earlier that evening. 'Of course,' he said, unaware that he was speaking aloud, 'we're looking in the wrong place.'

'I think that's fairly obvious by now,' the chief constable snapped, her stress and anxiety apparent.

'I said we were looking in the wrong place, that doesn't mean we're after the wrong target,' Nash replied. He pointed to the long, glass-fronted cabinet. 'That's the key to where we should be looking.'

They followed the direction of his pointing finger. Mironova was the first to make the connection. 'Got it!' she exclaimed triumphantly. 'That was what the man from the *Gazette* told us, wasn't it?'

'That's right, and I think we now know where we've to go next.'

Their second car journey didn't take nearly as long, but the tension, if anything, was even greater. They arrived in convoy at the point where the woods gave way to a sloping track that stretched gently towards the bank of the River. They pulled up as someone signalled them to stop by waving a torch to attract their attention. 'Police?' the man asked the driver of the leading ARU van. 'He's inside. It's Bryant you're after, isn't it? He's in there, but he's got hostages.'

'Right,' Nash emerged from the second car and took the man's arm. 'You stay with us, just to be safe.'

As the others spilled out of the vehicles, the man turned to go along with them, encouraged by Nash's grip on his arm. Nash let go, but walked across to the ARU leader and delivered his command in a tone that was no more than a whisper. Then he donned a flak jacket and told the others, 'It appears that Bryant is inside, and we think he has Becky and Dr Lloyd as hostages. I'm going to go in first, and I want you to edge forward towards the building until you have it surrounded, but don't get too close, we don't want to spook him into doing anything rash.' He looked at each of his fellow officers in turn to ensure the gist of the hidden message he was delivering had got home.'

'Mike,' Fleming said, 'I told you to—'

'Yes, ma'am, I know what you said. But the situation has changed.'

Fleming knew immediately Nash was trying to convey a message. He would never call her ma'am.

Then he looked at Mironova. She saw, in the faint light of dawn, the slight nod of his head towards the man who had stopped them. She bent her head fractionally to acknowledge that she understood and as the others moved forward, she waited, drawing Pearce back with a restraining hand on his arm until the two of them were at the rear of the raiding party, alongside two of the armed police, who seemed similarly disinclined to hurry.

Nash moved forward towards the front of the building, walking carefully over the uneven ground. The structure was little larger than a garage, but big enough for its purpose, he guessed. Beyond it, he could see the placid waters of the river, the slight current glistening silver in the early morning light. Nash reached the door of the building and paused for what seemed like an age to those who could do nothing more but watch and wait. Eventually, he took a deep breath and pushed at the door. It opened easily, although the creak as it swung on hinges that hadn't seen oil for many years sounded deafening. He took a step inside and stopped. He looked round at the occupants of the fishing hut. 'Hello, Paul. Everyone OK in here?'

It was difficult to judge which of the three occupants of the hut was the most surprised by Nash's sudden entrance. Bryant stood rooted to the spot, his mouth open in astonishment. To his right, Becky exclaimed, 'Mike' – her face lighting up with relief. She rushed forward and Nash held her close to him. 'Are you all right, Becky? Has that man harmed you?'

'I'm OK, Mike, she told him. 'Just a bump on the head. But that's thanks to Mr Bryant. If it hadn't been for him, things could have been far worse.'

Over Becky's shoulder, Nash saw that Marie Lloyd had moved protectively in front of Bryant and was standing, glaring at Nash defiantly.

'It's all right, Marie,' Nash told her calmly. 'I haven't come to arrest Paul.'

Nash saw Bryant's surprised expression. 'I think I've just about worked out what's been going on now, but I will need you to fill in a lot of the background, and I believe a search of this place might pay dividends too. If we find what I suspect will have been hidden somewhere in here, I think we'll be able to prove it conclusively.'

'Have you got him, then?' Bryant asked.

'Yes, he's outside, waiting for you to be dragged out under guard. Best not to disappoint him too much, don't you think? It's likely to be the last bit of fun he has for a long, long time, and I think you've earned the right to be there when I charge him.'

The raiding party waited, having got as close to the hut as

they dared. The tension was almost unbearable. After what seemed an age, Nash emerged, clutching Becky Pollard with his arm protectively around her waist. She blinked in the strengthening early morning light that contrasted with the gloomy interior of the place where she had been held captive. She looked round and saw her godmother. Releasing herself from Nash's grasped she ran forward, stumbling once on a tuft of grass, before reaching Gloria, who hugged her tight. Over Becky's shoulder, the chief constable saw the fugitive emerge from the building, along with the woman who had helped him to escape. She noted with interest that the couple were holding hands.

As soon as Bryant appeared, the armed officers raised their weapons, but Nash signalled to them to desist. 'That won't be necessary,' he announced in a loud, clear voice so that they could all hear him. 'Paul Bryant will not offer any resistance or threat.'

Towards the rear of the group, a man turned as if to move away, but found his route blocked by DC Pearce. The tall detective was more of a deterrent than DS Mironova, who stood alongside him. Even more discouraging were the two armed officers accompanying them, whose automatic weapons were pointed, not at Bryant, but in his direction. Unlike their colleagues, these two had not lowered their weapons on Nash's instruction.

As he looked round, the man saw Nash walking towards him. He listened in a daze as the detective spoke. 'Andrew John MacDowell, you are under arrest for the abduction and unlawful imprisonment of Rebecca Pollard. You do not have to say anything, but it may harm your defence....'

Several of the officers listening to Nash administer the caution looked at one another in surprise, which turned to astonishment as he ended by adding, 'I have to warn you that other charges will follow in due course. Other, even more serious charges.'

Big Mac looked round, desperately seeking an escape route, but when Pearce grasped his wrist and applied the handcuffs, the reporter realized that it was finally all over.

Justice had caught up with the real Woodland Strangler.

'I suppose I ought to have twigged a long time before I did,' Bryant admitted. They had brought him, along with Marie Lloyd, to the CID suite in Helmsdale.

The chief constable had whisked Becky Pollard away to Netherdale General as soon as she heard her goddaughter complain of a headache, and refuting all Becky's arguments. 'You're going to get checked over for possible concussion,' Gloria told her.

As Bryant began telling his story, downstairs, Sergeant Binns was completing the formality of booking MacDowell in and installing him in one of the cells.

'When I was in my last year at school there was a girl I really fancied; and it turned out she fancied me as well. Her name was Victoria Lindsay, although everyone called her Vicky. MacDowell was in the same year as me, and it was obvious he also wanted Vicky, but she wouldn't have anything to do with him. When she chose me, MacDowell was livid; so angry he picked a fight with me. I won the fight, but we were seen by a couple of the teachers. I was reported to the headmaster and slung out. Sadly, I also lost touch with Vicky soon afterwards. And although I've no doubt she also forgot me as quickly as I forgot her, I was really sad when I read years later that she had been murdered.' Bryant paused as sipped the mug of coffee provided for him and Marie by the detectives.

'When did you guess that MacDowell had framed you for the Woodland Strangler murders?' Fleming asked.

'The first clue was when I saw his name on a report the investigating police gave me. Quite ironic really. It had been compiled by a psychological profiler to reinforce their case. He spelled MacDowell right, which was about the only bit of the report that was accurate. Although I recognized the name, I'd no idea it was the same MacDowell I'd been at odds with at school. It isn't exactly an uncommon name. It was only when I saw him at Netherdale court, leering at me from the press gallery with that horrible gloating expression that I recognized him. He has changed a lot from when we were at school, and not for the better. I was able to put two and two together then. But of course, I had the advantage of knowing that I was innocent.'

Bryant looked across at Nash. 'Back in the hut, you said you'd just about worked it out. How did you do that?'

'There were a couple of things, really,' Nash told him. 'The first was only something that puzzled me, but when I realized the second part, it all fell into place. To begin with, when I read the case file from your original trial, I was puzzled that the police had been unable to recover any of the clothing or jewellery taken from the victims. These were obviously intended to be trophies, but they never turned up.'

He saw Marie Lloyd was looking puzzled, and explained. 'It was obvious that the Woodland Strangler had an obsession about the jewellery and clothing of his victims. Once you understand the compulsion that kind of obsession gives a killer, you'd know that he would want them close by him, so he could take them out and relive the moment, over and over again. Although the police searched everywhere connected with Paul they failed to find any of the stuff. That in itself wasn't enough to prove him innocent, but it did raise some doubt. Once I began to question the original verdict I was on the lookout for further evidence, and eventually I found it. Or rather I didn't, because once again it was something that was missing.'

Nash could see that everyone was baffled by this statement, and turned to Bryant. 'This was something I thought you might have picked up on. It concerned the way you were arrested. Big Mac went to the police with a tale he was supposed to have been told by a prostitute who had been assaulted, but managed to escape. The police were already looking for Kitty Prentice, who had been reported missing a few days earlier. That story led them to search the woods where the alleged assault on the anonymous informant took place. There they found the missing woman's body; did a DNA check on the semen sample retrieved from it, and got a match to you, Paul.'

'I simply thought they'd got the wrong man. I never doubted the assault story,' Bryant admitted.

'Neither did I, until I remembered that day in Netherdale court. Becky Pollard told me you'd been staring at her all through the proceedings, but you weren't. You were staring at the *Gazette* crime reporter, MacDowell, because you'd recognized him – and for that to have happened there had to be past history between you.'

'Ms Pollard's very attractive' – Bryant glanced sideways at Marie – 'but my tastes lie elsewhere.'

'Once I'd got that far, I began looking into MacDowell's past. I spoke to the officer in the West Midlands force who led the case, and he confirmed that as MacDowell refused to name his informant, the CPS had put pressure on them and instructed them to interview every working girl in the area. They did, but they were unable to trace the prostitute who was supposedly assaulted. That meant they only had MacDowell's word for the whole story. And why would he allow it to go so far as to cost him his job? The information had to be false – no witness; nothing. Like many people who tell lies, MacDowell made the mistake of giving too much detail. He said the woman who was attacked managed to escape because she'd learned self defence on a course run by the English Collective of Prostitutes. I checked with them and there was no such course. That meant the whole story had been concocted to frame you. And if he had an axe to grind, that would make the assault tale even more dubious.'

Nash paused and took a swig of his coffee, which by now was almost cold. 'I still had no more than a theory, and I was lacking a motive. Why would an established crime reporter with a good reputation want to frame an innocent lorry driver? It didn't make sense, until I spoke to the headmaster of your old school. He remembered you, and he remembered MacDowell too. He also told me you were dating Victoria Lindsay. As soon as I heard her name, it rang alarm bells, because she was one of the other possible Woodland Strangler victims. The headmaster clearly didn't like MacDowell, but he was forced to act after the fight you had with him. He thought expelling you would solve the problem, and so it seemed. Did you know that you'd broken three of MacDowell's ribs?'

Bryant shrugged. 'How could I, they expelled me, remember.'

'That finally established a motive. Revenge on you, and revenge on Victoria, the girl who had rejected him. She was the first of the suspected Woodland Strangler victims. Killing her must have given him the taste for it, but I suppose it was inevitable that the pressure would eventually get to him, and perhaps some of the investigations were getting uncomfortably close to home. The solution seemed ideal, I guess. Frame you, and he would be free and clear. However, once you were in prison, the Woodland Strangler's activities would have to cease. That remained so, until you escaped from prison which gave him the opportunity to strike again.'

'Why did he choose Becky?' Fleming asked.

'Who knows what goes on in a warped, obsessive mind? He had been working alongside her for a while, plenty long enough for him to become fixated on her, and once Paul was at large, he was free to act and satisfy his lust. Fortunately, we were able to prevent that.'

'What led you to the fishing hut? Bryant asked.

'MacDowell had supposedly been on a fishing holiday and couldn't be contacted. When we raided his house it was empty and his rods were missing from the glass cabinet. That made me realize we were looking in the wrong place.'

'So what happens now?' Marie asked.

'With regard to MacDowell? We'll interview him as soon as our forensic officers have completed their examination of his house and that fishing hut, plus his computers at home and at work. I really hope we find that missing evidence, it will make proving the case so much easier. With regard to you aiding and abetting the escape of a prisoner, that will be up to the CPS, but it may come to nothing.'

Nash paused, there was one unanswered question, but the subject was delicate. 'One thing interests me, how did you manage to evade capture all this time? We've had patrols out, searched every bit of woodland, all the barns, sheds, outbuildings, without even a trace of you. So where were you hiding?'

There was a long silence before Marie answered his question with one of her own. 'If I tell you, will you promise that it won't cause problems for anyone?'

'I think that'll be OK.' Nash glanced at Fleming, who nodded. 'Technically, I suppose if someone was hiding you they were harbouring fugitives, but as we're seeking to have your guilty verdict overturned, it would be churlish to pursue them.'

'It was a real stroke of luck,' Marie told them. 'When Paul told me about MacDowell, he asked me to find out where he lived. When I saw the address, I recognized it immediately. It wasn't difficult, being so rural, because the old lady who lives in the cottage at the end of the track alongside the road is one of my regular patients. I was on duty in the A and E department a couple of years ago when she was brought in with breathing difficulties. She went into cardiac arrest and I managed to save her and I've seen her on several occasions since. When I approached her, she was happy to do anything she could. I warned her she might get into trouble for it, but she didn't care. She said if it hadn't been for me she wouldn't even be here, so she said we could stay at the cottage. She even lent me her car so I could smuggle Paul away from the hospital, and later, to follow MacDowell. Paul thought that it would only be a matter of time before he did something to give himself away, but we didn't realize it would happen so dramatically.'

'The cottage was ideal,' Bryant added, 'because he had to pass the door every time he went anywhere. That was how we followed him and saw him attack Ms Pollard. We were too far away to intervene. So we tailed him and when he took her back to the fishing hut we knew we had to do something. We could hardly phone the police so we came up with a plan. Marie made a noise outside to distract him and when he came out to investigate, it gave me chance to get inside.'

Marie took up the story. 'I made enough noise to get him outside and then waved my torch about. I kept making a noise and flashing the light up the track so MacDowell was heading for the road. When I thought I'd given Paul enough time, I circled around and had just got back to the hut before you walked in.'

'What did you intend to do once you'd released Ms Pollard?' Nash asked.

'Erm, I don't think we'd thought that far ahead. We just knew we had to get her out of there. Taken her back to the cottage I suppose.'

'That cottage is really tiny,' Fleming said. 'Where did you sleep?'

Nash turned away to conceal a smile, but still saw Marie's blush. It wasn't helped by Jackie's, 'Oh, sorry, I didn't think.'

'We now have to decide what to do about you,' Nash told Bryant.

He was about to add something to this when the phone rang. Mironova answered it. 'Yes,' she said. 'What have you found?'

She listened, making notes from time to time. Thanks, let me know when you have any more details, will you?'

She looked at the others, uncertain how much to say in front of strangers. Receiving a nod of encouragement from Fleming, Clara said, 'That was Viv. The SOCO team started on the fishing hut first, and they've already found something they think might be important.' She smiled. 'That was their word, not mine. It sounds sensational to me. They've found one set of clothing in a plastic bag, all neatly folded, together with jewellery. There was a label on the bag, with the name Lindsay on it. They reckon there are a lot more bags they haven't got round to examining yet.'

'That sounds conclusive,' Fleming stated. 'Mike, you were in the middle of saying something?'

'We need to decide what to do about Paul, particularly in view of what we've just heard. Technically speaking, he should be returned to Felling Prison, but I doubt whether he's going to view that option favourably.'

'You can say that again. Especially as there's a contract out on me. I don't want to end up in more trouble,' Bryant said with feeling.

'I don't understand,' Marie objected. 'Why can't you simply release him?'

'It isn't as straightforward as that.' Nash smiled. 'For one thing, if we let him go without the public knowing why, there could be mass panic. However, more to the point, he has to remain in custody until we can get the courts to authorise his release on bail, pending an appeal against his conviction, at which we will of course offer supporting evidence. That will be necessary to clear his name so he returns to society without a stain on his character.'

He turned to Bryant. 'How would it be if you were to stay in the cells at Netherdale for the time being? You'll be more comfortable there than at Felling, and we could allow Marie to visit you every day, if she wishes. However,' he added wickedly, 'she won't be able to stay overnight, I'm afraid.'

Marie's blush was even more vivid than earlier.

'Now, if you'll excuse me,' Nash told them. 'I'm going to leave you with Superintendent Fleming and DS Mironova. You'll have to make statements covering everything that has happened since the hospital escape. Or almost everything,' he amended. 'I'm going through to Netherdale General to see how Becky is.'

The following Monday morning, when Clara walked into the CID suite, Nash was already at his desk. He was reading all the statements and supplementary evidence regarding the case. Nash had to vet them prior to their submission to the Crown Prosecution Service. She noticed that he looked tired. There was often a reason for this that Clara didn't care too much to probe deeply into, but somehow she didn't think on this occasion, his weariness was related to his hyperactive love life.

'Good weekend, Mike?' she asked.

'Not really. Not the finest I've ever had, that's for sure.'

'Why? What was wrong?'

'I got home on Friday night I'd been in the house about ten minutes when I got a call from the chief. You know Becky was staying at their house after she was released from hospital? Well, Gloria and Charlie were setting off on Saturday morning for a three-day visit to friend in Edinburgh, and they were planning to take Becky back to her flat on Friday night, but Becky got in a terrible state at the thought of being on her own; delayed shock I suppose. So Gloria asked me to help. I took her back to my place and spent the entire weekend reassuring her.'

'Reassuring her? That's a new name for it.'

'Anyway,' Nash continued, 'on Sunday she phoned her uncle and he's fit to return to work. So she drove her Mini round to Gloria's, locked it in the garage and she's going back to London tomorrow.'

That night would be the last Becky spent in Yorkshire. Nash had promised to take her to the train next morning and warned Mironova he wouldn't be in until lunchtime.

Late that evening as they went upstairs, Becky clung tightly to his arm. When they went to bed, she pulled Nash close.

Several hours later, he reflected sleepily that he was glad he'd had the forethought to tell Clara he wouldn't be in until late.

On his drive back from the station Nash reflected that this was the second time he'd taken Becky to the London train. Her return to the *Gazette* had caused an argument between them over the handling of the Woodland Strangler case, but at least they had parted as friends. Close friends, he thought remembering the previous night.

When he eventually reached the office, Clara's expression was sympathetic. 'Poor Mike. At least you'll get some sleep now you don't have to do all that reassuring,' she said with a grin.

****

210

About the Author

Bill Kitson, AKA William Gordon, is an established crime writer. His DI Mike Nash series is set in North Yorkshire; the county of his birth. Having taken early retirement from the finance industry he enjoys the challenge of writing both crime and general fiction, often with a twist of humour.

Having lived and worked throughout most of the North of England he is now settled in a small village on the edge of the Yorkshire Dales along with his wife and black Labrador. His writing never stops and when he isn't seeking inspiration from the surrounding countryside, he can be found in a small fishing village on one of the Greek islands, staring out to sea – laptop at the ready!

For further details go to www.billkitson.com